Praise for *A Scarlet Pansy*

"*A Scarlet Pansy* is essential reading for scholars and fans of Anglo-American queer literature. . . . To mix metaphors, this forgotten flower is quite a little gem, and Corber's editorial efforts are worthy of readers' deepest thanks and praise."
—*American Literary History*

"*A Scarlet Pansy* makes an important queer intervention in the historical record of how to be gay. It is a great pleasure to be brought out into pre-Stonewall gay culture along with the protagonist, and to see this combination of camp and sex."
—**Nicholas de Villiers**, University of North Florida

"*A Scarlet Pansy* is a queer romp of a read. . . . Corber's Introduction is excellent on the nuanced presentation of gender and sexuality in the novel, and he is especially good at locating the text alongside a range of other, more familiar queer novels and writers, from Wilde and Radclyffe Hall to Charles Henri Ford and Parker Tyler."
—*Modern Language Review*

"Fordham University Press deserves our gratitude for making available the original 1932 version of *A Scarlet Pansy*. . . . Editor Robert J. Corber stresses in his introduction the novel's importance for both transgender and gay literature."
—*Gay & Lesbian Review Worldwide*

A Scarlet Pansy

A Scarlet Pansy

by Robert Scully

Edited and with an Introduction
by Robert J. Corber

An imprint of Fordham University Press
New York • 2025

Copyright © 2016 Fordham University Press

Preface copyright © 2025 Fordham University Press

All rights reserved. No part of this publication may be reproduced, stored
in a retrieval system, or transmitted in any form or by any means—electronic,
mechanical, photocopy, recording, or any other—except for brief quotations in
printed reviews, without the prior permission of the publisher.

Fordham University Press has no responsibility for the persistence or accuracy of
URLs for external or third-party Internet websites referred to in this publication
and does not guarantee that any content on such websites is, or will remain,
accurate or appropriate.

Fordham University Press also publishes its books in a variety of
electronic formats. Some content that appears in print may not be available
in electronic books.

Visit us online at www.fordhampress.com/new-york-relit/.

Library of Congress Control Number: 2016936862

Printed in the United States of America

18 17 16   5 4 3 2 1

CONTENTS

Preface	ix
Recovering *A Scarlet Pansy*: An Introduction, by Robert J. Corber	1
A Note on the Text	25
Acknowledgments	27
A Scarlet Pansy by Robert Scully	29

PREFACE

Robert J. Corber

A DECADE AGO, WHEN I WAS PREPARING THIS EDITION OF *A SCARLET PANSY* FOR publication, I had little inkling of the moral panic over the visibility of trans people that would eventually emerge, let alone the role that such visibility would play in the rise to power of an authoritarian movement in the United States. Although I realized at the time that the proliferation of "bathroom bills" barring trans kids in public schools from using the bathrooms that corresponded to their gender identities was a sign that a backlash against trans activism was building, my primary goal was to correct a widespread misreading of *A Scarlet Pansy* as a "gay classic," despite the trans identity of its heroine, Fay Etrange. Such a misreading not only distorted the queer past by rendering invisible the trans men and women who were central to it, but it also erased the novel's significance for trans readers. My other goal was to complicate our understanding of queer literary history by making available to contemporary readers a novel written almost a century ago and long out of print that not only avoided stigmatizing queer life by portraying it as shameful, degrading, and empty of meaning, as so many other queer novels published in the same period did, but actually celebrated it.

Although I continue to believe in the importance of these goals, the campaign to eradicate trans people from American society undertaken by lawmakers, mostly in "red" or right-leaning states, has added new significance to the novel's jubilant treatment of its heroine. These lawmakers have prohibited gender-affirming health care for trans kids, banned trans girls from competing in girls' sports, enjoined public school teachers from teaching about gender identity and sexual orientation, and even threatened trans kids' parents with prosecution for child abuse. With the reelection of President Donald Trump in 2024, this terroristic campaign became national in scope. Within days of his return to the Oval Office the autocratic Trump followed through on his pre-election promises and issued a series of executive orders prohibiting trans men and women from serving in the military and declaring that there are only two sexes, male and female, as well as that a person's sex is immutable. Even the National Park Service quickly took action and removed all references to trans people from the Stonewall National Monument in New York City. Ironically, in so doing it expunged the identities of the very people who initiated the storied 1969 uprising commemorated by the monument.

In light of this virulent anti-trans backlash, the reissuing of this edition of *A Scarlet Pansy*, whose text is based on the original 1932 novel, could not be better timed. Its depiction of Fay's world makes clear that trans men and women have been a constituent part of American life since at least the early twentieth century and that their identities cannot be understood as the product of some newfangled "gender ideology" that "woke" or left-leaning public school teachers have inculcated in their students, as rightwing politicians have absurdly claimed. What's more, its descriptions of Fay and the other queer characters constantly scramble the categories "male" and "female." For example, when Fay is sixteen, she "could pitch as much hay as her father, could plough more land in a day, could lift heavier burdens," despite the femininity of her gender presentation. And when the crafty Mr. Fisher, who gives her a job after she has left home, seduces her, he clasps her "sturdy, muscular, hard-worked brown hand" in his "effeminately white, soft, weak" one before defiling her. Thus *A Scarlet Pansy* not only exuberantly

Recovering *A Scarlet Pansy*: An Introduction

affirms queer identities; it also validates the very "gender ideology" that has triggered moral panic and that the authoritarian right has attempted to stamp out. In Fay's world, a person's biological sex doesn't determine their gender identity; nor is their biological sex immutable, as the novel's consistent use of the pronouns "she" and "her" for Fay indicates. Because of this, I cannot imagine a more needed or felicitous treatment of queer life than the one in this remarkable novel.

New York City, 2025

Recovering
A Scarlet Pansy
An Introduction

Robert J. Corber

Largely forgotten since its publication in 1932 and out of print until now, *A Scarlet Pansy* is one of the most remarkable novels about queer identity published in the twentieth century. It offers an unusually rich portrayal of late-nineteenth- and early-twentieth-century urban queer life by recounting the sexual adventures of its transgender protagonist, Fay Etrange, to whom it refers throughout as "she," as she triumphantly makes her way in the world. The novel's exploration of the sexual underworld before the categories "homosexual" and "heterosexual" became firmly entrenched in American society may explain why it has failed to receive more attention. Its depiction of Fay's queer apprenticeship destabilizes the binary construction of gender and sexual identities. The little scholarly commentary that exists on *A Scarlet Pansy* has ignored this aspect of Fay's sexual coming-of-age and discussed the novel as a lost "gay classic." The novel's delineation of queer life certainly holds significance for gay readers, but this approach has marginalized its transgender content by assimilating it into a tradition of writing centered on gay

I

male experience.[1] But *A Scarlet Pansy* is first and foremost a *queer* novel—that is, a novel which explores a form of gender and sexual difference that cannot be identified as homosexual without drastically simplifying the history of sexuality. Recovering *A Scarlet Pansy*'s importance for both transgender and gay readers highlights its subversive treatment of the queer past, which scholars who have homosexualized Fay's identity and experience have overlooked.

Fay's initiation into queer life begins when she leaves the small town in rural Pennsylvania where she was born and moves to Baltimore in search of work to provide for her downwardly mobile family. Although her gender and sexual difference are obvious to everyone—including her father and brother, who pressure her to adopt a more "normal" gender presentation—she does not acknowledge them until the director of the YMCA where she is taking night classes seduces her. At first she is ashamed of her "unnatural" sexual desires and struggles to sublimate them in work, but when she moves to New York and discovers its raucous bohemian milieu, she immerses herself in it, befriends famed female impersonator Bert Savoy, and becomes the center of a closely knit circle of transgender men and women. In a queer reimagining of the Horatio Alger story, Fay quickly rises through the banking world, despite her transgender identity, and, having amassed a small fortune, she fulfills her ambition to become a physician. She has inherited from her mother a "love of service," and she hopes to discover a cure for gonorrhea, which she feels has been unjustly "fastened on mankind as a penalty for enjoying love." But the First World War intervenes, and she dies heroically on a battlefield in France while attending to the wounded American lieutenant with whom she has fallen in love.

Scholars have identified the period in which *A Scarlet Pansy* takes place as a particularly momentous one in the history of sexuality. Modern forms of sexual personhood emerged and steadily gained visibility. Fairies, transgender men who adopted a flamboyant, "tough girl" style of femininity and who engaged in sexual relations with conventionally masculine men, became fixtures in many urban working-class and immigrant neighborhoods.[2] The sensationalistic newspaper coverage of the 1892 trial and conviction of the middle-class transgender Alice Mitchell, who murdered her girlfriend Freda Ward when she refused to elope with her and yielded to family pressure by becoming engaged to a man, worked to conflate female same-sex desire, masculinity, and cross-dressing in the public imagination.³ In the wake of British writer Oscar Wilde's trial and conviction for gross indecency in 1895, similar scandals involving middle-class men in the United States encouraged the American public to view homosexuality as a distinct form of personhood linked to vice and corruption.⁴ At the same time, commercialized entertainment began to exploit the new forms of gender and sexual expression.⁵ Vaudeville, Broadway, and a nascent movie industry exposed mainstream audiences to the vibrant queer culture that was beginning to take shape in New York and other cosmopolitan centers by incorporating camp humor and other queer vernacular forms, albeit in ways that tended to reinforce negative stereotypes.

The period also saw the rise of a new science, sexology, that attempted to analyze, categorize, and regulate the new sexual identities.⁶ Sexologists regarded same-sex desire as a symptom of an inverted gender identity, and they made a distinction between congenital and acquired forms of sexual inversion. They viewed the congenital male invert as a woman trapped in a man's body and believed that his inversion could be read on his body—in his narrow shoulders, large hips, small or "under-developed" penis and testicles, and high-pitched falsetto voice. Ironically, the new science's biological determinism worked to normalize same-sex desire. Because the "true" male invert was attracted to "normal" men, his desire did not threaten to destabilize the binary organization of gender identities and roles but reinforced them. In the words of Richard von Kraft-Ebbing, the author of one of the key texts of sexology—*Psychopathia Sexualis*, published in German in 1886 and translated into English in 1892, the same year as the Alice Mitchell trial—male inverts were "nature's step-children," and although they should be prevented from reproducing, lest they pass their pathological "condition" on to their offspring, they deserved society's sympathy and understanding. Unlike the man who had acquired his inversion through loose morals and debauchery, the true male invert was born "sick" and could not control his "nature." Many sexologists advocated legal reform to protect inverts from blackmailers who entrapped and threatened to expose them. Most sexologists did not accept the view espoused by their more progressive colleagues that inversion constituted a harmless variation, but they agreed that congenital inverts needed treatment, not imprisonment.

Although sexological categories filtered into mainstream American society fairly rapidly and informed how even ordinary Americans made sense of their sexual desires, Fay and the other characters in *A Scarlet Pansy* have somehow managed to escape their pathologizing influence. They inhabit a world of polymorphous sexuality not yet affected by the new regulatory apparatus. Fay engages in sexual relations with cops, boxers, baseball players, sailors, and other stereotypically "virile" men, none of whom experiences his desire for her as a contradiction of his manliness or worries that their sexual relations will indelibly mark him as "abnormal." Indeed, in the world of the novel the understanding of homosexuality and heterosexuality as mutually exclusive forms of desire has not yet become dominant. Moreover, in making sense of their identities, Fay and the other characters draw on the categories developed by the sexual underworld rather than sexology: categories like "queen," "fairy," "pansy," "dike," "bulldiker," and "rough trade." These categories acknowledged a greater range of gender and sexual variance than those propounded by sexology and provided a much more useful taxonomy for negotiating the queer *demimonde*. Not surprisingly, when Fay encounters sexology during her medical training, the novel deflates the new scientific discourse's rapidly expanding authority to regulate sexuality by subjecting it to a campy send-up. Fay attends a lecture on "aberrant types" in which the professor illustrates his discussion of the male invert by clownishly imitating his effeminate behavior. But rather than convincing the students of the pathological effects of congenital sexual inversion, the professor succeeds only in arousing their desire, and once the lecture is over, they eagerly set off to begin their own "research" into deviant sexual practices: "When he had finished he had so enthused his entire class that they were ready to go downtown and start a laboratory course at once."

How do we explain this depiction of late-nineteenth- and early-twentieth-century queer life, a depiction that minimized the onset of the new system of sexual classification? By the time *A Scarlet Pansy* was published, the new mode of sexual regulation was more firmly entrenched in American society than it had been at the turn of the twentieth century, a development that reflected a backlash against the social and sexual experimentation of the Jazz Age precipitated by the Great Depression.[7] In the 1930s, social reformers blamed the collapse of the economy on the "excesses" of Prohibition-era urban nightlife, which encouraged "respectable" middle-class Americans to mingle with African Americans, working-class immigrants, and queers. Reformers were especially troubled by the "pansy craze," the popularity of male and female impersonators who titillated audiences in speakeasies, cafés, and nightclubs with their campy banter and flamboyant mannerisms. They believed that this common form of entertainment would further erode traditional gender roles and identities, already strained by the Depression, and they successfully pressured authorities to ban it in New York and elsewhere.[8] But despite their fears, "pansy" acts and humor often served to reinforce the boundary between homosexuality and heterosexuality by delineating more clearly the differences between queers and "normal" Americans.[9] Thus in the 1930s the regulatory divide between homosexuals and heterosexuals deepened with the result that "normal" men could no longer engage in sexual relations with queers without precipitating a definitional crisis that threatened to locate them on the "wrong" side of the divide. In setting *A Scarlet Pansy* at the turn of the twentieth century, its author, Robert Scully, indirectly challenged the consolidation of the new system of sexual classification. His representation of a milieu that no longer existed reminded readers not only that homosexual and heterosexual identities were recent inventions but also that their construction as mutually exclusive had resulted in a tremendous loss of sexual freedom.

Camping It Up: *A Scarlet Pansy*'s Queering of Gender and Sexual Identities

Although its title may have attracted readers curious about "pansies," *A Scarlet Pansy* did not assume that its readers were "normal" but rather positioned them as sympathetic participants in queer life. It was one of a spate of novels published in the early 1930s that explored the new constructions of homosexual identity.[10] Most of these novels were, like *A Scarlet Pansy*, written by unknown authors and published by obscure presses, which probably explains how they avoided censorship despite the Depression-era crackdown on queer culture. They included *Twilight Men* (1931), *Goldie* (1933), and *Butter-*

fly Man (1934), all three of which, unlike Scully's novel, exploited the pansy craze by providing readers with sensationalistic accounts of queer life. They enabled readers to experience the thrill of slumming without leaving the comfort of their own homes and reassured them of their sexual normality by situating them as titillated but detached onlookers of the sexual underworld. Although the protagonists of both *Goldie* and *Butterfly Man* start out as wholesome, middle-class young men who become morally corrupt only after their initiation into the queer *demimonde*, Armand, the protagonist of *Twilight Men*, is an effeminate upper-class youth whose artistic temperament already marks him as queer and foreshadows his sexual depravity later in the novel. Thus *Twilight Men* differed from *Goldie* and *Butterfly Man* in incorporating an older discourse of homosexuality that emerged in the wake of the Oscar Wilde trial and that associated homosexuality with decadence, effeminacy, and an aristocratic background. Despite this difference, however, all three novels tell basically the same story about Depression-era queer life. They equate homosexuality with an inverted gender identity and portray their protagonists as social outcasts doomed to lead lives of loneliness and despair. Unable to escape the *demimonde* and ashamed of their "deviant" desires, the protagonists begin to spiral downward. They are drawn into sordid and degrading relationships and eventually succumb to alcoholism and drug addiction and end up committing suicide or murder.

Inspired by Radclyffe Hall's *The Well of Loneliness* (1928), other novels about queer life published during the Depression sought to recruit readers for a progressive social agenda that included greater tolerance of the "third sex." For example, *Strange Brother* (1931) by "Blair Niles," a pseudonym for the popular travel writer Mary Blair Rice, focuses on the protagonist Mark Thornton's loneliness and despair and shows how unjust laws render him and other homosexuals who pass as "normal" vulnerable to blackmail.[11] *Strange Brother* was the only 1930s queer novel published by a major press, Horace Liveright, and reviewed by the mainstream press.[12] Its reform-minded approach to homosexuality would become much more common in queer fiction published later in the twentieth century. Although Mark has internalized the new sexual categories, his experience departs significantly from the sexological script adopted by Hall, whose heroine, Stephen Gordon, sees herself as a man trapped in a woman's body and therefore feels she deserves access to patriarchal privilege.[13] Mark struggles to construct an identity different from that of the flamboyant working-class fairies he encounters in New York's bohemian milieu, and he seeks moral legitimacy in a tradition of supposedly homosexual writers that includes Walt Whitman, William Shakespeare, and Edward Carpenter. Inspired by this tradition, he longs for a "manly comradeship" like the one exalted by Whitman in his Calamus poems—a relationship, in other words, that affirms rather than undermines his masculinity and therefore does not mark him as different from other men of his race and class. When he fails to establish such a relationship, he becomes despondent and like so many of the protagonists in 1930s queer novels ends up committing suicide. Thus in sharp contrast to the spectacles of depravity and dissipation in novels inspired by the pansy craze, *Strange Brother* treats queer life as the stuff of melodrama in a bid for the reader's sympathy.

A Scarlet Pansy's significantly different approach to representing queer life becomes clear in an early scene that satirizes middle-class slummers and in so doing prevents readers from approaching the novel as a slumming narrative inspired by the pansy craze. Fay's brother, Bill, who has moved to New York and with Fay's help obtained a position at the bank where she works as an assistant to the president, persuades her to accompany him and some friends on a slumming expedition to the city's red-light districts. First the group visits an "old place of disrepute" in Greenwich Village frequented by fairies, then a "hop-joint" in Chinatown, where everyone except Fay smokes opium, then a Lower East Side neighborhood so Bill can watch "the Jews overflowing the sidewalks," and finally another "fairy joint." Fay derives no pleasure from the party but remains a discomfited onlooker throughout, unable to comprehend the others' amusement and excitement. Narrated from her point of view, the scene compels readers to identify with her reaction. The scenes of the sexual underworld later in the novel once Fay has come out into queer life similarly discourage readers from adopting a voyeuristic point of view. By turns elliptical, campy, satirical, and allusive, they work to initiate readers into the queer world. Readers must fill in the blanks, translate queer argot, understand double entendres, appreciate camp humor, and decipher references to forgotten figures of the queer past such as Bert Savoy, whose "flaming" performance style deeply influenced early-twentieth-century queer culture; in short, they must possess an insider's knowledge of the queer world to make sense of what they are reading.

A Scarlet Pansy also differs from the novels discussed above in celebrating rather than condemning the outlaw sexual culture invented by queer men and women. Until her chaste romance with Lieutenant Frank at the end of the novel, Fay remains proudly a "oncer," a sexually promiscuous queen who avoids engaging in sexual relations with the same man more than once. Her only addiction is to cruising New York's streets and parks with her close friend and colleague Mason Linberg. She brazenly picks up cops on the beat, sailors on leave, and workers on their lunch breaks. Guided by the more experienced Henri Voyeur, who oversees her queer apprenticeship, Fay learns to accept her vagrant sexual desire instead of channeling it toward romance. Challenging the anti-homosexual discourse that permeated *Twilight Men*'s depiction of its protagonist, Fay's relationship with Henri restages Dorian Gray's relationship with Lord Henry Wotton in Wilde's scandalous novel *The Picture of Dorian Gray* (1892). But whereas Lord Henry embarks his youthful protégé on a life of sexual depravity that leads to his moral ruin, Henri Voyeur instructs Fay in how to achieve a rich and rewarding life. Indeed, unlike Dorian, whose corruption manifests itself in his ravaged looks at his death, Fay never ages or loses her attractiveness but dies, as the narrator campily informs us at the end of the novel, "at the height of her beauty—thirty-three years of age and looking ten years younger, as so many of her kind do for some queer reason." Fay's career as a physician and her desire to be useful to others further challenge the anti-homosexual discourse inaugurated by the Wilde trial. Fay not only successfully completes her medical training but also treats poor immigrant women on the Lower East Side, and when war breaks out, she volunteers for the Red Cross. Before she dies, she wills her fortune to Mason and instructs him to adopt two orphans, a boy and a girl, so that they can receive all of the advantages they would otherwise lack, and to tell them about their benefactor when they are grown, "the good if there is any, and all the bad, for I want no fictitious sainthood."

In fully embracing queer life, *A Scarlet Pansy* anticipated the better-known and widely admired modernist novel *The Young and Evil*, co-written by Charles Henri Ford and Parker Tyler. Published in Paris in 1933 in a limited edition,

Recovering *A Scarlet Pansy*: An Introduction

The Young and Evil was, unlike Scully's novel, banned in the United States, most likely because its publisher, Obelisk Press, had gained a reputation for publishing "dirty books."[14] Several scholars have identified *The Young and Evil* as the first American novel about queer life that took for granted its characters' homosexuality and refused to judge them, but this claim overlooks *A Scarlet Pansy*, published one year earlier. Like Scully's novel, *The Young and Evil* celebrates the sexual freedom of New York's bohemian milieu and attempts to dissolve the rapidly solidifying opposition between heterosexuality and homosexuality. Critics have justly praised the novel's experimental form, in particular Ford and Tyler's use of modernist techniques like stream-of-consciousness narration that work to compel the reader's identification with its queer characters.[15] It centers on two queer friends, Karel and Julian, who settle in Greenwich Village at the start of the Depression to pursue their literary ambitions. Like Fay, they inhabit a world seemingly unaffected by the new regime of sexual regulation, and their relationships with other men recall hers insofar as they resist categorization as either homosexual or heterosexual. The two novels also resemble each other in emphasizing the inventiveness of queer culture. New York's creative bohemian milieu enables Karel and Julian to make an art of their gender and sexual difference, and like Fay they participate in a fully elaborated queer culture, one with its own distinct modes of expression, types of humor, and sexual taxonomies.

Although Scully avoided the modernist techniques adopted by Ford and Tyler, he too experimented with the novel form. Fay's sexual awakening manifests itself in the novel's shifting style. Following her initiation into the queer *demimonde*, the stilted, old-fashioned language of the opening chapters gives way to the campier, more modern language of the later ones. Scully also rejected the narrative strategies of novels like *The Well of Loneliness* and *Strange Brother*, which had exposed the limitations of literary realism for portraying queer life, and opted instead for an episodic, loosely plotted narrative that lacked psychologically complex characters and was written in a style that paid tribute to queer vernacular forms. Its relatively open-ended and repetitive narrative was better suited to representing the waywardness of queer desire, its resistance to containment in the couple form. Unlike Scully, neither Hall nor Niles could imagine their queer characters' leading fulfilling lives without entering into marriage-like relationships. Their novels laid claim to the romance plot central to the realist tradition of novel writing to reinforce their pleas for greater acceptance of lesbians and homosexuals. In *The Well of Loneliness*, Stephen abandons her youthful lover Mary so that she can lead a conventional woman's life, married to Martin Hallam, a sacrifice that leaves her bitter about her fate as one of "nature's stepchildren." In *Strange Brother*, Mark falls tragically in love with the brawny Phil Crane, a naturalist, who does not reciprocate his feelings and who midway through the novel marries and embarks on an expedition to South America with his new wife, abandoning Mark to his unhappy fate. Thus in these novels queer men and women seem inevitably drawn to others whose sexual normality places them out of reach, and their desire emerges as incapable of fulfillment. When *A Scarlet Pansy* turns to the question of homosexual romance in its last few pages, it does so to parody and overturn the romantic conventions starting to coalesce in queer fiction. Fay's fate rewrites the tragic love stories in both *The Well of Loneliness* and *Strange Brother*. Although she falls in love with a conventionally masculine man, he returns her love, and she dies totally fulfilled, having discovered her "ideal," ironically in a chaste romance that requires her to sacrifice her life.

Scully may have drawn much of his account of the sexual underworld from *Autobiography of an Androgyne*, published in 1919 by a scientific press, intended for physicians, lawyers, and other professionals and available only by mail order.[16] A memoir of the pseudonymous Ralph Werther's life as a fairy, *Autobiography* offered vivid descriptions of the late-nineteenth- and early-twentieth-century *demimonde* rich in detail about queer gathering places and cruising spots. It also included explicit passages about Werther's sexual experiences discreetly written in Latin. Like Fay, Werther takes full advantage of the sexual freedom of the underworld and engages in sexual relations only with soldiers, policemen, and other "virile" types of men. He also retains his youthful good looks, despite his sexually profligate life. But the differences between *A Scarlet Pansy* and *Autobiography of an Androgyne* are striking, and Scully's novel can be read as a kind of retort to Werther's memoir. Unlike Fay, who openly expresses her gender and sexual difference, the middle-class, college-educated Werther leads a double life, carefully concealing his homosexuality from his "every-day circle."[17] He passes as a working-class fairy named Jennie June, and in what amounts to a form of slumming he undertakes nocturnal "rambles" in New York's working-class and immigrant neighborhoods in search of sex with "rough trade." Moreover, an avid reader of sexology, he has internalized the new sexual categories and informs his readers in the opening pages that he "is really a woman whom Nature has disguised as a man" (25). His elaboration of his transgender identity inadvertently exposes the misogynistic assumptions informing the new science. He claims to possess a female brain that has stunted his development: "If my business associates tell the truth, I am still a child nearly half a century old" (102). He portrays himself as vain, passive, dependent, and helpless—a powerless victim whose sexual encounters often end in brutal beatings and gang rape. His emphasis on the violence he and other fairies endure serves to reinforce his arguments for legal and other reforms, but it suggested that queer life was full of danger and hardship.

A Scarlet Pansy offered a much more complicated understanding of gender identity, one that indirectly challenged sexology's dichotomous construction of masculinity and femininity. In marked contrast to *Autobiography of an Androgyne*, its elaboration of queer identity destabilizes rather than reinforces gender binaries. Despite Fay's feminine gender presentation, we learn in the opening pages of the novel that "at sixteen she could pitch as much hay as her father, could plough more land in a day, could lift heavier burdens." Later in Baltimore where she works hauling coal, she easily keeps pace with the other laborers "and never guessed that they were trying to tax her staying powers." When Mr. Fisher seduces her in a Baltimore park, he clasps her "sturdy, muscular, hard-worked brown hand" in his "effeminately white, soft, weak" one, which suggests that at least outwardly Fay is more manly than he is. Her sexual encounters once she has come out further blur the boundaries between masculinity and femininity. She disarms her lovers' masculinity by remaining firmly in control of her relationships with them. Despite their virility, her lovers willingly comply with her desires and become her playthings: "Men were forever wishing to give her this, that, and the other thing." Some of her lovers even want to belong to her permanently. When she seduces a "strong and virile" cowboy on her "grand cruise" through the American West with Henri, he tells her, "I wish it was possible for us to marry. God! Wouldn't that be great?" Thus Fay defies classification as either masculine or feminine.[18] The scene in which she and Mason disembark for Europe, where they intend to pursue their medical training, underscores her gender ambiguity. The novel abruptly shifts point of view from Fay and her companions who are on board ship boisterously celebrating the marriage of convenience between Mason and the lesbian heiress Marjorie Dike to two bystanders on the pier observing them. When one of the bystanders wonders aloud who Fay and the others are, her companion has no difficulty pointing out Mason and Marjorie, but when she notices Fay, she is baffled and asks for a pair of binoculars so she can look at her more closely: "See that queer-looking woman in the mannish clothes and the very handsome young man and well, I don't know what the other one is, whether it's a man or a woman. Let me have your glasses a moment."

Despite its complicated understanding of gender identity, *A Scarlet Pansy* never acknowledges the extent to which Fay's experience as a fairy has been shaped by her racial identity, and at times it reproduces racial and ethnic stereotypes uncritically. In one particularly egregious passage, Fay rejects a Chinese vendor's sexual advances while visiting San Francisco's Chinatown because she fears she might contract leprosy from him, a reaction that reiterates the identification of Chinese immigrants with pestilence and contagion common in late-nineteenth- and early-twentieth-century American society.[19] In another passage, she makes a spectacle of racial difference by entertaining a roomful of prurient German aristocrats with her imitation of a "Negro girl nursing her half-white child." As its satirical depiction of white middle-class slumming discussed above shows, the novel could be quite scathing about Anglo-Americans' stereotypical views of racial and ethnic difference, but these two passages expose Fay's racial privilege without commenting on it critically.

Although *A Scarlet Pansy* indirectly challenged the sexological construction of same-sex desire, Samuel Roth, its publisher, promoted it by promising readers, "What THE WELL OF LONELINESS did for the man-woman, this most unusual tale does for the woman-man—only that the latter is a so much more wayward and more fascinating creature."[20] Such a claim suggests that Roth was more interested in capitalizing on the novel's focus on an illicit subject than on its critique of the new regime of sexual regulation. Roth had acquired a notorious reputation as a "booklegger" for publishing "sex pulps" and other forms of erotica, and he was imprisoned several times in

Recovering *A Scarlet Pansy*: An Introduction

the 1920s and 1930s for distributing allegedly "obscene" materials. But the renegade publisher also played an important role in the dissemination of the work of transatlantic modernist writers. He shared the frustration of Ezra Pound and other modernist writers with obscenity laws in Great Britain and the United States that constrained literary expression by preventing writers from portraying modern life realistically. He admired modernist literature for its potential to unsettle social and sexual complacencies, and he wanted to make it available to ordinary readers unable to afford privately published limited editions sold through subscription, a common mode of distribution for modernist literature, and he controversially reprinted experimental work that was in the public domain and thus lacked copyright protection.[21]

But Roth also sought to profit financially from the growing celebrity of "scandalous" writers like James Joyce and D. H. Lawrence, and when he published unauthorized and expurgated versions of Joyce's *Ulysses* and "Work in Progress" (fragments of what later became *Finnegans Wake*) in his magazines *Two Worlds* and *Two Worlds Monthly* in the mid-1920s, he became the target of an international campaign of writers and artists to ostracize him as an unscrupulous "literary pirate" who had violated the norm of "trade courtesy" that informally regulated the reprinting of literature that had not been copyrighted.[22] Despite the success of this campaign, however, Roth continued to publish work under obscure imprints like William Faro that pushed the boundaries of social and sexual propriety by blending modernist experimentation with a mildly salacious appeal. Thus his publication of *A Scarlet Pansy* reflected more than opportunism—a desire to capitalize on the public's voyeuristic interest in the queer *demimonde*. The novel conformed to his modernist project as both a publisher and a bookseller deeply committed to sexual freedom. It not only combined formal experimentation with an exploration of "taboo" sexual behavior but did so in a way that had the potential to unsettle stultifying moral and social codes. Given his values and commitments, it is hardly surprising that in 1939 shortly after serving a prison sentence for distributing obscene materials, Roth published an abridged and expurgated version of the novel titled *The Scarlet Pansy* under his newly created Royal imprint. The new version eliminated many of the original's vivid descriptions of the sexual underworld and added passages, most likely written by Roth himself, that linked Fay's bohemian coming-of-age to a nascent modernism by referencing George Moore's novels and James Huneker's musical criticism, which championed composers such as Richard Strauss and Claude Debussy. Reprinted several times in the 1940s and 1950s, this is the version of the novel that most readers have encountered.

Life's a Drag, Dearie: Reclaiming Bert Savoy's Queer Legacy

Although we know a great deal about *A Scarlet Pansy*'s controversial publisher and can reconstruct its literary and historical contexts, we know almost nothing about its author, whose identity remains a mystery. Roth's daughter, Adelaide Kugel, recalls that he was a physician "who dared not use his name to write about 'the love that dare not' in 1932 without losing some of his practice."[23] Despite her recollection, however, the contract for *A Scarlet Pansy* does not indicate that the author had adopted a pseudonym, whereas other contracts issued by her father for the Faro imprint in the early 1930s make clear when the authors had done so. The contract also listed the author's address as a post office box in Charlottesville, Virginia.[24] Combing through the American Medical Association's membership records, Roth's biographer, Jay A. Gertzman, has discovered a physician named Robert Emmet Scully who came of age in the period during which the novel is set and who had a connection to Charlottesville. Born in New Jersey, he attended the University of Virginia School of Medicine, was commissioned into the Navy's Medical Reserve Force in 1921, and eventually worked as a doctor in veterans' hospitals in Newark and Somerset Hills, New Jersey.[25] If in following the lead provided by Roth's daughter Gertzman has correctly identified the Robert Scully who wrote *A Scarlet Pansy*, it would explain the novel's reworking of *Autobiography of an Androgyne*, which the author may have encountered during his medical training, as well as his choice of profession for Fay and the detailed scientific knowledge displayed by the narrator.

The lack of definitive information about the author has led some scholars to speculate that "Robert Scully" was a pseudonym for the expatriate writer and publisher Robert McAlmon. The founder of Contact Editions Press, which published the work of Ernest Hemingway, Gertrude Stein, and Djuna

Barnes in the 1920s, McAlmon is perhaps most remembered today for his scathing portrait of the "lost generation" of writers in his memoir, *Being Geniuses Together*, which James Joyce acerbically called "the office boy's revenge."[26] But McAlmon also wrote a short-story collection, *Distinguished Air*, published in a limited edition in 1925, in which he explored expatriate queer life in an economically depressed Berlin following the First World War.[27] One of these stories, "Miss Knight," resembles *A Scarlet Pansy* in its incorporation of camp speech and other aspects of queer culture. It focuses on a working-class fairy down on his luck in Berlin, to whom the narrator sometimes refers as "she" and who like Fay cruises for "rough trade." The story emphasizes Miss Knight's resilience in the face of economic hardship and social isolation. A former chorus boy, he has copied his camp style from Bert Savoy.[28] Like the female impersonator, he wears a red bobbed wig when appearing in drag, and he repeats some of Savoy's trademark expressions, such as "Whoops, my dear" and "You must come over."[29] He also entertains the patrons of Berlin's queer bars and cafés by engaging in loud, vulgar repartee reminiscent of Savoy's. In this respect, he differs from Fay, whose camping has a subtlety and finesse that his lacks. When having exhausted his "repertoire of humor"[30] Miss Knight suddenly disappears from Berlin, the other characters speculate that he has committed suicide, but he turns up several weeks later in New York planning his return to Europe, thereby thwarting the expectations of readers trained by homophobic discourse to associate homosexuality with suicide and murder.

McAlmon's contributions to a queer tradition of modernist writing deserve much more scholarly attention than they have received, but it seems highly unlikely that the underappreciated writer was the author of *A Scarlet Pansy*.[31] His treatment of the queer world contrasts markedly with Scully's.[32] In *Being Geniuses Together*, he boasted that unlike Djuna Barnes, the author of the experimental novel *Nightwood* (1936), he treated his sexually variant characters "with complete objectivity, not intent on their 'souls,' and not distressed by their 'morals.'"[33] Although this narrative strategy hindered readers from deriving voyeuristic pleasure from the short stories, it also encouraged them to maintain an emotional distance from the queer characters.[34] Both "Distinguished Air" and "It's All Very Complicated," which was published the same year as *A Scarlet Pansy*, are narrated by male characters who do not identify as queer, which only reinforces this distancing effect; and despite his use of an omniscient narrator in "The Lodging House," McAlmon filters the story's action through the consciousness of its straight male protagonist, Harold Files, thereby positioning the reader as a sympathetic but removed onlooker of queer life. The stories also tend, perhaps inadvertently, to reinforce the identification of homosexuality and lesbianism with decadence by portraying queer life as sordid, desperate, and unfulfilled. McAlmon subtitled *Distinguished Air* "Grim Fairy Tales," which indicates his view of the queer characters. All of the characters in the stories belong to the lost generation of American youth, disillusioned by war and alienated from society, but the homosexuals and lesbians appear more forsaken than the heterosexuals who have the option of returning to a "normal" life. The ending of "Distinguished Air" highlights this difference. After spending a night slumming in Berlin's seedy queer bars and cafés, where they encounter cocaine-addled homosexuals and lesbians who fight raucously with each other and make unwelcome passes at them, the narrator and his companion Rudge Kepler, a cartoonist visiting from New York, vow, "No more nights like this—at least until the next time. It was really too depressing to see so much of a kind of life that one had not consciously helped to cause, and could not do much to alter."[35]

McAlmon's short stories also differ from *A Scarlet Pansy* in that they make no attempt to queer or destabilize the binary construction of gender and sexual identities. The contrast between Miss Knight and Miss Savoy, the character in *A Scarlet Pansy* based on Bert Savoy, throws this difference between the two authors into sharp relief. Whereas Miss Knight enables McAlmon to document camp and other queer practices, Miss Savoy functions in the context of *A Scarlet Pansy* to foreground the performative aspects of gender and sexual identities. Bert Savoy was openly homosexual, and his performances transformed how audiences understood female impersonation, which increasingly became associated with queer culture. Female impersonators like Julian Eltinge dazzled audiences with their ability to cross the supposedly immutable boundary between the sexes by magically transforming themselves into counterfeit women.[36] As a result, their performances served to reassure audiences of the differences between the sexes. By contrast, Savoy made no attempt to mimic a "real" woman. Unlike Eltinge, he did not engage in painful depilation or attempt to disguise his masculine bulk in fashionable feminine apparel but instead magnified it.[37] The critic Edmund Wilson famously described him as "a gigantic red-haired harlot, swaying her enormous hat, reeking with corrosive cocktails of the West Fifties."[38] Moreover, he communicated his homosexuality to audiences by introducing camp humor into his performances. Scully's portrayal of Miss Savoy emphasizes the impersonator's influence on queer culture, his creation of a widely imitated gender style that functioned as a signifier of homosexuality. Fay learns from Miss Savoy how to perform her sexual identity, how to communicate it to others through her gender style. She increasingly imitates Miss Savoy, repeating phrases like, "You don't know the half of it, dearie," made famous by the impersonator, and following her advice when cruising for trade. Thus Fay's femininity does not represent an expression of her "true" self but rather a performance designed to attract men willing to engage in sexual relations with fairies.

Because of the consolidation of modern gender and sexual identities, *A Scarlet Pansy*'s representation of the queer past may have unsettled post-Stonewall gay readers. In focusing on a fairy protagonist, the novel exposed the shared genealogy of the categories "homosexual" and "transgender," an aspect of the history of sexuality that is often repressed or disavowed because it threatens the normalization of contemporary gay male identities. Indeed, when Masquerade Books published an edition of the novel in 1992 under its BADBOY imprint, which like the Royal edition was titled *The Scarlet Pansy*, it attempted to erase this shared genealogy by masculinizing Fay's identity and adding several sexually explicit scenes. Fay became Randy, a change that shifted the novel's focus from gender difference to sexual pleasure and thereby aligned it with contemporary gay men's values and aspirations.[39] In breathing new life into the medical model of homosexuality, the AIDS crisis had intensified a desire long held by many gay men for assimilation into mainstream American society. Unlike the story of a "randy" gay male protagonist who comes of age in a world virtually unregulated by the hetero/homosexual binary, the story of the flamboyantly transgender Fay threatened to reinforce painful stereotypes that gay men in the 1990s sought to distance themselves from as they struggled for political and social equality in the face of the crisis. Such stereotypes opened old wounds by recalling the persistent association of homosexuality with gender deviance, an identification that many gay men were ashamed of and wanted to overcome. But in re-fashioning Fay's identity so it projected a more acceptable image of gay life, the BADBOY edition drained *A Scarlet Pansy* of both its transgender content and its radical conception of gender and sexual identities. These are the very aspects of the novel that will resonate most with today's readers. Ironically, in turning to the queer past, Scully's novel anticipated the queer future. Its treatment of queer life before the emergence of sexual categories and forms of personhood we now take for granted disarticulated gender identity from biological sex and erotic desire. In the wake of queer theory's transformation of our understanding of gender and sexuality, this truly remarkable novel may finally receive its due.

Notes

1. See Roger Austen, *Playing the Game: The Homosexual Novel in America* (Indianapolis: Bobbs-Merrill, 1977), 63–64; Byrne R.S. Fone, *A Road to Stonewall, 1750–1969: Male Homosexuality and Homophobia in English and American Literature* (New York: Twayne, 1995), 226–31; Jay A. Gertzman, "A Scarlet Pansy Goes to War: Subversion, Schlock, and an Early Gay Classic," *The Journal of American Culture* 33 (September 2010): 230–39; and Hugh Hagius, "The Mystery of *A Scarlet Pansy*: An Underground Gay Novel of the Lost Generation," typescript, 1982. Austen bases his discussion of the novel on the Royal edition, not the Faro edition.

2. For a detailed discussion of the figure of the fairy, see George Chauncey, *Gay New York: Gender, Urban Culture, and the Making of the Gay Male World, 1890–1940* (New York: Basic Books, 1994), 47–63. See also David K. Johnson, "The Kids of Fairytown: Gay Male Culture on Chicago's Near North Side in the 1930s," in *Creating a Place for Ourselves: Lesbian, Gay, and Bisexual Community Histories*, ed. Brett Beemyn (New York: Routledge, 1997), 97–118.

3. For more on the Alice Mitchell trial and its impact on popular conceptions of lesbian identity, see Lisa Duggan, "The Trials of Alice Mitchell: Sensationalism, Sexology, and the Lesbian Subject in Turn of the Century America," in *Queer Studies: An Interdisciplinary Reader*, ed. Robert J. Corber and Stephen Valocchi (Malden, Mass.: Blackwell, 2003), 73–87.

RECOVERING *A SCARLET PANSY*: AN INTRODUCTION

4. For a discussion of one such scandal, see John Howard, "The Talk of the County: Revisiting Accusation, Murder, and Mississippi, 1895," in Corber and Valocchi, *Queer Studies*, 142–58.

5. For more on this aspect of Progressive-era American culture, see Estelle Freedman and John D'Emilio, *Intimate Matters: A History of Sexuality in America* (Chicago: University of Chicago Press, 1995), 202–38; Chauncey, *Gay New York*, 301–30; Chad Heap, *Slumming: Sexual and Racial Encounters in American Nightlife, 1885–1940* (Chicago: University of Chicago Press, 2009), 231–76; and Kevin J. Mumford, *Interzones: Black/White Sex Districts in Chicago and New York in the Early Twentieth Century* (New York: Columbia University Press, 1997). See also Sharon R. Ullman, *Sex Seen: The Emergence of Modern Sexuality in America* (Berkeley: University of California Press, 1998), 45–71; and Laurence Senelick, *The Changing Room: Sex, Drag, and Theater* (New York: Routledge, 2000), 293–373.

6. For a detailed discussion of sexology, see Lucy Bland and Laura Doan, eds., *Sexology in Culture: Labeling Bodies and Desires* (Chicago: University of Chicago Press, 1998). See also George Chauncey, "From Sexual Inversion to Homosexuality: The Changing Conceptualization of Female 'Deviance,'" in *Passion and Power: Sexuality in History*, ed. Kathy Peiss and Christina Simmons (Philadelphia: Temple University Press, 1989), 87–117.

7. For more on this aspect of the Great Depression, see Chauncey, *Gay New York*, 301–54; Jennifer Terry, *An American Obsession: Science, Medicine, and Homosexuality in Modern Society* (Chicago: University of Chicago Press, 1999), 268–96; and Margot Canaday, *The Straight State: Sexuality and Citizenship in Twentieth-Century America* (Princeton, N.J.: Princeton University Press, 2009), 91–134.

8. For important discussions of the pansy craze, see Chauncey, *Gay New York*, 301–30; and Heap, *Slumming*, 231–76.

9. Heap, *Slumming*, 231–76.

10. For a more detailed discussion of these novels, see Austen, *Playing the Game*, 62–74; and Anthony Slide, *Lost Gay Novels: A Reference Guide to Fifty Works from the First Half of the Twentieth Century* (New York: Harrington Press, 2003). See also Christopher Looby, "The Gay Novel in the United States, 1900–1950," in *A Companion to the Modern American Novel 1900–1950*, ed. John T. Matthews (Malden, Mass.: Wiley-Blackwell, 2013), 414–36.

11. I should perhaps also include here the renowned puppeteer Forman Brown's fictionalized autobiography, *Better Angel* (1933), which he

published under the pseudonym Richard Meeker. Like Mark Thornton, *Better Angel*'s protagonist, Kurt Gray, feels as if he has been inducted into a "secret fraternity" when he discovers Walt Whitman, Edward Carpenter, and other supposedly homosexual writers and seeks moral legitimacy in their writings. But Brown's treatment of queer life differs significantly from that of Niles in that unlike her he can imagine a liveable life for his queer characters who are happily coupled at the end of his novel.

12. In publishing a novel that made a plea for greater tolerance of homosexuality, Liveright may have been emboldened by the decision of the New York Court of Special Sessions in 1929 that overturned the ban on *The Well of Loneliness* and allowed its publication in the United States.

13. Hall's novel famously included a "Commentary" by the sexologist Havelock Ellis that testified to the authenticity of its treatment of sexual inversion. For a detailed discussion of Hall's use of sexology in her portrayal of the heroine, Stephen Gordon, see the essays in *Palatable Poison: Critical Perspectives on "The Well of Loneliness,"* ed. Laura Doan and Jay Prosser (New York: Columbia University Press, 2001), 129–96. Hall's novel did not include any explicit discussion of Stephen Gordon's sexual desire, but it made a plea for greater tolerance of the "third sex," which probably explains why it was initially banned in the United States. For an excellent discussion of the censorship of the novel, see Adam Parkes, *Modernism and the Theater of Censorship* (New York: Oxford University Press, 1996), 144–77.

14. Interestingly, Horace Liveright, the publisher of *Strange Brother*, rejected *The Young and Evil* because he worried that its approach to queer life might lead to his prosecution for publishing obscene material.

15. See Joseph Allen Boone, *Libidinal Currents: Sexuality and the Shaping of Modernism* (Chicago: University of Chicago Press, 1998), 251–65; Looby, "The Gay Novel in the United States," 430–33; and Austen, *Playing the Game*, 59–62. For a detailed discussion of the novel's genesis, see Steven Watson, Introduction to *The Young and Evil*, by Charles Henri Ford and Parker Tyler (New York: Gay Press of New York, 1988), vii–xxxvii.

16. Several scholars have pointed to the similarities between the two texts. See in particular Austen, *Playing the Game*, 63; and Fone, *A Road to Stonewall*, 227.

17. Ralph Werther, *Autobiography of an Androgyne*, ed. Scott Herring (New Brunswick, N.J.: Rutgers University Press, 2008), 105. Hereafter all references are to this edition and are cited in parentheses in the text.

18. In one of the few scholarly discussions of the novel, Fone suggests that it never reveals the "truth" of Fay's sex, but this overlooks several scenes in the novel that clearly identify her as biologically male. See Fone, *A Road to Stonewall*, 226–31.

19. For a detailed discussion of this conflation in late-nineteenth and early-twentieth-century American society, see Nayan Shah, "Perversity, Contamination, and the Dangers of Queer Domesticity," in Corber and Valocchi, *Queer Studies*, 121–40.

20. Quoted in Jay Gertzman, *Samuel Roth: Infamous Modernist* (Gainesville: University Press of Florida, 2013), 119. Publishers frequently cited *The Well of Loneliness* in their advertisements for queer novels. For example, an advertisement for *Goldie* proclaimed, "Not since *The Well of Loneliness* has the delicate theme of sexual inversion been handled so artistically." Quoted in Austen, *Playing the Game*, 69.

21. On this aspect of literary modernism, see especially Lawrence Rainey, *Institutions of Modernism: Literary Elites and Public Culture* (New Haven, Conn.: Yale University Press, 1998).

22. For a detailed discussion of Roth's problematic career, see Gertzman's indispensable biography of the publisher, *Samuel Roth*. The norm of "trade courtesy" compelled publishers to compensate authors when they reprinted work that lacked copyright protection. See Robert Spoo, *Without Copyrights: Piracy, Publishing, and the Public Domain* (New York: Oxford University Press, 2013), 32–49. Spoo points out that the charges of literary piracy against Roth were technically false because he published only material in the public domain.

23. Quoted in Gertzman, *Samuel Roth*, 119.

24. Book Contract, 3 February 1932, Box 42 Folder 13, Samuel Roth Papers, Rare Book and Manuscript Library, Columbia University Library.

25. Gertzman, *Samuel Roth*, 119–20.

26. For more on McAlmon's life and career, see Sanford J. Smoller, *Adrift Among Geniuses: Robert McAlmon, Writer and Publisher of the Twenties* (University Park: Pennsylvania State University Press, 1975). McAlmon shared Samuel Roth's intense dislike of Joyce and the other modernist writers who organized the campaign against the controversial publisher, which McAlmon pointedly refused to join, and he may have sought out Roth when he returned to New York from Paris in 1930 to find an American publisher for his work and was met with repeated disappointment.

27.   In 1932, McAlmon published one other short story with a queer theme, "It's All Very Complicated," set in Paris and centered on a transgender lesbian. Robert McAlmon, "It's All Very Complicated," *Contact: An American Quarterly Review* I (February 1932): 64–79.

28.   Some scholars have suggested that McAlmon modeled Miss Knight on the homosexual abortionist Dan Mahoney, who inspired Dr. O'Connor in Djuna Barnes's novel *Nightwood*, but judging from McAlmon's descriptions of Miss Knight it seems much more likely that he based his portrayal of the drag queen on Savoy. See Andrew Field, *Djuna: The Formidable Miss Barnes* (Austin: University of Texas Press, 1983), 138–41; and Edward N.S. Lorusso, Introduction to *Miss Knight and Others*, by Robert McAlmon (Albuquerque: University of New Mexico Press, 1992), xx–xxii.

29.   For a detailed description of Savoy's performance style, see Senelick, *The Changing Room*, 315–18. For a virtual catalogue of famous Savoyisms, see the interview with Savoy in Ashton Stevens, *Actorviews* (Chicago: Covici-McGee, 1923), 113–18.

30.   Lorusso, *Miss Knight and Others*, 19.

31.   In addition to the reasons elaborated here, I should also point out that the author of *A Scarlet Pansy* displays an intimate knowledge of queer gathering places and cruising spots in both New York and Philadelphia at the turn of the twentieth century, which it seems unlikely McAlmon could have had, because he did not arrive in New York until 1920 and never lived in Philadelphia.

32.   It is also worth noting that McAlmon's fiction was widely admired for its spare, documentary style, and it is difficult to imagine that he could have written *A Scarlet Pansy*'s florid, campy prose.

33.   Robert McAlmon, *Being Geniuses Together 1920–1930*, revised and with added chapters by Kaye Boyle (San Francisco: North Point Press, 1984), 134.

34.   McAlmon's "objectivity" is surprising, given that he claimed to be bisexual "like Michelangelo, and I don't care who knows it." Quoted in Smoller, *Adrift Among Geniuses*, 212. He also attacked Hemingway for treating homosexuals in a "vulgar orthodox manner" in *The Sun Also Rises* (1926). Quoted in Smoller, *Adrift Among Geniuses*, 211.

35.   Lorusso, *Miss Knight and Others*, 53.

36.   Eltinge aggressively asserted his masculinity offstage to counter rumors that like Savoy he was homosexual. He participated in several well-

publicized boxing matches and although he never married, he entered into highly publicized engagements with several women. For more on Eltinge's homosexual panic, see Ullman, *Sex Seen*, 45–71.

37. Senelick, *The Changing Room*, 317.

38. Quoted in Marybeth Hamilton, *"When I'm Bad, I'm Better": Mae West, Sex, and American Entertainment* (Berkeley: University of California Press, 1997), 145.

39. Its cover made clear the differences between Randy and Fay. In sharp contrast to the frontispiece of the 1933 edition, which contains an illustration of an epicene male youth, inspired by Art Nouveau illustrator Aubrey Beardsley, the cover of the BADBOY edition displays an unshaven young man with long sideburns and a square jaw who could pass as the Marlboro Man.

A Note on the Text

The text of *A Scarlet Pansy* presented here is based on the original 1932 William Faro edition published by Samuel Roth and out of print since 1933. Teetering on the edge of bankruptcy in the early 1930s, Roth may have copy edited and proofread the novel himself, and like many of his other publications, it contained numerous typographical and punctuation errors, which have been corrected. The novel also contained two chapters numbered 9, the first marked "a" and the second marked "b," presumably to save the publisher the expense of having the novel re-typeset starting with Chapter 10. This too has been corrected. *A Scarlet Pansy* has an unusually complicated publication history, and it is worth recounting it briefly to highlight the importance of this new edition, which in reprinting the original text recovers the novel's literary and historical significance, which later editions have obscured. Shortly after Roth declared bankruptcy in 1933, the Nesor Publishing Company issued a pirated version of the novel based on the Faro edition, but it has been out of print since the late 1930s. In 1939, after serving a prison sentence for distributing obscene materials, Roth issued a new edition of the novel titled *The Scarlet Pansy* under the Royal imprint that differed from the original version in crucial ways. The controversial publisher eliminated many of the original version's richly detailed descriptions of the queer *demimonde*, probably to avoid inviting another prosecution. But in expurgating the novel, he eviscerated its critique of the modern regulation of gender and sexual identities.

A Note on the Text

In 1992 Masquerade Books issued a version of the novel under its BADBOY imprint also titled *The Scarlet Pansy* but based on the original version rather than the more widely available Royal edition. Nevertheless, it resembled the Royal edition in that it fundamentally transformed the novel's meaning by updating Fay's story for a readership eager to achieve the normalization of gay male identity. In restoring the original version, the new edition of *A Scarlet Pansy* published here rectifies these modifications and distortions.

Acknowledgments

I want to thank Robert Spoo and Jay Gertzman for their generosity in sharing their knowledge of Samuel Roth and identifying sources I might otherwise have overlooked as I pieced together *A Scarlet Pansy*'s complicated publication history. Don Pease and Steve Valocchi read a draft of the Introduction, and I am grateful for their comments and suggestions. I owe a special thanks to Zayde Antrim, who was an ideal interlocutor as well as a generous reader; her probing questions helped me to clarify my arguments. I also want to express my deep appreciation to Richard Morrison for his enthusiastic support of the project from start to finish.

A Scarlet Pansy

by Robert Scully

I

Fay Etrange lay dying on a battlefield in France, dying in the arms of the man she loved.

Young Lieutenant Frank, much younger than herself, tenderly drew her closer. At that time he did not sense that she had sacrificed her life to save him. Though she had revealed her true self, in his gratitude for her recent ministrations he thought he loved her. Perhaps he did. Perhaps he was even broad-minded enough for that. At least in after years he was heard to speak reverently of Fay.

Fay was beautiful, had always been beautiful, from babyhood onward. Whatever feature is to be admired in a babe, she had possessed: skin of the softness and bloom of a dainty blush rose; eyes of deepest blue; ringlets of spun gold. And later, at the age when growing girls are thin and gangling, she had been pleasantly rounded and winsomely lovely. Even at the time of her death, when she was well past thirty-three, her beauty had not begun to fade, but with each year had seemed to take on an appropriate maturity. Best of all, she had never realized that she possessed beauty. She had studied her mirror but little, except when making up for some grand function. This was due to an overwhelming interest in others and in objects about her, a trait manifested early in life.

Though Fay belonged to the emotional type, nevertheless, she was possessed of a marked interest in science. Thus her life had developed along complex lines.

At the age of five years, Fay had suffered her first sexual trauma, a thing so revolting that she resolutely thrust it from her mind, and it only recurred to her and was vividly recalled in after years when she sought for a full sequential explanation of the development of her dream and love life.

Fay was born in a quaint little white cottage at Kuntzville, in the lower Pennsylvanian hills. Here she lived with her father, mother, two sisters and her brother William. Her parents were of that superior type which in a past generation had been called so proudly "good American stock."

Her father's farm was large. In summer the little child roamed freely about the flowered fields and beneath the immense trees of the nearby woods. One rainy day she chanced to run to the barn for shelter. Here, unseen, she discovered two neighbor boys playing at what they conceived to be mannish practices. Fay was fond of the older of the two, and a few days later, meeting him alone in the woods, asked what he and Jack were doing in the barn and told him what she had seen. The boy, Fred, at once sensed the possibility of disgrace from a childish tattler. Raising his fist threateningly, he asked, "Did you tell anybody, anybody a-tall?"

"No, I didn't tell," Fay fearfully assured him over and over.

"Then I'm a-goin' to make you do somethin' too, so you dassn't to tell."

He directed. In terror Fay complied.

"Now you're wusser 'n us," Fred taunted. "An' don't you dast to tell nobody!"

So forceful was he, and so terror stricken was the child, that she never did tell her elders. Later on in life, when she had run across so many people who never knew when to cease babbling, Fay was glad she had learned to keep silent.

Of course psychologists of some schools will insist that this early trauma laid the foundation for all of Fay's later escapades. Was it that, or was it the constant seeking after an unrealized ideal, an ideal conditioned by some inward physical development not readily discernible through externals? However that may be, her first loves were idealized, and each disillusionment was followed by a sense of keen self-condemnation and by a long period of hopelessness before again attempting to grasp happiness through love. If they later became more frequent and promiscuous, perhaps it was because of the attempt to find in the many a summation of the attributes which love craves.

From the time of her first childish episode at five, until late in adolescence, she had no further frankly sexual experience. She did have frequent "crushes" in her first contacts at school, and these, as with all children, were sometimes directed towards the young, sometimes towards mature people; sometimes towards her own sex, sometimes towards the opposite sex. Aside from her physical beauty, she was always a marked child, never interested in the games of other children, always dreaming, so absorbed with some inner urge that she often seemed stupid to normal children. Yet her school fellows always went to her for advice and sought her out for aid when lessons were difficult.

Fay loved all animal life, human or otherwise; the difference was only in degree, and this motivated her future career. From her mother she inherited a love of service. As much as possible she followed that good woman about on expeditions to nurse sick neighbors, or to render other kindly offices, though the father demanded much of Fay's time for work in the fields or about the barns.

Early Fay learned to feed the smaller stock and to nurse any sick baby animals. As she developed sturdily, she was obliged to give her time and strength to the rough field work, doing quite as much as her older brother Bill. She would have preferred to be with her mother in the house, doing womanly tasks, cooking, sewing, beautifying the home, but her father resented any such attempts. Thus the instincts that were normal to Fay were somewhat thwarted in her home life.

The years of work, school and play sped by. The village school and the town high school were soon finished. Then the need of earning money was forced upon her. Debt had piled up. The summer after finishing high school, Fay worked side by side with her father and brother Bill, ploughing, planting, harvesting. At sixteen she could pitch as much hay as her father, could plough more land in a day, could lift heavier burdens. She was strong and healthy. But there was that in her cheeks, her eyes, even her hair, that proclaimed her sexually different. Mentally there was a hidden unrest, dimly perceived by her brother Bill, who resented her difference from the common herd and frequently taunted her on her manner of speech or her graceful movement—the antitheses of his boyish ideal.

Fay realized that the farm was not her place. She determined to go to the nearest large city, which happened to be Baltimore, to make her own way at least, and to try to stand as a buffer between her family and the hardships of the world. With Fay, thought was quickly followed by action.

'Twas a dull day in February when Fay left home, left it to return only for such dreary events as family funerals. After the hard summer's work on her father's farm, or about the community, doing whatever she could to earn a dollar here or there, harvesting crops, picking fruit, peddling produce of all kinds to the neighboring towns, her efforts had failed to do more than pay her share of the expenses at home and provide a rather scanty cheap wardrobe. The most important thing was that she had learned to work, to work hard, and to be independent of others. So she was off to Baltimore. Money! The family must have money! She must hasten and earn. She could not bear to see her mother becoming more bent and tired-looking, denied many of the necessities and most of the pleasures of existence, for Fay's affection for her mother colored all of her early life.

The sun was sinking as the train which was to bear Fay away pulled into the station at Kuntzville. Any sentiment she might have called up at this parting was dispelled by the presence of a neighbor's boy, who was going to the nearest small town to take a job, and attached himself to her. They sat together on the train. He urged her to stop in the town where he was going and to attend a theatre and afterwards go to a dance hall, explaining in great detail how "a fellow can pick up a girl." But Fay's mind was on essentials. At the railway junction they parted.

Fay had to wait an hour for the Baltimore express. A dowdy old woman sat beside her, asked, "Where you goin'? How long you got to wait?" and finding that the wait was ample, started out to sing a saga of the family Ritter. Once Fay interrupted to get a drink of water. On her way to the cooler she observed a well-dressed man looking at her intently. It was but a moment before he was at her side offering assistance, seeking to engage her in conversation. She sensed something wrong about him. Perhaps he was a pickpocket! But he was not a pickpocket. Fay hurried back to the old woman. This first meeting with a strange man was almost prophetic. For the rest of her life she was to meet his kind, wherever and whenever she travelled—always seeking her and the favors she could bestow.

At last the Baltimore express arrived, and Fay and her small packages were stowed into half of the seat of a day coach. The car was dimly lighted by gas. Every seat was filled, and it seemed to Fay that each occupant was possessed of a distinct and repellent odor. All of them were untidy and most of them more or less dirty. Fay felt a sensitive recoil, which but accentuated the loneliness that was beginning to well up within her.

The train jerked along. Fay alternately waked and dozed and dreamed horrible dreams. At dawn they dragged into the suburbs of Baltimore. There was no snow, but the ground was bare and frozen; the air was smoke-befouled and the landscape dreary; it all formed an unpleasant contrast to the clean wintry aspect of her snowclad Pennsylvania hills. When she alighted from the train she felt a damp chill which was more penetrating than the dry cold of the higher country. She left the railway station and looked about her. Already the sun, which at peep of day had promised gay sunshine, was beginning to be obscured by a dull grey fogginess, bringing twilight at early morn.

The city was bewildering.

For several blocks Fay could see only warehouses, freight stations and horse-drawn drays going back and forth. A long way up the street, and in the direction which most of the travelers pursued, higher buildings were in evidence. She reasoned that there she would more likely find a stopping place. As she started forward, a policeman who had observed her hesitancy stepped up and asked, "What's botherin' you? Don't you know the town?"

"I would like to find a place to board," she explained in her too musical singing type of voice.

At once he was all kindness and waved his stick in the direction of a spire with the admonition "Keep that thar spire in sight and right besides it you'll come to the Y. There they c'n tell you of plenty places."

Fay picked up her suitcase and started forward, while the cop muttered to himself, "Nice lookin' youngster. Nice lookin' country youngster."

How disagreeable the air was to Fay! Those were the days of horses, and all cities reeked of the odor of equine effluvia. Then too, sanitation in general was not so good as today. In the poorer parts of towns a smell of horse, sewage and garbage prevailed.

Fay picked her way carefully across the street and onwards toward the spire that was to be as a beacon to her for the next year. She arrived at the Y, a building of brick with a low, arched doorway placarded, "You are welcome." Fay smiled. She entered and approached the nearest desk. The professional welcomer arose and initiated her to the usual overly ardent handclasp. Questioning, he learned her mission and piloted her to an official for enrollment as a new prospect of the Christian welfare workers of the city to guard and watch over, and, if possible, bring into the fold of the righteous.

The official was a thin, wrinkled, sallow, sandy Scotsman, bent and spectacled, half-bald, a man of about thirty-five, of the type Fay later learned to classify as "born old." He greeted Fay effusively: "We are pleased to welcome you to our midst. You refreshing young country people, you buoyant adolescents who bring an air of health and verve with you! Our cities would decay unless they were replenished and constantly rebuilt by the fair youth of the countryside." Fay listened with amazement. Much useless language was an unfamiliar thing to her. Sandy was very flattering and patted her arm. Then he gave her a list of boarding houses "on the approved list," and spoke gushingly of the hope of seeing her again and the hope that she would avail herself of some of their night classes. Night classes! The very thing she had hoped for! There was no fee for finding her a boarding house but there was a fee for filing with the employment agency. She learned, too, that there were other employment agencies, and with anxiety also learned that a young person who is without specific training in some one branch of work "is very difficult to place."

Fay found a boarding house, a dark, dingy, ugly house, not too clean, situated on a street which was still respectable but which abutted on the edge of the less reputable part of the city. The landlady was a small dark Virginian of lovely manners but of shabby attire. Fay noticed the unaired smell of the house as she was guided to her room on the top floor. The room had one window, and that opened on an airshaft; there was a shade but no curtain. There was a small bed, a washstand with a tarnished-looking bowl and pitcher, and a single chair. She was instructed that when she needed better light to turn on the gas. The landlady illustrated. The sickly flicker seemed to add to rather than to dispel the dreariness of the dimly lighted room. The linen, though recently washed, looked grey and unclean. The carpet was spotted and dirty. The room's one virtue was extreme cheapness. The landlady quickly recounted the advantages of her house and its location and added a brief description of the good companions whom Fay would find there; these included "a splendid young man from the Eastern Shore"; a farmer-politician who was a member of the legislature; a wonderful young man who was a sewing machine agent; Mr. Strong, who was a boss carpenter (and, incidentally, the lady's secret lover, as Fay later learned); and Mr. Shorthorn, who was a motorman. Fay would meet them all at the evening meal. Meantime, she could pay a week in advance and make herself at home. "At home!" Already she loathed this place, as she was to loathe all of her city dwellings for the next five years to come—cheap, dirty, depressing. The landlady was all kindness. Truth to tell, generosity had and always would be her undoing. She gave shelter and food to those who failed to pay; she gave love to those who used it and failed to reciprocate. She looked at Fay with pity and sympathy. So many had she seen come to the city, only to be transformed into hardened, selfish human animals. To Fay's anxious inquiry about prospects for work, the lady assured her: "No one who wants work will fail to find a job." She cited case after case of her young men who were "successes," young men who had come from the country and taken positions in offices and factories and in a brief two or three years become head bookkeepers or chief clerks or foremen of departments—and gone to live elsewhere. She ended, "Yes, indeed, you will find work and success."

It was to be but a brief time before Fay would forget that Mrs. Foreman was a slattern and incompetent and remember only that she was the embodiment of generosity. Later in life, when Mrs. Foreman's bright prophecies of success had in some degree been realized, Fay was to meet the cream of American society and titled Europeans aplenty; but never did she meet one who was always such a perfect exemplification of kindliness and good manners as was this little dark Virginia woman.

At the evening meal, Fay met the assembled paying guests. She listened to them, avid to learn. Years later she could recall that supper of ham, cabbage, corn pone and talk, much talk, and afterwards a banjo badly played, and games of euchre before a pungent-smelling soft coal fire in an open grate in the "parlor."

At bedtime Fay counted her depleted hoard, which had shrunken to less than ten dollars.

2

To anyone who has ever been stranded in a strange city, this part of Fay's life would seem familiar. Her second day she made three rounds of the Y, the employment agencies and every shop and office within a certain district of the city. The third day was like unto the second, with the exception that she invaded the blocks adjacent. The fourth and all the days up to the end of two weeks were the same, and still there was no work offered to her. Hope steadily sank. Her lovely face became drawn and pale from terror. The landlady had not yet asked her for another week's rent. The beginning of the third week was at hand. She had scarcely tasted food, feeling that she had no right to eat that for which she could not pay. She hurried from the house. It was her lucky day. At her third call, a coal dealer told her he would give her work. He looked at her closely and seemed to sense that she was in dire need of employment. Fay could never decide whether pity or the desire to take advantage of her necessity induced Mr. Rush to give her a job. But she was thankful for an opportunity to labor, even at the pittance offered her, which allowed a margin of fifty cents each week after all expenses were paid. At once she took her place in the line of laborers. In those days all coal was handled by means of shovels and barrows. For Fay was young and had always worked hard, and muscular effort did not trouble her. She kept pace with Irish Mac and Black John and never guessed that they were trying to tax her staying powers. That night she hurried home joyfully to tell the good news of having found something to do. After that it did not seem hard to ask

Mrs. Foreman to give her credit for a week. And in the coalyards Fay passed two years, a brief part of that time at hard manual labor, till her office value was discovered.

It was shortly after Fay began working in the coalyards that her first love experience in Baltimore occurred. Queer too, to one knowing Baltimore!

Fay realized that she must do something to procure more remunerative work. She talked it over with her friend, the practical Sandy. He advised her, "Take up some night study, both for intellectual betterment and to find profitable social contacts."

Fay laughed at the idea of "social contacts." Sandy laid out a business course for her—bookkeeping, shorthand, typing. Before she enrolled for the classes he suggested that she come up to his rooms and look over some of the books and give further thought to the matter.

Bashfully Fay followed Sandy to his room in a tower. She had no feeling of insecurity, but she did experience a deep feeling of embarrassment. Sandy gave her a book and pinched her cheek playfully as he excused himself, ostensibly to go down to his desk, but in reality to see if the coast was clear. Sandy was not bold enough to attempt a quick seduction, but he was so madly enamored that he had worked himself up to the state where he dared, at least, to attempt an awkward kind of lovemaking. By degrees, and by book after book, he arrived at the point where he had courage to sit down and put a loving arm about her shoulder. She endured! Physically the man was repulsive to her, but at that time of life she was not experienced enough to know what to do. She could only blush. Her embarrassment was not yet complete. Suddenly the gym instructor, wearing rubber-soled shoes, bounded into the room. His only remark was, "Oh! did I interrupt you?" Then tactfully he fled. Fay disengaged herself. On her way homeward she pondered the incident and felt regret that she could not reciprocate Sandy's very evident love—he had been so kind to her.

Shortly afterwards, Sandy was transferred, and Fay heard veiled gossip of his suspected misconduct with others.

She took up her night courses with determination. Thus she occasionally met the gym instructor, who always looked on her with a kindly eye, too kindly. Fay could only return his wordy salutations with a bashful nod of her head and a deep blush. She did not read aright the yearning that was in his eyes. But she was becoming more accustomed to city ways and also more accustomed to the admiration and attentions of all types of men.

One Sunday, when visiting a military camp and watching the men march by, one jocose militiaman yelled, "Look at pretty standing there by that tree." At once the whole company took up the refrain, "Pretty! Say there pretty!" And one called out, "Oh, you peaches and cream, meet me tonight in the moonlight"; another one—"Oh, you fairy, will that complexion rub off?" "Razzing," she learned to call such conduct later on in life. At that time Fay was so innocent that she did not grasp the evil intent that lay behind their words. But she was beginning to realize that she was different from the majority of her sex.

3

WHEN THE COMMERCIAL COURSES WERE COMPLETED, the Y, ever anxious to advertise, held a "commencement," at which the prize pupils wrote somewhat familiar business dictation on a blackboard, displaying their accomplishments to the assemblage. The business men, the chief contributors to the Y activities, thus could see that their money had been well spent. Fay, all blushes as usual, and more beautiful than ever, did her part along with the others of her classes, and felt a perfect fool while doing it.

Mr. Rich, a banker, with an eye to pulchritude as well as to efficiency, asked for an introduction to Fay and straightway offered her a position in his bank, a leading one in Baltimore. She demurred, well knowing that she was not sufficiently expert to do good work.

Fay was entirely ignorant of all the possibilities that lay behind such an offer. Then she did not know that her beauty would offset poor typing; that one glance of her lovely eyes would give the banker a rejuvenating thrill for which he was willing to pay high. A knowledge of "Johns" had not yet been vouchsafed to her. At that time, a compliance which she would have shunned, a very little compliance, not even surrender, would have gained for her not only an ample income, which she could have done through the formalities of earning, but would also have provided her with a home, a course at college, or any of the better things which she craved. She had not the cupidity to take advantage of all these possibilities; nor had she any thought that such compliance, even to complete surrender, would soon be yielded to another in return for nothing but remorse, heartbreak and a sense of shame.

The next evening, Mr. Fisher, the successor to Sandy, called Fay into his office to learn why the business opportunity had been refused. She explained to him that her work as a typist was too far below the standard required. This was his opportunity. At once he suggested that she do extra copying for him evenings; he would pay her liberally. Fay, ever eager to improve, and also earn, gladly consented.

She began the next night. After she had been working an hour, Mr. Fisher came to her desk and suggested that she come with him to a nearby restaurant for a "bite," and then return to finish her work. Innocently Fay exclaimed, "But I cannot afford to eat at such an expensive place."

"This time you are coming as my guest. Now, don't refuse!" he urged her.

She accepted, her heart thumping wildly from an excitement which she did not understand.

There was music at the restaurant, music which she loved. This brought the topic into their conversation, and Fay spoke of her own modest achievements as the church organist at Kuntzville, while Mr. Fisher in turn told of his courses in Boston, courses both in music and painting. Fay was awed.

To the haunting strains of a Chopin waltz they left the restaurant. Fay was more pleasantly excited than she had ever been before. The typewriter seemed to bound along magically when she returned to her task. By nine o'clock she had finished. Mr. Fisher came to the doorway. He complimented her on the work she had done, then asked pleasantly if she would like to hear him play, and suggested too that they try a duet together. He explained to her, "I have to go out your way to see a sick man and I'll call a cab afterward. You'll arrive home just as soon as if you relied on the cars." He was a man prolific with plausible schemes. Poor, lonesome Fay! Happiness seemed to beckon. Innocently she thought Mr. Fisher the most considerate man she had ever met. He was considerate enough; considerate of every angle and possible move in a dangerous game. Too, he knew just when to be reassuring and just how far to move. He wanted Fay in his arms, in his own room, behind locked doors, but he sensed that any inopportune suggestion might startle her and drive her beyond his reach. He led her to one of the semi-private parlors. There she waited while he went for some books of music and some of his drawings. He returned quickly. Without comment he turned to a difficult Chopin nocturne and played with the ease of the born artist. The man had been properly schooled. His playing was far beyond anything Fay had theretofore heard. She was entranced.

"Why are you not a concert pianist?" she asked, spontaneously paying him a high and deserved compliment.

"I have tried that too," he answered, "but the work with the boys of the Y gives me more satisfaction than concertizing would yield. Besides, I have some means of my own and do not have to submit to all the unpleasantness of travel and the inconveniences of public life."

Then he asked her to try a duet. She read quickly enough, but all of her musical work had been at the organ, and she was not at ease at the piano. Mr. Fisher was surprised when he learned of the disadvantageous circumstances under which she had acquired that knowledge. She begged him to play more. Wily one, he chose Liszt's "Liebestraum" and for an encore Chopin's deliciously sentimental waltz, Opus 70, No. 1.

Then it was time for the ride home. He directed the driver to go by way of the park. It was moonlight, nearing the full of the moon. Fay was strangely moved by this evening full of unusual delights. Mr. Fisher was not crude. When the cab rolled around a curve he pressed against her and observed that she did not find it unpleasant and breathed a little faster. They neared her door. He started to shake hands. As he felt the intensity of her grasp he lifted her hands to his lips.

He did not embrace her, only held her hand tightly as he helped her from the cab. Solicitously he asked if she could come the following Saturday night and finish the task she was engaged upon.

That night, before sleep came to her, Fay pictured herself in Mr. Fisher's arms, being kissed on the lips instead of her hand, as her old friend, the family doctor, had kissed her when she was a tiny child. Her thoughts reverted to the doctor who, from a neighborhoodful of children, had singled her out for his special favor—always she had possessed this uncanny charm for men.

4

Saturday, the end of a week filled with backbreaking, muscle-torturing labor!

Monday, under the broiling sun, they had begun the task of unloading a fleet of coal barges, and even the office force had been impressed. Fay held her end up with the most robust of them. All day long, hour after hour, she formed one of a line of laborers trundling barrows of coal. She did her work smilingly, for she knew that at last she was to leave it and advance to a more profitable occupation.

Most lovers of beauty are not good workers or good students; they are commonly of the type that loves to look on. There are a few exceptions, but even these are usually capable only of sustained effort along their chosen lines. Fay could work either mentally or physically, and continue at it, till others would be exhausted. Her subsequent career was due to this ability.

But the hopes that sustained her that day had no concern with ambition, but with an all-consuming emotion—love. Love comes to all who are normally constituted (and to most of those, alas! who are abnormally constituted), comes in some guise or other. The one who loves reeks not of ambition; when love begins to wane, perhaps then ambition may influence and degrade.

Fay had not yet tasted real love, unless her childhood adoration of the family physician could have been termed love. Even at the age of four, she had gone to sleep of nights thinking of the handsome doctor and wishing he was there to take her up in his arms and kiss her while she looked into his lovely eyes. All day Fay was buoyed up by her dream of being with her trusted friend of the Y, after the day's work was finished.

At last the week's labor was over. Fay hastily bathed beneath a hose, donned her street clothes and hurried to the boarding house which she called home. There she completed her toilet, doing everything over and over, that she might be the more presentable.

The street cars seemed to creep. At last the Y was reached, and then her courage failed her as she bashfully stammered that she wished to see Mr. Fisher. Soon he sauntered up and greeted her in a casual, disarming manner.

They went to the lovely old Southern Hotel and entered the cool palm room. While Mr. Fisher handled the terrifying bill of fare with ease, Fay scanned one after another of the items, all so highly priced. Secretly she was looking for something cheap. Pressed to state a preference, she made the usual decision of the socially inexperienced and murmured, "I'll take whatever you do."

So began Fay's first acquaintance with hors d'oeuvres, cold chicken soup, lobster à la reine, salad and Russian dressing, and biscuit Tortoni. Even the bread, though still bread, was different and seemed all delicious brown crust.

In the interlude between the musical numbers, they talked of things beautiful. When they had finished, Mr. Fisher suggested that they go to the park and sit under the trees and listen to the orchestra. Moonlight and music! Nothing could have given Fay greater pleasure or made greater appeal to her romantic nature.

On their way to the park their hansom passed an automobile. Mr. Fisher expressed his envy of the possessor of such wealth and trappings. Poor Fay! At that moment she envied no one; she possessed the greatest thing in the world.

Twilight faded quickly. By the time they had reached the park, her sturdy, muscular hardworked brown hand was grasped in his effeminately white, soft, weak paw. She thrilled to this touch. Well he sensed this and was satisfied—for the time being. Then they left the cab and wandered out into the park beneath the trees. Here they found a secluded bench. The music drifted to them and answered for language. They were half in shadow, and when the full moon passed behind a cloud he wasted not this opportunity but put his lips to her neck in a caress that aroused all of her passion. Impulsively she threw her arms about him, and for a moment their lips were pressed in a passionate kiss. An ecstatic waltz was being played, just suited to their mood.

He drew her away from the bench to the shadow cast by the trunk of a great oak, and with that at his back he sat on the ground with her head cuddled against his chest. The music had ceased. The crowd had left. A gentle breeze sprang up and fanned them. The moon sank from sight, and the darkness stole upon them as he kissed her ears and whispered his desires.

She seemed sunken in a stupor of acquiescence, an automaton as without volition as a subject of hypnosis. Thus began her degradation. Morally, from then on, she was to go down, down, down.

Not till he had completely defiled her and sated his lust did she come back to her normal self.

Then she moaned in anguish of spirit at her debasement. Nor could consolation be derived from the realization that she had experienced no pleasure from her compliance, but seemed to have been goaded on by forces which demanded her complete abandonment to another's will. So strong is instinct!

Fay's emotional reaction was violent and frightened even Mr. Fisher, practiced seducer of the young though he was. She shuddered with horror! Now she realized that she could with justice be called the loathsome name which at times and with horror she had heard the coarse workmen use, a name from which she recoiled.

"Think what I have done!" she exclaimed over and over again.

Mr. Fisher tried to induce forgetfulness by caresses calculated to arouse a new compliance. But Fay arose and walked madly towards the gates of the park. He caught up with her. All attempts to engage her in conversation were met with the reiterated plaint, "Think what I have done! Think what I have done!"

She did not shed tears, too tortured by conscience even for that. She wished to escape from him, from herself. A homewardbound street car, the last for the night, came into view. Madly she ran from him and scrambled aboard.

It was two o'clock when she reached her home. She tried the front door. It was locked. She was ashamed to ring. Huddled on the doorstep, she slept and awoke when the milkman made his rounds.

She walked down the street till she came to a leaky fire hydrant. There she washed her face and hands and freshened her appearance as best she could. At seven she knew the landlady would be up for the early breakfasts. She went back with the morning paper, entered by the back door, went to her room, rumpled the bed to make it appear used, came down and announced that she had decided to go to a special early church service.

Then she stole away to the park and hidden there slept till her wearied body was refreshed.

She awoke to realize that she must adjust herself to a new conception of her personality.

5

A week of dreadful self-realization dragged by. Fay worked with a zeal which should have brought exhaustion and sleep, but did not. Her self-respect had been annihilated. In her need to regain her self-esteem, she decided to see Mr. Fisher again and talk with him of the horror which she now felt for her conduct. She wondered if even he still respected her. So with the coming of another weekend she went to the Y. There Mr. Fisher received her with unusual warmth, for he had begun to have some fear of the consequences of his most recent seduction, the sudden disappearance of his new sweetheart and the ominous silence. Thus his welcome was perhaps more fervent and his expressions of pleasure at seeing her more sincere than they would otherwise have been. His manner alleviated to some extent the ache within her. She regained a part of her old-time composure.

As he shook hands he said, "Wait while I finish some work and then we can go to the Southern and dine."

"But I'm not hungry."

"You will be by that time. So wait for me!"

"Very well."

Soon they were at the Southern, and as they talked things over in a none too specific fashion, his lightness of manner helped her to forget and seemed to bring back some of the atmosphere of things as they were before "the awful deed." She was almost happy again. The soft lights, the delicate food,

A Scarlet Pansy

the lovely music and the skillful flattery of the subtle Mr. Fisher dulled the thoughts of the act which had so cruelly wounded her soul.

During a lull, when the music stopped, she looked up at him and murmured, "Then you do still respect me?"

"Why, of course!" he made quick reply. "That was nothing. I love you more than ever."

"How good of you to say that; you don't know how tortured I have been all the week. I did a terrible thing!"

"You mustn't feel that way about it. You have harmed no one. You are feeling morbid about something that is perfectly natural—to you!"

Then he proposed a play, a gay hodge-podge which was then classed as a comic opera. He knew that a series of fresh impressions would help to deaden these too sharp reactions.

In the theatre, a pressure of knee against knee, and handclasps in the dark, were all that were needed to kindle anew the violent infatuation which Fay had conceived for him.

After the play they walked for a while, and he told her of the acting he had seen in New York, of the operatic singers he had heard, and of the symphony concerts, at one of which he had substituted as pianist. Cleverly he piloted her by a roundabout way to the vicinity of the Y, and then he abruptly suggested that she come up to his room, adding, "There we can talk over all the things about which we feel so bad."

By that time Fay had forgotten to feel bad. For the moment, at least, she was perfectly happy. The Y was dark, and he let himself in with his latch-key. Guiding her by the hand, carefully they tiptoed up the stairway to his den. Then he adjusted the windows and curtains and turned on a rose-colored light which put them in shadow but illuminated the room sufficiently—for his purpose. He led her to a great old-fashioned comfortable sofa, and with his arms about her and his lips kissing her that tantalizing kiss on the nape of her neck, he drew her down to him.

He spoke in a tender tone of voice: "Now tell me just why you feel so bad. You know I love you, don't you? And you love me. And after all love is the only thing in the world that matters. You don't feel so bad now, do you? Aren't you happy with me?"

And Fay was everything he suggested, eager to coincide with his opinions and just as happy as her love for him had first made her.

With his skill, and Fay's hypersuggestible state, the culmination could only be as before, an almost automatic compliance with his desires, succeeded by a return of normal self-assertion in which she again felt her debasement and defilement. It is always thus with people who have been highly idealistic. Even marriages are sometimes shattered by the too sensitive attitude of one of the partners. Curiously, she did not blame him then; not till much later.

With horror Fay regarded herself in a great mirror on the opposite wall and burst out, "Oh, I am going away. I am going away where this can never happen again. I do not know why I do this. I must not do it. I must not!"

She outlined a plan for going to New York—New York, for reformation!

Fisher, perhaps a little conscience-stricken, tried to give her good advice. He even suggested introductions to people in New York, people who might be of value to her.

She rose suddenly and held out her hand to bid him a stiff, formal good-bye. He, probably thinking it appropriate to carry out the role of devoted lover, drew her close and gave her a farewell kiss, but now he avoided her lips—only a cold pressure to her brow.

Fay left him, fired by determination to rid herself of a loathsome practice. She had the feeling that sensitive "sinners" often experience, that her character was stamped upon her face.

Then began the attempt to cultivate a new outward self.

6

SUNDAY MORNING FAY DECIDED TO ATTEND THE CHURCH TO WHICH THE BANKER, Mr. Rich, belonged, and to meet him after the service.

She was in the vestibule as he came out. Mr. Rich greeted her more than cordially and presented her to his wife and daughter, both of whom were impressed by Fay's good looks. Later they made flattering comments about "the handsome Yankee." Fay asked permission to call on Mr. Rich at his bank the next day, and the happy man, thinking that at last he was to have a loaf, a delicious loaf, float back on the waters of philanthropy, gladly assented.

Fay lingered to hear the organ. It soothed her, as it always had.

Monday dawned hot, bright and clear, as so many Baltimore summer days are. Fay donned her best clothes and arrived rather late at the coalyards. The "boss" was late too, and all of the workmen were standing about, waiting for orders. Briefly she told them that she intended to leave Baltimore and go to New York. Irish Mac burst forth: "So that's what's eatin' ye? I though' all that stoodyin' was doin' somethin' to yer brain!" And all, with one quip or another, which they deemed killing wit, told her they knew she had been planning something new. In their rough way they had been kind. Though it was a relief to escape from the phase of life which they represented, still she felt a twinge of sorrow at leaving even such friends, and an unaccustomed emotion crept into her voice as she bade them farewell.

What was late for these laborers was early for the banking house, and Fay arrived there before the portly, redfaced, reddish-haired, successful Mr. Rich.

There was a marked stir, an exaggerated attempt at activity when Mr. Rich arrived. Because he was so anxious to please her and give such unstinted evidence of it, the junior officers and clerks regarded with wonder this young person who could work such a transformation in the usually flinty old goldworshipper.

Mr. Rich ushered Fay, almost with menial servility, into his private office. He seated her in a chair, closed the door and then with one hand on her shoulder and the other on her knee and with the look of a cannibal on his face, gloatingly asked, "So you have come to take the position I offered?"

Fay read that look instantly and replied, "It is imperative that I go to New York. I came to see if you could give me some introductions. When I arrive there I must find work without delay."

"But you are not leaving today?" grieved the banker. "Can't I prevail upon you to accept a position here?"

"No, not in Baltimore."

"Then do promise to visit us at our home for a few days before you go," he urged.

Fay thought quickly. She realized that if she was to have his influence she must accept his invitation and favor him with her society, the luxury for which he hungered. With him she felt safe; knew well that he could never induce her to yield to him; could not overpower her through her emotions. He was a different man. She felt no attraction for him. Too, she was vaguely aware that she could "wind him about her finger," so to speak, though she had no desire to do so. She did not feel curiosity as to just how far he would dare to go. She did not follow that thought far, for she knew that no matter what his goal was, it was not hers too. So she accepted.

And while he was still tasting the joy of having her with him, she deferred not, but possessed herself of a sheaf of letters of introduction which any high financier might have been glad to have.

Thus, Fay became a guest for three days in the home of a member of Baltimore's so-called "aristocracy" and drove and rode with the unsuspecting wife and daughter. The old banker played his part with surprising self-repression, considering the ardor of his desires. He had lived long, and perhaps had become used to being thwarted. One does! Then too, he had no intention of jeopardizing his chances of success by too hasty avowal of his purposes, and he could not read this cool, apparently self-possessed young person who appeared never to have been awakened sexually.

His usual plan was first to kindle a firm friendship, and when sufficient obligation had been imposed, to force friendship a step further. He spoke of meeting Fay in New York. She assured him, "That would be nice."

There was no danger of this friendship getting out of bounds. For three days Fay kept Mr. Rich talking of affairs of commerce, learning what she could that might be of service in a business way. And he, with such a willing auditor, enjoyed to the utmost expanding his ideas. Fay had not yet learned that the most subtle flattery one can give is to listen intelligently. The old man was happy he was being understood; he was being looked up to for his wisdom. The more flattered he felt, the more maddening became his infatuation; even his wife and daughter laughingly commented on his crush.

The daughter, Lola, with that frankness which is so often a part of the charm of young southern people, and also with that sagacity which is a part of the endowment of the socially successful, endeavored to interpret Fay.

The last evening of the visit, after Fay had been playing the pipe organ for them for an hour, Miss Rich urged her to go out on the balcony and enjoy the cool breeze. She looked at Fay earnestly, then spoke frankly: "Do you know, Fay, you are wonderfully attractive. There is even something thrilling about your voice. I do not believe you realize fully how fascinating you are, and it is not alone because you have good looks but because of some quality in you which I cannot define; mother feels it and so do I, and you have simply infatuated dear old father. With it all, I believe you do not know yourself; not yet. Some day you will awaken and if you do not become self-conscious, you will have your own way with everyone."

Fay slowly raised her eyes, sat erect, drew a deep breath, scarcely compressed her upper teeth against lower lip, then let escape a sigh. Slowly she relaxed, leaned back in her chair, gazed afar off, and simply remarked in a tragic voice: "I wonder!"

Never did she forget that remark: "You do not know yourself." It served to increase her desire to understand this new self which seemed to be developing with maturity. She felt a certain shyness and to hide it went back to the organ and played largo, a *nachstücke* and even part of a sonata which lent itself to organ. Fay had the gift of feeling music and making others feel it too. The old French strain often shows itself that way. At Mr. Rich's request she ended with a medley of "oldtimey" songs, then quietly wandered back to the balcony as if in a dream. Something new, a half-vision, had come to her.

The next morning the adieux were said. Mr. Rich himself offered to drive Fay down to the depot. He chose a roundabout way through the ever fateful park, and stopped the horses where the view was best. He told Fay how much he had enjoyed her sojourn with them and added, "You were wonderful last night. But then you are always wonderful. It is a part of you to be that." His emotion overcoming him completely, he threw his free arm about her and drew her to him in a fierce embrace. Over and over he repeated, "You don't know how I love you! You don't know how I love you! I'd do anything for you." And when she remained calm he added, "Oh, make me happy, make me happy for just a little while. Don't go away. Stay here with me! I've loved you ever since the first time I saw you. I've never loved like that before."

Fay had read him aright, but she had expected no such sudden outburst in broad daylight in a public park. She did feel sorry for the poor old man. Her own suffering had been so great 'twas easy to extend pity to him and, for the time being, forget that what he called love was nothing but mad lust. She petted his flabby, fat hand and assured him that she liked him very much; that she would never forget him; that she would write often and would surely come to see him again, and urged him to visit her in New York at any time. Fay kept her word later, but Mr. Rich never bothered to go all the way to New York to visit her. When Fay again went to Baltimore she found Mr. Rich had consoled himself with someone more amenable and also much more convenient.

The rest of the journey to the train continued with more decorum. Mr. Rich insisted on presenting her with a ticket to New York and a seat in the Pullman. When she hesitated to put herself under what she felt to be a financial obligation, he waved her objections aside: "But you have given us your society, your music and the inspiration of your presence."

Not to prolong the embarrassing situation, she accepted without further demur. It was a relief when the train pulled into Mount Royal and she had left the man.

Fay turned this episode over in her mind. Was she always to be pursued by some man? Then the only hope of escape was the cultivation of the utmost reserve. Quite unconsciously she was laying the foundation for one of the greatest charms of any person. She suppressed herself; a faint smile took the place of laughter, and thus she forever escaped that prevalent bane, the society grin.

7

No sooner was the train well in motion than a rather oldish, prosperous-looking, somewhat overfed man seated himself near Fay and tried to engage her in conversation.

Quickly youthful beauty is observed by the sensation hungry! The man made Fay uneasy. She did not wish to be abrupt or rude; that was not a part of her nature. She did sincerely wish to be rid of the individual. He detected her lack of experience and hoped evidently by persistence to break down her polite, but none the less determined, resistance to his advances.

She excused herself and went to the washroom to brush her teeth. No sooner had she come back to her seat than he returned to the attack. Four drinks of water, two brushings of teeth and constant unnecessary attention to her toilet still failed to dislodge this unwelcome suitor. Fay's voice made her conspicuous. Even the porter had observed her—and watched her to see what would happen. When she next went to the washroom, the porter suggested that perhaps she would find it agreeable to visit the observation platform. She followed his suggestion.

There was but one empty place. In going to the seat, Fay found it necessary to pass others and spoke, excusing herself.

When loose males are gathered together their tendency is to dwell on anything even remotely feminine which presents. Fay's voice was a challenge. She had not yet learned to control it; in fact never did succeed in controlling it absolutely. It was a revealing voice!

A Scarlet Pansy

The men became boisterously offensive, all but one, a travelling salesman who suggested that the sun was hot and that a chair inside might be more comfortable. Then, looking at his watch, he suggested luncheon. Fay accepted the invitation, anxious to escape the pointed remarks of the other men. Her sharp ears did not miss the comments that followed her departure: "Unless I miss my guess, that's one of them!"—"Too good to be true!"—"How would you like to meet that in the dark!"—"My Gawd, Percy, did you notice that voice!"—"Easy to pick up too!"

In the dining car the salesman exchanged cards with Fay; his read, "Henri Voyeur, Ladies' Hats." The name was as French as her own. He was to prove a valued acquaintance. Mr. Voyeur confided, almost apologetically, to Fay that he had tried various lines of trade but that ladies' hats seemed to be the one for which he was fitted.

"Oh, well," he said, "one must be satisfied and do that for which one is best fitted, no matter what that may be."

Then he told her in a very low voice, "I understood you even before you had come out on the platform—your gait! You are inexperienced. You do not yet understand yourself! But you'll have to learn, and you may as well begin at once. You say you are going to New York. That city will crush you unless you master it, and a thorough knowledge of life is the only thing that will give you the upper hand. You must learn to be quick at repartee. A wise one would have made those men feel ridiculous."

Then he dashed into a description of phases of the night life of New York, just as wild then as now, in some respects wilder, and much more open, wide open. "Reform" had not yet struck the town. He described the old Hay Market, which might have lived up to its name in a distant past, but which at that time was a market where the merchants were hot young men and the merchandise somewhat tarnished women.

Fay said, "That doesn't interest me."

"I didn't think it would, but I wished to feel you out—to be sure. I think I know just what pleasures would appeal to you in New York."

"Pleasures? I am not going to New York to seek pleasure. I'm going to seek work and opportunity."

"You'll find plenty of both, and sometimes when you are tired of work you'll seek pleasure, the same as the rest of us. In New York it is sometimes even possible to combine work and pleasure." He laughed mischievously. "Better let me wise you up. I'm not after you, but others will be. Not my type! Don't be afraid of me. All I want is companionship. You'll need a straight friend; you'll need plenty of friends. Better let me help you out. I remember the mistakes I made when I first came to town. No use your making them too. I understand you completely. Your voice tells me everything."

"My voice? Again my voice!"

"Yes, your voice; too soft; too genteel; too caressing. There's not a man back there who's not wise to you. Don't be afraid to open up to me. I look on you as a sister."

Fay shuddered. Were her recent experiences as an open book to others?

There are some natures marked for definite experiences, marked clearly and absolutely. Hers was one of these peculiar personalities!

As they entered Jersey City, they finished their long drawn-out luncheon. Before they parted she had promised to let Monsieur Voyeur hear from her again.

So Fay entered the great city, with the doors of one type of society open to her and with precious letters of introduction to the men of the financial centre.

8

SETTLED IN A BOARDING HOUSE IN THE OLD TWENTIES OF NEW YORK, Fay was quickly swallowed up by the town. Easily she found a position as stenographer to a bank president, Mr. Rule, a man who appreciated one who could take dictation rapidly and accurately and spell correctly without the aid of a dictionary or prompting from the valued and highly paid other clerks who had their own duties to perform. Also Fay had the ability to relieve him of practically all letter writing, once she had absorbed his style. As time went on the banker found Fay invaluable and later on took her with him again and again on his summer trips to Europe.

Fay was quickly classified at the bank as a queer sort; and the other clerks let it go at that. Her employer took her for granted. She did not interest him any more than any other efficient clerk. The Baltimore banker's letters vouched for her. That was enough. Outside of paying the bills of his society wife and daughter, the banker was interested in a member of the Floradora Sextette. Fay was a cog in his machine.

At the boarding house she was popular because she could now afford to be generous with money and further because she was possessed of an innate desire to please and make others happy. People circumstanced much like herself, they were not overcritical of others. Most of them were poor. Their entertainment consisted of walks along Fifth Avenue, watching their "betters"; conversation in the boarding house parlor; innocent games of cards and an occasional evening when some visitor would drop in who could play and sing.

A man named Bryant occupied what the landlady styled "the back parlor room." His formal education had been obtained at one of those newer denominational western colleges, St. Something-or-Other's. 'Twas not of good quality, nor of much depth. Superficially he could pass for a gentleman.

Through Fay's good offices a clerkship had been found for her brother Bill in the bank where she was employed. Bill and Bryant soon became devoted friends. They were entirely congenial. Bill seemed to hark back to his Irish ancestry; had little ambition for aught but pleasure; would accept only what came easily; drank too much; saved nothing. As a family asset his value had been nil, whereas generous Fay was ever sending money and gifts home. Always Bill was borrowing small sums of money from Fay which he never repaid and for which she could never get up the courage to ask him. His overdrinking and his improvidence had worried both Fay and her mother. Fay had not yet learned that this type of man sometimes marries, changes, settles down to business and becomes one "of the backbone of the country," as intolerant as any of the other members of a well regulated "Christian" community. She disapproved entirely of Bill's lack of thought for the family welfare. She did not realize yet that he as strongly disapproved of her, seeming to sense in her the latent sexual aberrations which would shame him before his male companions. Already he was objecting to her voice, constantly admonishing her not to talk, or to change her voice and talk like other people. Fay did talk like other people, but not the other people he meant.

Bill approved entirely of Bryant, because Bryant appeared to have a wide knowledge of worldly affairs. For the same reason he approved of Fred, one of the other clerks at the bank, a somewhat older man who had made the mistake of marrying one of the spoiled-virgins of his small Connecticut town. Bill, Bryant and Fred, along with Fred's somewhat dissolute wife and her bosom friend, a kept woman, made wild parties about town. Fay did not dissipate—then. Dissipation interfered with ambitions, and her ambitions, though difficult of fulfillment, were by no means petty.

One Saturday night, wishing to rouse Fay out of her serious mood, and desiring too her financial contributions to the entertainment, Bill insisted

A Scarlet Pansy

that she accompany them on a slumming tour. Finally she consented. She anticipated no delight in the thing; drinking was nauseating to her. But downtown and the great East Side were being featured in the papers, and slumming parties were then beginning to be the vogue; she succumbed to the urgings of the party. The tour embraced an old place of disrepute in MacDougal Street where Fred's wife seemed quite at home and called various of the males "Lily," and "Maude" and "Fanny," all of which seemed to titillate most of the party. To Fay it seemed common and low. The place was dirty and the air stifling. She was glad when Fred suggested that they go on down to Chinatown. There they ate Sino-American messes and then went to a "hop-joint"; such dives were fairly open then. Freely Fred and his wife smoked opium and Bryant and Bill even took a few puffs "just to see what it was like." Fay refused and longed to leave the place and get the trip over with. But then they must see East Broadway and the Jews overflowing the sidewalks, and after that Fred announced what was to be the crowning event of the evening, a visit to a "fairy joint" in Chrystie Street.

They came to what was apparently an ordinary saloon, but instead of entering the main door they stepped through a side-door and followed a long narrow hall which finally gave on a brilliantly lighted back room. On the face of it, the place appeared orderly. The usual beer was served, with a soft drink for Fay, and then Fred's wife pointed out to them the various characters of the place. There were men and boys who called themselves "Kitty," or "Minnie" or "Maude" (a favorite name). By way of being sparkling they indulged in imitation spats with each other, exchanging all the vile epithets of the gutter and brothel. Fred's wife giggled, and though she said, "Ain't they awful," she was delighted.

At an adjoining table sat a handsome dark-eyed refined-looking young Jew. His seat almost touched Fay's, and when a waiter, to make more room, pushed the table back a few inches further, the young man's chair was tilted, and he fell heavily against Fay. He apologized, and that paved the way for a few remarks. Fay was conscious of an aesthetic attraction which the man had for her. When he excused himself and went elsewhere, she remarked, "What an unusual man to be in such surroundings. He really seems to be a gentleman." Fred's wife giggled at this "good one" as she informed Fay just what the young man was. From that time onward Fay was discreetly silent. She was glad when the party broke up; glad to leave the half-besotted and half-doped Fred and his wife.

Fay was beginning to find Bill unsettling. So one fine day she announced her intention of living alone, that she might study in peace. Bill, despite his somewhat irregular social life, was doing well at the bank. She had done all she could for him. He needed her no longer.

Up near one of the colleges, Fay found a tiny room. She enrolled for all of the evening courses they would permit her to carry. Now she was joyously happy. Every spare moment was filled with useful endeavor. Thus the time sped.

9

FAY WAS PROGRESSING. The language courses at the university night schools brought promotion at the bank also. Then too, she was learning of favorable investments. Her savings were beginning to amount to a substantial sum.

And because of her position others were beginning to ask her advice about investments, seeking a "tip" about one stock or another. She pondered this. Her earliest training at the bank had taught her not to disseminate information. Finally illumination came. Patiently she cultivated the acquaintance of the small local tradesmen. They wished to make money rapidly. So did she, and she had the opportunities but not the capital. Finally, she evolved a practical, safe and honest plan. Whenever she saw an occasion for a quick safe turnover, she would approach one of the tip seekers, borrow the five hundred or thousand dollars which he had saved to gamble with, give him her note and promise to share the profits of the investment with him. The details she kept to herself. In due time, six weeks, a month, or even a shorter period, she repaid the loan and gave the lender the interest and a fair share of the profits. It was not long before she was able to control a fair amount of capital. She never traded on margin. It was all safe, sure.

Fay was generous. Soon she was able to do all and more than she had planned for her mother and the family and was looking forward to the gratification of her own ambitions.

She had almost forgotten her Baltimore episode. When it did recur, she no longer thought with love but with contempt of the man who had humiliated her; the man who instead of seeking the best within her had sought only to debase her. There is a fundamental difference between true love and passion. The one looks deeply into the soul of the beloved, tries to read aright and aids in the unfolding of the best within that person; the other seeks only to lead on to physical sensation and emotional enslavement. But try as we will to forget that we are sexual beings first and other things afterwards, we usually end only in deceiving ourselves, and the more deeply we are deceived the more in danger are we of suffering disastrous consequences. Fay had ceased to acknowledge sex. She failed to realize that it was as much the sex attraction of the orchestra leader as the beauty of the music which attracted her to certain concerts; also she failed to realize that a man's shoulder, his legs encased in puttees, a certain dark Vandyke beard, were all powerful fetishes to her. She was frank in her outspoken admiration of the musician's conducting, of the mounted policeman's appearance astride a horse, of the masculine beauty of one or two physicians whom she occasionally met in society. She thought "studying types" in public conveyances was an innocent pastime; its disguised sexuality was well hidden from her.

She again changed her abode and went to live at a boarding house where her piano teacher lived. Here she also met other musicians and people either studying or interested in music. It was long since she had seen her brother Bill, who had been transferred to an uptown branch of the bank. A student's concert was scheduled. Fay was to play, her first appearance in the role of pianist. She thought to surprise Bill. He was always proud of anything which tended to exhibit the family in a favorable light. She invited him to dine at the boarding house and attend the concert. He came. He gave short answers to her and to everyone else; he was churlish. After the concert, when pressed for an opinion, he expressed himself forcefully and to the point: "The music was fine, but these men are a bunch of sissies. Such lisping I've never heard before, and you talk like them. Do you like such people? God, sometimes I wonder whether you are going to be one of them! How can you stand that old bearded lady (referring to a physician who was also a guest that evening)? Get educated, but get out of this. And change that damned voice of yours; it's getting worse instead of better. I heard some of the boys down at the bank telling about the bunch you hang out with."

Fay was crushed. Her sexual transgression had not endowed her with the ability to read people and thus sift the worthy from the unworthy. Besides, she could not change herself; she could not see herself. Her only defense was, "Well, Bill, God made us all. Blame him!"

Afterwards she thought, "Can Bill be right?" She reviewed her list of acquaintances. None of them meant much to her. She determined gradually to withdraw from them and to cultivate new circumspect acquaintances. Instead of drifting socially she would apply the same careful tactics that she used in her business life.

So Fay decided to call on Henri Voyeur and ask his advice. He told her briefly, "Be yourself and to hell with the rest of them! You are as you were born. You will never change. You may deceive others—quite unlikely; you may even deceive yourself, very likely—but innately you will be the same."

Fay's dearth of social life outside of the office turned her to the theatre for diversion. There, quite unconsciously, she lived the part of the heroine and in the actress identified herself as the one held in the loving embrace of the stage lover. She was having many, many love affairs; true, all vicariously, but through them she was perhaps laying the foundation for the promiscuity which she was later to manifest.

The process of acquiring a desirable social position in New York then was a difficult and also a painful one. Now, thanks to night clubs, dances and more or less open doors at country clubs, and co-mingling at various affairs, it is easy. Then there was one main channel, church work and its associated charities.

At an early age, even before her misfortune in Baltimore, Fay had ceased to accept the validity of her mother religion, relinquishing one idea after another as childish and much on a par with the fables regarding Santa Claus; this had led in turn to a critical examination of some of the offshoots of the faith. Electing to take religion as one of her college courses, she had obtained a wide knowledge of the teachings of the East. Practically all began with assumptions of infallibility, which, though unproven, the disciples then proceeded to teach as basic facts. Their leader, she found, ignored the selfish reasons which led them on and caused them to set aside reason and endeavor to inculcate blind faith. She had no faith. She could see no reason to have faith. She was happier without it. Nothing was explained ultimately; why accept puny, childish explanations? Certainly this attitude gave her great mental freedom, and her logical-mindedness probably saved her in the end from the frightful and hopeless remorse from which so many of her kind forever suffer, and which even she underwent for a time. Fay then turned to some of the newer manifestations of religious faith, wondering if there was any comforting knowledge they could give her. She listened to long harangues on spiritism, on theosophy, on new thought, on "X-science," on Hindoo "philosophy." What was good and useful in them she found reduced to two very simple practices—self-control and auto-suggestion—the rest was harmful. They did not teach her a tithe of the wisdom she found in a study of psychology.

Mentally Fay was fearless and not afflicted with the cowardice which obsesses the great majority of human beings and causes them to fear the logical conclusion, always devastating to the previous childish ideas with which the thought of the whole race is cluttered. The teachers of new religions she found to be wholly selfish and their followers of the suggestible, emotional type. The combination was less satisfying than the organized and regulated practices of the old religions bodies.

It is well recognized that religious experience and sex are closely interwoven. The wild outcroppings which manifest themselves at intervals in some of the newly inspired cults but serve to bring out this feature of religion more clearly.

It is probable that Fay was unconsciously seeking sexual experience and that her desires disguised themselves as yearnings after truth.

Deliberately setting aside her lack of faith, she again took up attendance at the church of her childhood. She accepted no part of the tenets, but she revelled in the pageantry and the music. She laughingly told one of her acquaintances of a Sunday morning that she was on her way to a performance of grand opera. "In the morning? On a Sunday? What grand opera?" he asked. "High Mass at St. M's," she answered. Though superstitions no longer bound her, things aesthetic exercised a greater and greater sway over her emotions.

She affiliated herself with some of the church's charity workers. It did her good to be of service to others; also she met many congenial souls. To one of these, Theodore Wemys Cocke, a young Englishman, she was strongly drawn. The man, who was somewhat older than Fay, had left home to seek opportunities in the less fettered America, where one can embrace trade, or anything except openly recognized fraud, and be highly respected for any financial success. Quite unaccountably to Fay, but not to the Englishman, she found herself on some committee or other with him.

Mr. Cocke's ideas were quite as liberal as her own, but the social call had always kept him from making any out and out break with the church.

There was the usual groping after topics of mutual interest. Their thoughts ran much along the same lines. Perhaps Fay's mind led her more toward an interest in abstract science, while he fancied applied science. Both loved art, or rather objects of art, both loved music, both loved the theatre. So together they visited all of the good things with which New York abounds. Mr. Cocke, except for the Englishman's manners and accent, was anything but British; in fact, he was more of the French type, dark, intense, quick in his decisions and actions. His suavity was delightful; his *savoir faire* was phenomenal. He had travelled extensively and had the ability to relive and retell and make others share his abundant experiences.

Fay began to feel that all of her scant leisure was ill-spent unless she and Teddy were together. They called each other up on the 'phone at luncheon time and made appointments; they telephoned at five, and later dined together if possible. Fay did not acknowledge that this was love, but spoke openly and much of their friendship. Love, and its peculiar manifestations in Baltimore, had meant so much disillusionment, that she refused to admit that love could touch her again. Teddy had been born promiscuous-minded; he had the faculty of being in love with many at the same time, an accomplishment which if not natural, can be acquired in time. To him love was an amusement. Perhaps it should be so for many people. His affair with Fay was but one of three he was developing at the same time. Even to himself he admitted that he loved Fay most. Despite the fact that he was showing marked and rather expensive attention to a youthful member of an English theatrical company, he sought Fay whenever possible and applied himself only enough in the other quarters to keep interest alive. He found Fay delightfully economical and valued to the full her ability to get the utmost for the minimum of expenditure. With this as excuse, he changed his place of residence to her boarding house. Perhaps he was becoming impatient and wished to hurry to the climax and then pass on to yet untasted, but imagined, other joys.

At last Fay awakened to the fact that she was in love. She was very happy. This was such a pure love. She had been disillusioned and defiled before, but past experience should serve as a warning. With youthful idealism she vowed to keep this love on the highest planes of purity and not suffer it to be dragged down by lust. Often she would say to herself, "Love is the greatest thing in the world." So it is. Perhaps even chemistry is love, or perhaps it is the other way about.

10

It was an early fall day, one of those crisp, sunny, cheerful days when New York seems to blossom in anticipation of the greater winter season; a time when all are freshly costumed; when the business houses flaunt anew all their temptations; when there are new plays in town; new faces invading old haunts; when the town in every way seems to take on added life.

Fay had been transferred to the private home of the president of the bank. Her duties had become progressively fewer and more important. Her time was almost her own during the briefer business hours. She was even able to arrange a few day courses at the university, some early and some after business. With greater leisure she even found more time to give to love. She found herself thinking of Teddy between her tasks, planning everything with reference to him; Teddy wanted to see certain shows, she provided the tickets for the following Saturday; Teddy liked her best in dark blue, she bought blue; Teddy did not care for this and did not care for that; Teddy! Teddy! Teddy!

Teddy had invented a new type of automobile. He was anxious to try it. Also, this day, he was anxious to get Fay out into the secluded romantic country where he could feel more free with her. In the city there was the ever-present crowd, at the theatre, at the restaurant, on the street, anywhere. Even the halls of their boarding house were constantly being invaded, and there was no opportunity to caress at ease. He knew intuitively that Fay would have to be won unsuspectingly—taken unawares.

So this lovely fall day he planned to try out his automobile and also to try out Fay. He suggested a run up the Hudson. The novelty of the thing was appealing. Fay was tingling with excitement, the thrill of her new love, the sense of novelty, the stimulation of the wonderful fall day. Life seemed glorious. She would love Teddy always and he would love her and that would be all there was to it, love, love, love—purest love!

They turned from Thirtieth Street into Fifth Avenue. Fay waved gaily to several acquaintances. Any automobile was a novelty then. She felt a pleasant sense of importance in being different from the crowd, an admired and envied something different. They passed through the park, over to the Drive and up the Hudson where the foliage was all brilliant reds, yellows, oranges and purples. Teddy's car was a success. 'Twas a glorious ride, of wonderful distance—for those days! They were far out in the country. They arrived at an eminence where the view of the Hudson was superb. Here Teddy halted. They alighted to enjoy the scene and also to have a picnic supper.

The dead, dry grass, sunned all day, was delightfully warm. They sat down. The sun was beginning to redden the sky. They ate their sandwiches lingeringly and quietly. Words seemed unnecessary. Fay's face, as she gazed on the beauty about her, wore a look of exaltation. The sunlight on her short, curly hair turned it to reddish gold. A faint happy smile played about her lips.

Teddy too was affected by the scene. Also, he was experiencing the happiness which comes from satisfied achievement. He was stirred by Fay's youthful beauty as never before. Also, he had become increasingly aware of her excellence. For the time being he thought himself capable and eager to renounce all other loves for the sweetness of this, the most entrancing affair of his life. There are times when sex dominates completely. Such a time had arrived!

As the sun sank, a chill wind sprang up. Teddy went to the car for robes, one to sit on, the other to wrap about Fay. As he enveloped her slender body with the robes, he closed his arms about her, and meeting no resistance gave her a long lingering kiss.

"Oh, Teddy, Teddy, how I love you!" she whispered, though there was no one to hear had she declaimed it aloud. Almost she swooned in his arms.

Teddy, to do him justice, had never been so much in love as at this moment. He kissed her over and over again and they made repeated avowals of their love, just as all lovers do.

The sun set in a glorious burst of flame that encompassed the whole horizon. They were alone; the world, the entire world, seemed theirs. As the sun disappeared from sight, the moon came up casting its dark blue shadows. He pleaded. The almost hypnotic compliance invaded her. She felt no emotion other than the compulsion to do his bidding.

The ride home was very quiet. Teddy was beside himself with joy. Far from feeling satiation, his experience had served to make him more truly in love with her than ever. On every possible occasion he stole one hand beneath the robe and caressed her.

He came into her room to bid her good-night. Then he took her again into his arms and gripped her body madly as if, with such vicelike force, he would fuse them into one being. God! How he loved her!

"Teddy," she whispered, "you do love me, don't you?" and when he answered that he loved her more than ever she begged, "Then don't let me ever forget my better self again!"

He laughed as he said, "Oh, you've been there before. You're too good at it."

"Stop, stop," she whimpered. "Go away before I hate myself and you too."

Puzzled, he gave her a perfunctory embrace and hurried to his own room.

For hours Fay lay awake thinking alternately of her love for Teddy and her new fall from grace, with its accompanying sense of shame. But this time she was calmer in the face of self-realization.

II

THE NEXT MORNING, Sunday, Fay felt ashamed to meet Teddy at breakfast, and planned to remain in her room. But Teddy's action showed that he experienced no such qualms. His attitude was entirely matter of fact. He was in love with Fay, and he cared not who knew it or what others thought; this was Fay's affair and his; it was for them to seize happiness when it presented, in whatever form it presented, and make the most of it as and while they could. In after years he was wont to relate with pride that this was the great love affair of his life. True, he was ten years older than Fay and also came from more sophisticated people. Ten years more of experience did much to develop Fay's character; at the end of that time she would have been quite a match for Teddy. Complete revelation had not yet come to Fay. To too many it never comes at all; else the world would be much more tolerant and kindly.

Teddy arose bright and early. Fay could hear him whistling in his room above, whistling gaily. What would he think of her? Would he tell on her? She had forgotten to make him promise not to tell. She was terror stricken at the possibilities. As she sat gazing into space, imagining all of the horrors of such a situation, she was startled by a knock on the door, followed by Teddy's cheerful call: "Hello! Are you coming to breakfast?"

"In a minute!" she answered as she realized thankfully that he still desired her companionship. She put the finishing touches to her toilet, then opened the door. "Come in Teddy!"

He stepped into the room and closed the door quickly, then gathered her into his arms. She did not resist but welcomed this demonstration of his continued interest in her. "Teddy," she murmured, "Promise me that you will never tell anyone about yesterday!"

"Of course not! That is for me and you alone to know. But you take things too seriously," he whispered as he kissed her ear. "Don't you wish to make me happy? Are you not happy loving me? Let us make the most of life while we can. I love you. You love me. What else matters! Now come along and eat breakfast."

So they went down to the dining room, and Fay found enjoyment in the luscious late peaches with cream, the hot waffles and the coffee which "Jinny" set before them. "Jinny" too could have told a tale of love—of loves, of many loves, in which conscience had not been the least bit troublesome to her. She had survived them and had been and still was happy. After all, we are beginning to question whether repression, with its frequent dire consequences, is the desired thing which the priesthoods of all nations would have us believe it to be.

Teddy wished to rush off at once to church so they might enjoy the music together. With their automobile, it was almost a triumphal tour to the church of St. M's, where the music and pageantry at that time were unrivalled and where the senses were lulled into sweet dreams which answer well for religious sentiments when one is too advanced in thought to accept either Judaism or any of the teachings of its many, and even more childish, Christian offshoots.

The music was exquisite. Fay was ecstatic. All through the service she and Teddy held hands under the overcoat thrown across his knees. They did not accept communion; they never did.

They dined in the park, a special dinner in celebration of their happiness. The afternoon they spent driving up and down the avenue in the novel car, astonishing the onlookers and earning the curses of the cabbies whose horses had not yet become accustomed to the new-fangled machine. At night they returned to their boarding house, tired and happy. Teddy, perceiving that he must not proceed too fast and too suddenly with Fay, or perhaps satisfied enough with his conquest, gave Fay a chaste goodnight kiss as they parted in the hallway before her door.

12

EXCEPT FOR AN OCCASIONAL SIGH at the thought of her peccadillo of the afternoon along the Hudson, Fay was wildly happy during the following week. Teddy gave her every evidence of being in love with her, and she in turn loved him—in fact thoughts of him almost excluded all others. Every evening they met for a short turn on the avenue in his new car, and later they would always slip into Café Martin for Teddy's "nightcap."

Already Teddy was planning for another weekend. They would run up to New Haven in his car, see a theatrical tryout and put up with mutual friends there. He proposed this one evening as they were walking home from the old barn where he stored his automobile. Fay snuggled close to his side. She agreed that it would be delightful but added, "You must promise to be good, Teddy. Our love must be kept above all sordidness. We must keep it ideal and pure." Teddy, having never experienced the novelty, acquiesced. Joyfully Fay exclaimed, "Oh, Teddy! I never thought love could be quite so beautiful. I am the happiest person in the world." Then, "We are the happiest people in the world," she amended.

In sex matters Teddy was quite unmoral. His opinion was that what people do with each other is only their own personal concern, a tenet which seems to have become more and more a part of the teaching of the present generation, when one is likely to hear sex, normal or abnormal, openly discussed by adolescents at fashionable luncheons, or tea dances, or between dances at an evening gathering. Teddy lived for the joy of the moment. Kindly, and certainly a gentleman by instinct, he would not intentionally have hurt anyone. He had been spontaneously attracted to Fay, and she was attracted to him likewise. It was all very simple. Thus he reasoned. Saturday came. Fay had never visited New Haven before. She was eager with anticipation; almost she fluttered, her movements, unrestrained, taking on the mannerisms which are so revealing of one of her kind.

It was another perfect fall day. The ride was enjoyable from almost every point of view, despite the fact that roads had not yet been improved to their present smooth stage. They arrived in good time and wandered over the campus. They visited some student friends of Teddy, and though these admired some of Fay's characteristics, they laughed, one and all, at the unusual timbre of her voice once she was out of earshot. Perhaps Fay, a little forgetful and excited by the novelty of everything, failed to repress what her brother Bill had characterized as "that damned voice."

They had luncheon. They attended a frat dance. They hurried to the theatre. The play was the premiere of a musical piece which later became famous. The young men and women of the cast had been chosen not alone for their singing and dancing ability, but also for their pulchritude. Teddy was outspoken in his admiration of the physical attractions of various members of the cast. Fay felt a quickening sense of jealousy, admitted their good points, and then gushed forth in praise of some of the wonderful Yale men they had met earlier in the day. Teddy sensed her jealousy, and she was annoyed with herself for the ill-suppressed emotion.

After the theatre, they rejoined some of Teddy's college friends and together went to a rathskeller, a haunt of the students and the theatrical people. Teddy was busy acting as toastmaster. Fay was neglected and a trifle bored. To make the time pass more pleasantly she engaged in conversation with a young instructor who was seated at her left. This man had made his own way in life, even as Fay was doing. He drew her out, her true self, as no one else ever troubled to do. He was interested to hear of her college extension work, of her desire to give up business and earn a degree in science. Mr. Wright, of the many men who were attracted to Fay, was drawn not by sex, but by the quality of her mind. He gave her valuable advice, outlining easy ways for the accomplishment of her ambitions.

The evening wore along. Fay did not drink. Teddy, though he carried his liquor well, was unduly exhilarated. He was sufficient master of himself to realize this and suggested that they take a long walk before appearing at their friend's apartment. They wandered out into the country. The houses were fewer and fewer. Teddy removed his hat and complained that his head was hot and throbbing. Sympathetically Fay laid her hand to his brow. As she let it drop he caught it to his lips—

"How sweet you are, Fay!"

She nestled close to him. In a moment their arms were about each other. His kisses were wild and furious. This time Fay felt a mad desire for compliance, a conscious enjoyment.

More calmly they walked homeward. As they bade each other good night she said almost lightly, "Teddy we must stop being naughty." To this he answered, "We only obeyed something stronger than ourselves—instinct." He was quite sincere when he added, "I only love you all the more for it."

During the night Fay heard a stealthy tapping at her door. She understood. Without hesitation she opened it.

Thus began their more intimate clandestine relationship.

13

FAY WAS CONTENTED AS SHE HAD NEVER BEEN BEFORE. With her emotional life thoroughly satisfied, the quality of her work both in business and at the university improved. For the time being, at least, she had let go her inhibitions. And with that there was a noticeable slight change in her personality; more and more frequently her voice broke beyond the bounds of proper restraint. One day she chanced to meet Bill. She was happy to see him, fluttered gaily up to him and burst out rapturously, "How wonderful to meet you, Bill. You are looking perfectly marvelous." She took a turn about him as if to look him over well. "For God's sake, keep quiet!" was his answer. "Why can't you act natural?"

His rebuff hurt. She had been so sincere. But she understood perfectly—perfectly at last. "Very well, Bill, goodbye," she said in a low, heartbroken tone of voice.

Fay felt his condemnation. It symbolized to her that of the rest of the world. She had sacrificed much for Bill and in fact for all of her family. The thought came suddenly that all this counted for nothing. The iron began to enter her soul.

Slowly she walked homeward. After dinner Teddy came to sit with her in her cozy homelike room. He observed her depression, noted the lack of her usual buoyancy, her quiet and absorption. Fay sat staring straight ahead, lost in deep sad thought. He kissed her with what was meant to be compassion, but when Teddy kissed Fay this meant the arousing within him of fiery desire. As his caresses became more intense she begged, "Not tonight, Teddy, not tonight. You ridicule my conscience. I do not know what it is, Teddy, whether it is conscience or a sense of loss of self-respect. I must get away from all of this, Teddy. I'm going away."

He knew how firm she could be; that anything he might say would not shake her decision. He had begun to love her madly, to the exclusion of all other love episodes. He felt the need of her. He couldn't lose her. He protested that they would keep their relation one of purest friendship, but she must not go. He shed tears. He promised her what to a mercenary person would have been tempting gifts. Not one move did he leave untried. He threatened to follow her. At last he realized that for the time being his pleas were useless. He kissed her and left.

The next morning Fay arose much earlier than usual. Quickly she packed her bag and trunks. More bulky belongings she left behind to be sent for later. She hailed a hansom, then the common mode of conveyance about the streets of New York, and asked to be taken to the —— Hotel. After she had registered and given a few directions regarding her luggage and boxes to come later, she turned to follow the bellhop. As she did so the room clerk gave a knowing wink to one of his fellows. Fay happened to catch this reflected in a glass. "Does everybody see me as I am?" she thought. Then defiance came to her support—"Well, I'm as God made me, if there is a God, or whatever it is that creates human mistakes."

A dreadful week of remorse and loneliness followed. The day's work now seemed arduous. She looked and felt ill. A pompous young physician who had his bronze sign prominently displayed at the entrance of the hotel, observing Fay, announced, "There's a praecox case," knowing that though his auditors would not understand they would marvel at his erudition. But Fay was not "a praecox case." Her mind was keen, sound and sharply analytical.

Habits once formed are difficult to break unless something especially engrossing is substituted. Teddy had become a habit. At the end of a week, Fay cast conscience, or remorse, or whatever it was, aside, and as abruptly as she had left returned to the boarding house—and to Theodore Wemys.

14

TEDDY GREETED FAY WITH TEARS IN HIS EYES, succeeded by violent sobbing as he gathered her into his arms.

The Christmas season was approaching. Teddy begged Fay to let him know what he could get for her. The vanity of testing his infatuation, more than desire of possession, prompted her to name some extravagant thing which she did not need. Teddy brought it the next day. After it was received, she did not experience the satisfaction which she had anticipated. Somewhat remorsefully she told him, "Teddy, I really did not wish you to spend so much money on me. I only wanted to see if you were willing to do it. Take it back." He of course did not fathom her whims, and felt wounded. Probably from that time the inevitable estrangement set in. Teddy had sacrificed to make this gift. He felt that it was not appreciated. Their conduct towards each other, from then on, began to be less even. There were lapses of politeness on both sides. Teddy's attentions began to wander to others. Fay began to have more fits of remorse. At the end of the winter she suddenly left him again. This time she put so much distance between them that return was more difficult. She spent a wretched week of loneliness. At the end of that time her craving for some sort of affection was so great that she felt almost beside herself with longing. The weekend took her to Boston for the bank. Saturday afternoon she attended the Philharmonic concert. On the way to the hall she was more than once conscious of being noticed by attractive men. She wept quietly through the more sentimental numbers of the concert. She must have love. She could not live without it.

As she left the concert hall she made up her mind. This time she did not bother to return to Teddy.

Her new friend complimented her on her sophistication. She shrugged her shoulders and threw out her hands in a Frenchified gesture as much as to say, "What's the difference?"

Her work held her in Boston for the following week. She did not even seek to find her new lover again, but night after night, handsome substitute was followed by handsome substitute in a careless succession of experiments.

At the end of the week, when she returned to New York, from her new lodgings she telephoned to Teddy quite casually—"I'm back; you may as well come up."

15

TEDDY CAME. He was very considerate, very tender, but not excessively emotional as on their former reconciliation. They spent the afternoon driving, stopping for tea at the lovely old Jumel Mansion. After tea they took a walk along the Drive, drinking in the fresh spring air, feeling elated by the beauty of the season and the renewal of their companionship. They discussed the future. Fay admitted that she thought she understood herself better and could be happier than before. As they passed along the Drive, Fay began to indulge in what, at times later on, was almost an obsession with her, the studying of the various types they saw. So absorbed did she become in watching the face of one well-dressed, tall, Vandyke-bearded man that Teddy asked sharply that she stop staring at people. Reproofs from Teddy too? Oh, well!

They agreed, after much discussion, to take an apartment together and at once set out to find a furnished place. This they located somewhere in the Fifties, cozy, not too expensive, and convenient to the life of the town.

Shortly afterwards the bank president sailed for Europe, practically making Fay free for the summer. So habituated was she to routine useful occupation that time hung heavily. Summer courses at the university were not yet open. She decided to take private lessons in French, German and Spanish. The best teachers were within easy walking distance. April and May are lovely months in New York City; even early June, before the parks have become sere, gives one the feeling of living in an enchanted land. Fay spent hours afoot, going from one place to another. She had formed the curious habit of carrying on two distinct trains of thought, almost simultaneously. She lived a life of actualities and a dream life. In this dream life she was successful, financially at ease, the centre of a deferential admiring circle of people. Curiously she never pictured any real women in this circle.

The avenue seemed full of gay people those days, persons as happy as she. At intervals were stationed the mounted traffic police. Their splendid figures, their neat, well-fitting uniforms, their highly polished puttees protecting perfectly formed legs, the thigh outlined by pressure against the horse's side, all combined to make a picture which she found irresistibly appealing. She found herself looking for the mounted police. She formed preferences for one or the other. She thought of the Aztecs with their idea that the men astride of horses were some kind of god, and she smiled to think that her poetic sense was interpreting these horsemen in the same light. She liked especially to view the officers from the back, the torso, the carriage, the outline of the leg all accentuated.

In Boston one of her experimentals had been with a handsome, muscular, athletic young Irishman, a cop in plain clothes, off for the evening. She had felt a peculiar satisfaction in giving her caresses, an intensity of excitement which Teddy, perhaps too refined and not sufficiently virile, had failed to arouse within her. She found herself, when admiring these lovely young policemen, reverting to the Boston experience and wondering about the possibilities with these men too. That was only occasionally. She was too busy with her studies to give too much thought to them. She found herself laughing when she compared these virile types with so many of the men she met daily, teachers of French, or Spanish, or German, or music; or overly fat brokers and business men—all a bit physically degenerate.

June came, and with it all classes ceased. Of course later she would enroll for the summer sessions at one of the universities. Teddy knew she would be busy at the summer schools and suggested that they take a trip together before that time. "We'll call it our honeymoon," he said.

The forerunner of the Tin-Lizzies was made ready. They were to have two weeks of June along the Hudson, the Mohawk Trail and the Adirondacks. The first days were delightful. Teddy was trying a speedometer which he had invented. Whenever it registered a new fifty miles he stopped and kissed Fay.

He was very playful—in the beginning. One week had sped by. They had been very happy. Perhaps they had been too unrestrained. Certainly satiety breeds enervation, and enervation breeds antipathy, the reaction of the wearied body in its attempt to repair itself.

They had reached their goal, one of the pretty lakes with which the Adirondacks abound. They camped on a grassy slope.

Fay was tired. She felt nervous, irritable and dissatisfied with herself as much as with Teddy. His continued insistence led to rebellion. Suddenly she burst forth, "You think of me for one thing only! You do not even respect me! I hate you! I hate everything!"

She started away. He called to her and when she did not turn cried out angrily, "Then go, damn you, and don't ever come back."

She ran at first, then settled down to a steady walk. It was miles to a railway. That was no task. Her overwrought nerves needed the relaxation which exercise would give them. After she had covered a mile, Teddy overtook her with his machine. But she would not ride with him. He pleaded to take her wherever she wished to go. He knew it was fifteen miles more to the railway station. Her only reply was, "Keep away from me. I never want to see you again." Even though she would not talk to him or ride with him, he kept her in sight. He would not leave her unprotected till he saw her safely at the railway station.

Aboard the Pullman she sobbed most of the night. She put Teddy out of her mind. She felt that she was grieving for a dead self, an idealized better self.

In a city as big as New York, one is quickly lost. It was years before Fay saw Teddy again. In the meantime her point of view had shifted completely. It was on 125th Street. Teddy was so intent that he did not see Fay. She laughed gaily as she looked on and saw him trying to "make" a blonde. She thought "The same old Teddy, bless his heart, and up to the same old tricks."

16

FAY WENT TO WORK WITH A VENGEANCE when the summer session opened at the university. The work at the bank was slight. With the consent of the president she had broken in an assistant, a young, ambitious man from Brooklyn, who was able to do the work as well as she could. Her conscientious services were appreciated, and the officials gave her permission to take six weeks of leave without pay; this covered the summer session at the university.

In view of her record in previous courses, the dean gave her permission to carry an almost impossible number of points.

Fay's reaction from the Teddy-episode, far from unfitting her for intense mental applications, seemed to have left her brain in so receptive and sensitive a condition that she could grasp her subjects with one reading or one hearing. She did the best scholastic work of her life; her accomplishment was so remarkable as to attract the attention of the dean. At the end of the session he called her to his office. He complimented her on her successful performance and asked what was her incentive. Finding that she was not attempting to make up points flunked at some other college, he tried to fathom the reason for her industry. "Surely," he said, "you have some definite aim in view in studying so systematically?"

Fay had a well-defined aim, but even his kindly sympathy could not induce her to put "the goal of her ambition" into words. He suggested that if finances were bothering her, the university would see that she had ample opportunity; they would give her a scholarship if she would enroll as a full-time student. "That will make your financial burden an easy one to meet," he assured her. He was astonished when she revealed the extent of her more than ample funds. A fortunate investment the past spring had netted her a clear one hundred per cent profit. Several other turnovers of her capital had brought the amount up to an even fifty thousand dollars. She felt safe. But until she had achieved a measure of success in her chosen field, she had no intention of telling anyone of her plans, not even the dean. None other than a psychologist would have been able to understand her motive in giving up what was already a successful business career for a life of drudgery in a difficult branch of science.

So she thanked the dean and fled quickly to take advantage of the one day of vacation which remained.

The need of relaxation pressed upon her. She decided on a trip by the dayboat for West Point as being the most restful recreation she could have. She chose a deck chair on the shaded breeze-swept deck and at once fell into a heavy sleep, from which she was awakened half an hour later by the boat swinging from the dock. A little self-indulgently, she thought smilingly of the summer's studies. Suddenly she realized that she could scarcely recall any part of the work she had covered. Puzzled, she groped in her mind for the key which would unlock remembrance, but to no avail.

Two boys of about twelve were standing near. One had a fishing rod and a basket. The other carried a common old tin can. As if in answer to her wondering gaze, the larger of the two announced, "We are going fishing when we get to West Point. Buddy has the worms in the tin can. Don't you want to see the worms? We got up last night and took candles and went out on the grass and grabbed them before they could get back in their holes." With that he picked out "the greatest biggest one" for prideful exhibition. At once Fay began to chant inwardly—"The common earthworm, lumbricus terrestris, is one of the most interesting of all the species which we will study in this course. In it you see a perfect exemplification of hermaphroditism, that is, both male and female, perfect in every sense, in the one body. You will do well to remember this as you study the higher species and compare what you see today with the rudimentary appendages which will be found even in man. Those of you who will study medicine will find that the human female has an appendage designated the clitoris, which is the analogue of the male penis; conversely the male has within him the analogue of the female uterus. By some authorities it is even held that the hidden hermaphroditism of some human individuals accounts for various sexual vagaries. The female organs of lumbricus are complete; likewise are the male organs. Mutual cross-fertilization probably always takes place. Some of you may be fortunate enough to find two specimens in your day's supply that are copulating. If so, you will observe that the more cephalad organ of the one is joined to the more caudad organ of the other, and vice versa. That is, they do not lie head to head and tail to tail, but the head of each is directed towards the tail of the other. The embryos . . . ," etc. She recalled the entire lecture, word for word, every question, every answer, the dissection with the aetherized worm stretched out on waxed plates; every detail up to the end of the lecture hour. Then there was a balk. She could not remember what came next. Uneasily she left her chair to stroll about. Passing a French couple, she caught the word "aller." At once she seemed to hear the effeminate old French professor intoning—"Les parties principales du verbe aller," and that lecture to its close. She laughed to herself. "You press the button, we do the rest. Anyway, it's evidently still there. I didn't spend my money for nothing at the knowledge factory. I'll not worry about it."

When the boat stopped she elected to remain at the Point instead of going further up the river. She climbed the hills to the old fort and later lolled about beneath the shady trees surrounding the parade ground. She was disappointed; there was no drill. Instead, a group of young officers was engaged in polo. How wonderful their poise astride a horse; how beautiful the muscles of their arms! Nearby stood a group of tall young men in service uniforms. Their slim erectness, their slender legs encased in shining puttees made their usual disguised sex appeal, which Fay acknowledged to herself only as admiration for physical development. One of them looked her over critically, almost superciliously. "I'm an earthworm," she thought. "Lumbricus terrestris! Army officers! What connection is there between army officers and earthworms and myself?" Her mind wandered to her course in zoölogy as she pondered the relationship which exists between all forms of living matter. One of the young officers whispered to another as he looked at her. Then she failed to notice them further. She became engrossed in the polo again and tense as she observed a difficult play. Gradually she became aware of a uniformed man close beside her. He was not a commissioned officer. He spoke. Evidently he was trying to become friendly, or else wished to appease his curiosity. Without any self-consciousness, Fay answered all of the questions he so laboriously led up to and by the end of half an hour had informed him that she was there for the day only; that she did not visit the place frequently; that she knew no one, either of the enlisted or the commissioned personnel; that she came there only because the excursion trip happened to offer the Point as a stopping place; that she held a position in a bank and still had one day of leave; that she could smoke but did not care anything about it; that she did not drink, though she had liberal ideas on that, and in fact on all subjects, that she had no booze with her, she did not think drinking a wise habit; that this, that that. That she would not care to meet any of the soldiers, they were too crude; that she did not think she would care to know any of the cadets, they were too immature; that she was not especially anxious to meet anyone socially, officers or otherwise; that she did not think she would care to have him look her up when he came to New York, and she added with veiled sarcasm, "My time is too taken up with things of importance."

Fay was really too tired at the time to fathom his motive in asking her all these questions. She did remember seeing him later talking to one of the group of officers, then looking at her, and when she reviewed the episode thought, "They saw me as I am; they were after me. God! They must think themselves tempting!" In later years, retelling it at an afternoon tea in New York, one of the tempting buds of the season volunteered, "They wanted to make you."

"Not at all," corrected the hostess, every inch a woman of the world, "they wanted to get her!"

The return trip to New York was quiet, blissfully quiet and uneventful. She took the then new subway home. She crawled into bed and slept as if drugged.

17

FOLLOWED A BEAUTIFUL FALL. Fay was assigned anew to the bank president's uptown library. The work was confidential. She learned of accumulated dividends, uncut "melons." All this formed the basis for wise investments. No longer had she anything to fear financially. And now, when she was able to do so much for her mother, she received word of her sudden passing away. Fay was alone! Her brother Bill had taken pains to estrange the other members of the family.

Fay enrolled for extension courses to fill out certain subjects required for the major work of her life, unless her subsequent love episodes, adventures, conquests, should be considered the major work of her life.

Even with a busy routine, at intervals a kind of loneliness invaded her. This proved disturbing. Work, activity, theatrical entertainment, music, art, nothing quite submerged the vague longing which possessed her.

She found herself studying types again. Fay now realized that she had fetishes, as she had learned to call them—Vandyke beards and strong-looking men with thick matte skins and closely shaved blueblack beards showing through the skin attracted her especially. She found herself comparing one type of man with another, on the street, in the bus, on the El, in the subway, at the theatre, wherever she might be. She found herself anew yearning for comradeship. But she determined that this time there would be no enslaving infatuation connected with her life.

She bethought herself of Henri Voyeur. At intervals she had run across him in the Waldorf-Astoria, and they had occasionally attended the theatre together. She called him on the telephone. Henri had always found Fay unusual, agreeable, and to him entirely congenial. He responded at once.

The banker subscribed to countless theatrical and musical performances, as well as to the opera. Always Fay had tickets, as many as she could find time to use. She and Henri formed the habit of going to these entertainments together. Henri never presumed. He was not in the least interested in Fay physically. Together they satisfied that craving for intellectual companionship which is needed to complement all lives, and which, alas! is not always found in one's immediate family, or even in marriage. Henri too had the habit of studying and admiring types. They compared notes. They became frank and outspoken. Fay told him in detail of her affairs of the heart (and head) and vowed she was through with all love forever. To this Henri responded, "I hope this is true, Fay, but my experience leads me to believe that those of a certain type will continue to seek the ever evasive and baffling happiness of love, and not finding it in one affair will, as the years go by, take the bit they can find in one place, and the bit they can find in another and thus pick up here and there in their lives sufficiently varied experience to make in the aggregate enough to satisfy." He confessed to his own promiscuous adventures. Fay drew back from becoming again a slave of sensation. "No, Henri, I have gone too far already," she told him. "I shall never play at love again. I realize what I am. I must reform. I've had enough!"

"Fay," he warned, "if you mean that, you will have to cut out all friendship with the people to whom you are attracted. You will have to live as a hermit. You cannot even see me. Your conversation with me always turns to this subject. You are seeking a vicarious enjoyment. You can only satisfy your cravings by indulgence. There is no happiness in this so-called sublimation. For your own sake I hope that you can live without love, for society is not organized with a view to the exceptional individual and makes no allowances for the variation from the conventional type. If you can forswear your own kind, you may not be exactly happy, but you will at least breathe more easily. Even now you are interested in various men without acknowledging it to yourself. Why do you comment on the splendid physique of the traffic squad, for instance? I think you deceive yourself."

It was shortly after this that Fay and Henri began to habituate the gay Bohemian places of the town. A famed chop house was one of them. Here, after opera, they frequently sat to nibble a sandwich and have some innocuous drink. Not long after they took to supping at the place, Fay observed a dark, moustached, unusual man at a nearby table. She tried to place him. Finally she remembered; she had seen him at one of the parties which she and Henri had attended in the basement of a 55th Street apartment house where the famous and beautiful Lillian Russell and other well-known theatrical people lived. At that time the society blackmailer was beginning to make his appearance again in New York. Fay looked at this sleek, expensively dressed man. There was much that was unusual about him. Then she remembered more; she had seen him at the opera too. She called Henri's attention to the fellow. "Looks like a grafter to me," Henri remarked curtly. The man did look the part. Fay dismissed him from her mind.

The next Friday evening, forgetful of her resolution to reform, Fay dropped into the 55th Street place. It was a rainy night. Few people were there. The dark chap of the chop house was sitting by a window she had to pass. She was startled. He looked up laughing as she carefully rearranged her white drag and said, "What frightened you? You needn't be afraid of me." When he smiled and when he talked, his face was transformed.

Fay felt that she had shown her feelings too plainly. She retorted gaily— "The only thing I am afraid of here is a cop. Hope there'll be none tonight. But why should I be afraid of you?"

"To prove that you are not, you must have supper with me after the opera next Friday instead of with your friend, the one you call Henri. I wish to know you better. For a long time I have been wishing to speak to you, but did not dare. I am Billy Pickup. Almost anybody who steps out the least bit in society knows all about me. God knows I'm notorious enough. You've heard of my father too, I am sure. We are stopping at the Holland House this winter. I hope you are going to be generous and make it possible for us to see each other again."

Fay knew his father, had met him in the bank frequently. She studied the young man's face a moment; the eyes, the nose and forehead were the same as those of the father; the mouth, somehow, was different, not so strong, not so determined. Small wonder the fellow could dress exquisitely! Quite safe! She accepted.

When she told Henri he blurted out, "Who'd have thought it. So hard to tell the genuine from the imitation these days. I've heard of him. He gives remarkable parties, the gayest in town. If he invites you, don't fail to attend, for you'll meet the very elite of our young set."

Friday night came. There was a double bill. Fay came in late for *Il Pagliacci*. She had called young Pickup on the telephone and told him to look for her. He was sauntering about the lounge when she entered. Billy insisted that she come to their box. As the act started and the house was in darkness, he placed his chair close to hers, grasped one of her hands and pressed it tensely. Fay's emotions were mixed, but the flattering satisfaction of being desired by Billy Pickup probably was dominant.

By the time they had reached Jack's Restaurant, where they were to sup, they were like old friends. Pickup appeared to be madly infatuated, but that meant nothing, for infatuations new and frequent were a commonplace in his life. At first Fay was rather indifferent emotionally, but his long practice in lovemaking had schooled him in the art of insidious flattery, and as a love affair is in great part founded on self love, 'twas not long before Fay thought she was again in love and that this time she had found the idealist she sought. Certainly the sentiments he expressed made her idealize him. Candidly she told him of her heartbreaks and how she had forever forsworn all love. Then he promised to be true to her if she would be his. She believed him.

The next morning, feeling expansive, at breakfast Billy planned an elaborate party for the following Saturday night, to be in Fay's "honor." He enumerated the string of notables who would be present. Fay left him, walking on air. Surely the gods were being good to her.

18

FAY BY THIS TIME HAD ABSORBED THE NEW YORK CUSTOMS and indeed no longer looked on herself as anything other than a New Yorker.

To while away the afternoon, Fay lunched at the Waldorf-Astoria, then went to a haberdasher's for a gift for Billy Pickup and also something for herself.

Billy had bidden Fay to bring Henri along. The party was to begin at eleven-thirty, after theatre, and of course would last all night. Fay knew that most of Billy's crowd would attend the Empire, where a musical comedy was the attraction. Several of the cast would be at the party. She and Henri attended the Empire too. Fay was surprised to see how many of her New York acquaintances were present. She had not realized how much her circle had widened since she and Henri had taken to frequenting the resorts of a more Bohemian character.

In the foremost row she saw Billy Pickup. She hoped he would come to the lobby during the interact, so that she might present Henri. Fay observed that Billy kept his opera glass pointed almost constantly at one member of the cast. She was surprised, perhaps a little jealous. When the intermission arrived, Billy did not come to the foyer; instead he went back stage. She knew what that meant. She spoke of it to Henri, who sagaciously remarked, "You'll end by taking whatever comes your way, enjoying it for the moment, and doing as the rest of us do. Surely you realize by this time that these affairs can lead to no lasting bond. Why these infatuations are so intense they burn themselves out to a finish almost as soon as curiosity is satisfied. Take your love where—and how—you find it. Enjoy! Pass on! Then you'll never be lonesome or unhappy. Be in love with love. You may as well realize that the failure to hold a lover is as much due to the inherent defect in yourself as to the unfaithful tendency of your sweetheart. Be like me—a oncer. Love often and not too hard; don't take your emotions too seriously; then they'll not get the best of you."

It did not shock her. She was changing in her attitude toward life.

The play swept on to a glorious finale, and even then they did not succeed in joining Billy Pickup.

The party was to be held in the studio of Mr. (and Miss) Painter in East 69th Street. Fay hurried, as she did not wish to be late. Billy had not yet arrived. The artist Painter, then beginning to be known for his murals, was acting host. Already there was a more than lively crowd, all drinking, singing and dancing, and doing other things too that suited their fancy.

Painter welcomed Fay with, "I suppose you are Fay Etrange. Billy told me to expect you with your friend."

Henri was presented, and then Painter with a wave of his hand announced, "A new friend of Billy's. Make yourselves acquainted!" That was the end of all formalities. Then he turned to Fay and said, "You will attend my costume party next week, won't you? Everybody in our set who is worth knowing will be there. The sky's the limit. You can wear much, or nothing. Several of my models will be there too. Promise me you'll come." Then he whispered in Fay's ear, "You come early."

Someone was playing, one of the old-fashioned things, a waltz, or a two-step, or a turkey trot, whatever it was the style to dance then. Everyone danced, with frequent breaks for drinks and followed almost invariably by the choice of a new partner. The reigning Earl of the season, quite the most betitled human object that England had sent out heiress-hunting for some time, danced frequently with Fay.

"My God!" she said to Henri afterwards, "What use can a real woman find for a thing like that?"

"They can use their titles, can't they?" Henri laughed.

In the midst of the hubbub, Billy arrived, as one of the girls expressed it, "dragging in something lovely"—a handsome young Irishman, a member of the fire department. The fireman seemed a bit abashed at finding himself in this hilarious crowd of such a different level from the people with whom he usually associated.

Billy rushed up to Fay with, "So glad you came," kissed her and then passed on, forgetting both her and the fireman. His ideas of the duties of a host were rather unusual. He seemed preoccupied and left each guest to make the best of things and amuse himself. With the arrival of the theatrical contingent the reason for this preoccupation became evident—the star of the company had arrived. Much later in the evening Billy came back to Fay and said, "You are going to stay after the party, aren't you?"

Fay, not to be outdone, answered boldly, "Why, of course. What did you expect I came to the party for?"

Off dashed Billy. That was settled. He must look out for his newest conquest—"See that someone does not grab it away from him," said the worldly-wise Henri.

Certainly to be promiscuous was the keynote here. Fay shrugged her shoulders as she confided to Henri, "I'm in it now, so here goes."

A slender dark young Jew from California, just out of college, claimed her for the next dance, which seemed to resolve itself into a grappling contest. Fay complimented him on the power of his biceps, and he begged to see her soon. The type was new. She liked him, even if she did not love him. He kissed her hungrily, and though she felt no actual reciprocation of his passion, neither did she feel any repulsion, but rather a pleasant sense of excitement. He wished to monopolize her. She feared ennui. A little of such intensity went far.

Then a French singer, an unusual blond, claimed her for a dance. At once he told her that he loved her, protested that it was love at first sight. She took his declaration lightly; it was only after meeting him many times afterwards and learning that her indifference had wounded him that she realized that he had been quite sincere. Then she felt a kind of gratitude, perhaps a bit of pity which is akin to love. The poor chap had left his beloved Paris and accepted an engagement in New York to forget the disappointment of his first love gone wrong. He too was learning.

The young fireman sought Fay. The party was as novel to him as to her. They got on famously. He told her of his life in the Fire Department and insisted that she visit the "Hook and Ladder" and meet some of the boys. After a drink together he began to be affectionate. She enjoyed him; his speech, his mannerisms, all so different.

"Let's have another drink," the fireman invited, "and then let's go out on the balcony. I want some lovin'."

But Fay did not want "some lovin'" just yet and pretended to be interested in the playing of a young lawyer. The lawyer asked her if she played too. So she sat down on the piano bench beside him and made a medley of parts of Chopin waltzes suitable for dance rhythm. The lawyer followed with his right hand an octave higher, leaving his left free to embrace her. Billy Pickup saw them. "Having a good time?" he called out. "Remember what you promised me!"

The lawyer seemed not to mind. "You'll give me a chance too, sometime, won't you?" he asked.

Fay was in the mood to promise anything, even if not to fulfill all the promises made. "Oh, I'll try you out," she answered. That seemed to satisfy for the time being.

Thus she passed from one to another. Love was taken lightly. It was nearing time to go. She rejoined Henri, who asked, "Are you converted to my way of thinking yet?"

"Perhaps a little bit."

"Remember the French saying, 'One only loves.'"

"Implying?"

"That the other accepts. It's this way in life. You love me; I love somebody else; somebody else loves another; another loves still another, and so it goes on ad infinitum. Therefore why take your loves so seriously? Why even in marriage you don't suppose a woman takes the man she loves, do you? No, she marries the man she can get. If she happens to love him too, so much the better. Be adaptable. Take what you can get."

It was nearing four. Some had left. Fay had not seen Billy for the past hour. She and Henri went after their wraps. On a divan a couple were writhing, their lips glued together. On the way out they passed one of the bedrooms. The door was open. There were noises! Luckily, the lights were out. She called to Henri—"Let's escape."

On the way home they laughed gaily. "Did you enjoy it?" Henri asked.

"Of course, in a way. It was exciting. I'm going to meet that Jewish man again and the fireman too, sometime. We're invited to Painter's party next week, a costume affair; let's go."

Fay's Boston experience had been her initiation into, and this evening her confirmation in, promiscuity.

19

The next Saturday night, Fay and Henri attended Painter's costume party. Fay determined to follow the artist's advice and wear either much or nothing. She chose to wear nothing—or practically nothing. To be sure, her skin was protected by a coat of copper-bronze paint, and she had a magnificent head dress of eagle plumes and a scanty bunch of feathers suspended from her waist by a deerskin belt. She was beautiful.

The guests were much the same as at Billy's party. Painter was entranced. He piloted her about the rooms constantly calling attention to her lovely back, insisting that she must pose for him. She promised. Why not?

Fay knew he wanted her; but there was no appeal. He was handsome, but his posture was too slouching, his features too soft, and there was a weakness to his face, more evident when he smiled than at any time. His voice too lacked the deep mellow timbre which she was learning to demand. To Henri she confessed, "I can't see him as a lover. As a jolly comrade, yes, but nothing else. How can I circumvent what I know he will demand?"

"That's easy enough," replied Henri, "tell him you are afraid you have caught a disease. That will stop him if nothing else will."

Fay laughed. "Then I would be out of society entirely, wouldn't I?"

The funniest and also the most pathetic member of the evening party was a scion of the famous Rhinelander family, not yet noted for its miscegenation. Fay observed a fat old woman whose corset stays must have scourged her for her sins. The woman's entire mode was exaggerated. Her face had been "enameled." The profuseness of her makeup but accentuated her wrinkles. Her hair was dyed that usual dark brown sticky-looking mess which so many aging dames affect. No doubt their impaired vision prevents them from seeing the imperfections of their artifices.

The funny old creature was made more ludicrous by a combination of brown ostrich feathers, tipped with orange, sweeping over her head and floating down her fat back, the whole contraption held in place by a diamond-studded band which encircled her head. Her gown was intensely décolleté and of a vivid robin's egg–blue velvet. She carried a bejeweled lorgnette and with that would indicate her prospective conquests.

Her method was simple. She sidled up to the host: "Present that young man to me," pointing with her lorgnette.

Then began her almost unvaried siren's song: "I've been watching you all the evening. I am sure you are someone unusual, and I wish to know you well"—this with a coquettish smirk. "I'm very fond of young men and know just what they like. I want you to come and see me. I have excellent wines and cigars. And, tee-hee, when you play with me you are safe, for I have influence with the police department."

Then she would draw out a tiny pencil and a notebook, open to a blank page and require her "prospect" to enter his name, address and telephone number. The scheme evidently worked for her. She was always surrounded by a group of that blondish half-feminine type which is forever dancing along the edge of society. She was known to be immensely rich and though niggardly in making repairs to the tenements which she rented to the poor, she was notorious for her lavishness with her lovely young men.

Henri laughed as he said, "You see why it's necessary that some have great wealth?"

The husky young fireman, who had been present at Pickup's party too, volunteered, "God! She can't touch me. She looks like the plague. Me for you Fay, any time you want. I give myself away. I don't have to be bought like a flossy dame in a fancy house."

"Thanks. I may wish to take advantage of your offer some day," she answered.

Miss Savoy, the notorious impersonator, came sailing by, in grand drag. She gave an appraising glance at Fay, then rushed up, bursting forth in her quick excited manner. "Oh, you sweet, innocent-looking thing! I adore you. You're quite the most beautiful person here. Have you yet committed the unforgivable sin? If not, you must let me teach you!"

"What is it?" asked Fay.

"Well, there are really two of them, one for men and one for women. But I know them both. Dearie, I'm certainly glad you are poor and have no clothes to wear. It makes you show off your beautiful body. Now me, I have to dress extravagantly and be the village cutup to get any attention. Nevertheless, I get it, dearie, all I want. Your mother [referring to herself] is here to tell you that. Come around and see me when you've nothing else to do." Miss Savoy passed on.

Painter's three models came in wearing veils, pink, light blue and delicate green. But still Fay continued to be the belle of the ball.

An anomalous-looking masculine woman, Miss Bull-Mawgan, and her inseparable friend, Elsie Dike, dropped in, "Just to look at the scenery," said La Bull-Mawgan in her deep masculine type of voice. Really, she had her eye on the models. But Elsie always kept close to her friend for fear that some of the money would be spent on another one. Though it was an evening party, both wore mannish riding clothes. La Bull-Mawgan stepped up to Fay. "Really, my dear, I can't tell whether you are a boy or a girl. I wish I knew."

"Well, don't call me either; just call me it," hinted Fay delicately.

"But it does make such a difference, you know," said La Bull-Mawgan. "I'll find out from Painter. He'll tell me." She passed on, followed by her Elsie.

Just then the policeman on the beat entered. He had been apprised of the entertainment by Robert, Painter's butler, and dropped in to have a bit of the liquid cheer which was being so freely served. Fay had often seen him on the Avenue and been struck with his magnificent masculine beauty. Of course he was Irish, or of Irish descent. What wonderful lovers they are, those Irish. Connoisseurs say they are the best, but mercenary. He called to Fay, "Hello, little one, come and help me drink this!" He smiled and showed perfect even teeth. His eyes were blue-grey, set off by dark lashes and brows; his hair almost black; his skin smooth, blond, tinted pink, with blotches of red on the cheeks, along the jaws and at the edges of his ears. His hair had a wave like an artificial marcel. His height, his erectness, his deep voice all made an irresistible appeal to Fay. She was infatuated! She knew she could not resist him, in fact no longer wished to resist him. Evidently she appealed to him for the time being. She would take what the gods so kindly offered at the moment. She went to him. She permitted him to make the advances, for they prefer it that way. He found the air hot and oppressive and piloted her to the back stairway. Luckily, no one else had discovered it. He opened his overcoat and shared it with her. She cuddled against his warm body. She could feel the beauty of his tense muscles. "Do you like me, kid?" he asked. Intuition prompted her to reply in his idiom: "Bet yer life I do."

"Do yuh want me?"

For answer she wrapped her arms about him and rested her head against his chest. The fragrance of his body thrilled her.

She felt no remorse. Before they returned to the others he said, "What about lending me five dollars?"

Fay was more discreet than penurious. Beneath her deerskin belt she had a wad; she made the loan. Shortly after, she and Henri left.

Fay met the cop again on the avenue the next week. He greeted her coldly. "Don't hang around. I got a regular girl; works for Miss Gool. Goin' to get spliced nex' week. Fix you up with a couple friends of mine. What say? There comes the boss! Beat it!"

She walked away wondering what his friends would be like.

In telling Henri of it later she said, "Do you suppose one cop is just as good as another?"

Fay had not even been hurt by the policeman's bluntness.

She began to speculate as to whether she were a typical masochist.

At last Fay had reached the stage where she could laugh not only at others but at herself too—the most saving accomplishment one can possess.

20

FAY WAS VERY BUSY FOR MONTHS, working hard during the day and attending classes evenings and at odd hours. Once a week, when Saturday came, she permitted herself relaxation. Almost as regularly she brought to a conclusion some flirtation started during the week. Since she did not drink or smoke to any extent, she found that about the only exhausting experience was loss of sleep. So she formed the habit, advised by Henri, of "flopping" at five of a Saturday, sleeping till either eight or nine, relying on food later in the night to make up for the lost dinner. She tried out various types of men. But more and more she found herself drawn toward the athletic type. She told Henri, "They are amenable, these athletes—very!"

Also Fay attended many boxing bouts and thus became acquainted with delightful young pugs from all walks of life. Too, she became acquainted with many college men, sometimes by introduction, quite often by the simple ruse of asking the direction to some nearby place. As the spring advanced she attended the Saturday afternoon baseball games. Quite often, learning at which hotels the players were stopping, she would dine there with some of her friends. In a city like New York a professional outdoor athlete can be recognized almost invariably. The baseball players in particular have a very tanned skin, unusually clear bright eyes, very erect carriage, expensive clothing, and a short snappy jerky gait which betrays their quickness of action. All of their movements are swift. Fay tried turning her head with the same speed with which the ball players move. The jerk which resulted made her dizzy and gave her a headache.

Fay's earliest experience had been with men of the intellectual type, muscularly soft; of too soft speech. Now she began to judge her men by two outstanding characteristics: the tones of their voices and the cleanliness of their teeth. With the years, Fay acquired greater charm. She spoke little, only sufficient to keep a man talking about himself, his favorite pursuits, his hopes and ambitions. Her wide knowledge of business, her keen appreciation of the true values of life (outside of her questionable love game), her college experiences, all made her desired and respected by these men. They were proud to be loved by her. They would end their description of Fay, "She's been brought out—good and proper—but she's worth knowing."

In summer many of Fay's conquests were made at the bathing beaches. In a swimming suit her own remarkably symmetrical build was shown to perfection. Her muscles of steel, beneath skin of velvet, showed to their fullest advantage. Like all of her kind, she looked younger than her years—innocently young. One of her ruses on the beach was to get in the way of a ball, be struck and then, "poor kid," be properly pitied.

Frequently she would swim out to the life savers, look at them and smile. Often as not a life saver is a young Greek god taking this means to save up money to attend college in the fall. They do not make overmuch. An invitation to dine and go to a show after the day's work means just so much more ahead. They start out meaning to be companionable; they end by becoming violent lovers, temporarily, at least. Fay found that the more virile the man, the more readily he succumbed to her open advances.

Sometimes Fay would cross a street where a lovely young policeman was stationed. A simple query as to the location of some nearby place would be the entering wedge. Then she would ask, "By-the-way, what do you smoke? I'll bring you a cigar on my way back." The fictitious errand accomplished, she would return. The next day, or a few days later, she would again pass his way; this time she would have the cigar ready. They were now old friends. Each day would make them better acquainted. By the end of a week, a trip to a theatre, or to some summer resort, would be arranged. In telling one of her boon companions of some of her adventures, the less-practiced one remarked, "But I should be so afraid of policemen. How do you broach the subject to them?"

"I don't," answered Fay, "they broach it to me."

"And I suppose you use the language of flowers?"

"Yes, dearie, scarlet pansies!"

Fay Etrange had become a oncer—that is, she was through with a man after one experience.

One Sunday, having spent the afternoon at one of the beaches with Henri, he suggested that she accompany him to a restaurant in what was beginning to be popularly called "Greenwich Village." Fay had never heard of the eating place before. He described it as "an Italian dump where not the foods but the people are what you go to enjoy," and added provokingly, "Wait till you see for yourself."

First they stopped in the basement of the old Brevoort, where at that time one of the gayest and most interesting crowds gathered nightly. From there they went to Tenth Street and west almost to noisy Sixth Avenue. They descended into a basement on the south side of the street, passed through the kitchen and emerged into what had been a backyard but had been converted into a galleried garden. They chose seats on the balcony, close to the railing, where they could both see, and if desired, also be seen. Fay remarked, "It seems very ordinary."

"Wait till they drink some Italian red," said Henri, "then you'll get more than an earful. No one has come here yet and gone away saying that he did not get more than his money's worth."

A fat, pudgy, old, grey, grinning man raised his glass to drink to Fay. She smiled over the brim of her own glass, "Just to keep in practice of being naughty," she informed Henri. Then the old man motioned for them to join his table. Fay shook her head no. A friend of the old man called out to him, "Oh, behave, Jack, be yourself! Can't you see it's fish?"

Billy Pickup entered. Fay went below to have a word with him. As she passed a table at the foot of the stairs, one of the two sitting there nudged the other and spoke audibly, indicating Fay, "Ain't it grand?"

"Grand?" said the other, "It's most marvelously gorgeous. I'd like to make it." She feigned not to hear.

Fay had recently finished a course in abnormal psychology. In this restaurant she saw, with the exception of the actually psychotic, practically every type she had studied about. There were bulldikers with their sweeties; fairies with their sailors or marines or rough trade; tantes (aunties) with their good-looking clerks or chorus molls, and all singing, gesticulating, calling back and forth, in a medley of artificial forced gaiety. An effeminate young man shrieked in an assumed falsetto, "I see a mouse; let me get up on a chair. Protect me, protect me! I demand, I must have protection."

"Ah, sit down, yer rockin' the boat. You've mixed your drinks!" a young sailor cautioned.

Another, when opportunity came as the racket subsided temporarily, minced, "Gawd knows my name is pure. Your calumnies are unwarranted. Don't you insinuate anything about me. I don't have to be insinuated about. My life is an open book. I'm a broad-minded woman. The world sees me as I am. Whoops! I should worry!"

Evidently some sailor had befouled a reputation, for Fay heard someone shriek in falsetto, "Sailor boy, if you don't take back those indecent words, I'll bring my longshoreman over here and he'll almost choke you to death. He's big enough. He's done it to me several times. At first I thought I'd never get over it."

The bulldikers, with few exceptions, were more quiet. But there was one blonde, "Dolly," they called her, not more than seventeen, pink-cheeked, exquisite, extremely neat in collar and tie, a mannish coat, and a short tight skirt. As she removed a boy's hat she revealed beautiful hair combed straight back like a college man's. Fay was attracted to this miss. The blonde was sufficiently inebriated to be talkative. She walked up to Fay and began, "Listen, dearie, this is no place for you. Go back where you belong. I know high-grade people when I see them. Used to be one of them too. You don't belong here. This life has got me; don't let it get you!"

Here sailors came with their "boy friends" hoping they would meet some unattached girl and run away with her, meantime having their food and drink and not paying for it. There was a continual din, a coming and going, a visiting back and forth between tables which would not be permitted in an uptown place. There was the most open lovemaking between people who should not have given themselves away in public.

Acquaintances met, rushed madly up to each other, embraced, kissed. One gushed, "Sweetheart," another, "Dearie." A verbose queenly one burst forth to her sister, "You're looking most marvelously grand. I declare the way you keep your youth and beauty is a source of wonder all along Broadway. You must give me the secret too. Of all things, I must be young."

A marine, overhearing the last sentence, called out, "Young, I don't want 'em young, I want 'em experienced." "And with money too, don't forget the price!" suggested the boy friend who was with the marine.

An absurd old man went to the piano and begged someone to play his accompaniment. The sole song in his repertory was, "When You and I Were Young, Maggie." His appearance was greeted with hoots and screams of "Maggie! Maggie! Maggie!" some in hoarse male voices, some in truly feminine voice, but by far the most in shrieking falsetto. He sang, and at the end of the lines where "Maggie" occurs, there were bellows and screams as everyone "Maggied." He finished with éclat; the applause was thunderous. Then that part of his exhibition complex satisfied, he quietly went over into a corner to get drunk. "He works in a livery stable," a queen volunteered.

After a lull, with time between for drinks, a fat Jewish boy, with a high-pitched voice, delivered a patter song, with exaggerated rolling of eyes, shimmying movements of shoulders, swaying of hips, wriggling and overdone femininity, as he sang, "I cannot make my eyes behave, nor my lips either."

Here one heard fruit, banana, meat, fish, tomato, cream, dozens of everyday words used with double meaning. With their voices pitched high and in imitation of the effusive type of woman, the guests declaimed with the utmost exaggeration possible, what they had to say, each and all trying at the same time to be the centre of interest. They burlesqued all life. This they designated "camping," and to "camp" brilliantly fixed one's social status.

It sounded very amusing on first hearing.

Another time, yielding to her curiosity, Fay again visited the place. She found that most of the remarks, which at first she found funny, were repeated over and over, borrowed, loaned and never repaid, till she was reduced to boredom.

Henri summed it up. "Be liberal! Perhaps it's natural to them; what is natural to them may not be natural to another. Imagine them married. What would their offspring be? Probably even more erratic. Perhaps they are fulfilling their destiny by not marrying. Did you ever consider that? I often think that people who do not wish to have children should not be criticized, for probably there is some basic instinct which prompts them not to be parents. Perhaps they are really not fit to have children."

Henri and Fay ended by discussing marriage in all its phases, polygamy, polyandry, monogamy, and Henri advanced the idea that "This is a hell of a civilization which does not permit each type to live its life as it sees fit."

They discussed illegitimacy, and Fay laughingly quoted, "There are no illegitimate children; only illegitimate parents." Then she went on to describe the lamentations of her last lover, a mutual acquaintance, who had been adopted when a child, and so did not feel sure who his parents were, and was wont to intone tragically, "To think that perhaps I am the child of some couple's night of pleasure." "As if," said Fay, "we were not all the result of one couple's night of pleasure, whether we are born in or out of wedlock. And thank God they got at least that amount of pleasure out of life."

21

By this time, Fay had become addicted to cruising, as it is vulgarly called, deliberately walking the streets for the purpose of flirtation and the ultimate culmination of flirtation.

She narrowed her choice down to one type: the tall, hugely muscled, blondish man with abundance of wavy, lustrous hair, bold blue eyes and healthy glowing skin. The so-called Irish eye, deep blue, with long, black, curling lashes and dark well-formed brows would set her heart to beating madly.

In this classification fell most of the many professional athletes, many pugilists, many young skilled mechanics, and by far the greater number of the American physically perfect.

Sometimes, after her evening classes, she would saunter down Broadway and pick up "something nice" for a half hour's diversion. She was always well-stocked with funds these days, and sometimes, when in a great hurry, not wishing to spend time on entertaining, would say, flashing a bill, "I have not time to invite you to eat or to have a drink. Would you be offended if I offered to make it possible for you to seek entertainment?" Even if she did not make such an offer, as often as not the prostitute that is in most men, would lead her choice to ask, "What's there in it for me?" A bargain would be struck. Henri reproached her one evening: "Fay, you are absolutely brazen."

"No," she gave back answer, "just matter of fact. Substitute the word 'adroit' and you may be right."

"I wish I had your nerve."

"Nerve? It does not take nerve to say the correct thing sweetly and flatteringly at the right moment."

"Illustrate, please!"

"Last night you saw that man give me the glad eye?"

"Yes, and you reciprocated with an agreeable smile."

"Just so!"

"What did you say when I left you?"

"First I'll tell you what I did not say. I did not ask the time, nor say it was a pleasant evening, nor 'what do you take me for,' but I did say, 'Certainly it is pleasant for one as lonesome as I am to receive such pointed attention in a city as big as New York.' Now, I could have said that much with perfect propriety to a plain clothes man. Did that commit me to anything?"

"Then what did he say?"

"He said, 'You looked at me first!' And I smiled, very, very, very, very sweetly and answered, 'But who, getting one glance at you, could help studying you. Surely you must realize that you are an uncommonly well-built and fine-looking man.' And he said, 'Not so bad to look at yourself.' Now that certainly was making progress. So I queried, 'Not so bad to look at?' and then I added, 'But I am very bad to be with; very, very, very, very, very bad to be with. I'm a very, very, very naughty person—sometimes.' And you know, Henri Voyeur, how I can lisp that word very! I used my voice, my eyes, my hands and my facial muscles to express myself. And then he asked, 'Just how bad can you be?' I answered him with another question, boldly putting it up to him, 'Just how bad would you want me to be?' 'The sky's the limit with me,' said he. I thought he was a peddler, so I questioned him further: 'The sky's the limit with you, and for how much?' 'I don't sell anything,' he retorted, as offended. 'Neither do I,' I hastened to assert. We bantered back and forth and I managed to keep him laughing. It is almost axiomatic that if you can make a man laugh with you, and not at you, you can make him do almost anything else with you that you wish, but be sure it is a genuine laugh, for if it's imitation, that man is dirt! Anyhow, he turned out to be a gorgeous lover, and, oncer that I am, I could almost bring myself to the point—"

"Yes, the point, of course!"

"I don't mean what you mean, but have it your way! I could almost bring myself to the point of reindulging him, were I not to see him too soon. But

A SCARLET PANSY

that is impossible. He does not live here, but lives away down in Texas, and he wants me to visit him there sometime. Evidently he's rich. Really, he is a friend worth remembering. He insisted on giving me this ring as a memento."

"Did he have to insist very hard?"

"Oh, be your age!"

"You have all the luck."

"If I do, it's because I'm discriminating. When it's necessary I can be coldly indifferent. There are types that need that too."

Henri changed the subject. "Come on! There's just time to step into Café Martin and see if it's lively."

Alas! Café Martin is no more. It occupied almost a whole block and extended on 27th Street from Broadway to Fifth Avenue. The Broadway side held the café and the Fifth Avenue side the restaurant. That night the orchestra was demonstrating a "novelty." The three pieces had been augmented by Caruso, not in person, but canned Caruso. The effect was not bad. The voice was loud, and the rasp of the phonograph was covered by the instrumental accompaniment. Radio music was only being dreamed of then.

Henri and Fay had no sooner stepped through the doors than they received signals from table after table to come over and be guests. It was at Café Martin that the catch phrase, "You must come over," originated. Queer, too, how many of these people were strangers, and in other surroundings would not have been so free and easy. But such was the atmosphere. In those days of legalized traffic in the demon rum, and his little brothers and sisters, cousins, uncles, aunts and grandparents, an evening's entertainment could be comparatively inexpensive.

Henri and Fay joined a group of Wall Street people; the men were talking of trade, the women of housekeeping—the price of meat or fish and how they made their beds; how much they paid a truckman, or a plumber or a bricklayer, and how much went to the iceman.

At an adjoining table was a group of near-boys and girls, camping madly. It was agreed by the circumspect and censorious who were present that the conduct of the people at the adjoining table was unseemly for such a place. That was before the circumspect and censorious had consumed their whiskey-sodas, their pousse cafés, and other concoctions that delighted them. After the drinks, the rules of etiquette were completely reversed, so much so that eventually the whole crowd was "bounced," if one might apply such a vulgar terms to any happening in so elegant a place as Café Martin was. Anyway, they finally "whoops-my-deared" themselves out of the place. Before that happened one of them remarked, "I'd like to have a party with that, wouldn't you, Sammie?" pointing at Fay. "I wonder if I could make it?" Fay shook her head a violent no. Then he addressed her directly, "Why not?"

"Firstly, because I like my companions to be entirely sober; secondly because there's no appeal." ("It" had not yet been invented; that's a postbellum word.)

The reigning Earl of the season came in, looking rather seedy. He had not yet married into millions. Fay admired him for his clever wit. He was an original; reserved in public, but behind closed doors 'twas another story; there he was the most brilliant and scintillant, always the life of the party. Indeed, it was from the Earl that the world-wide famous Prince learned toe-dancing and how to "strut his stuff."

The entire assemblage was gay. One very emotional young lady, a real woman, wishing to satisfy her exhibitionism, called aloud, for all to hear, "I simply have to dance." She climbed atop one of the tables and danced, a very brief dance, lasting only the time it took the maitre to walk from the other end of the room.

At Martin's the window shades pulled up from below, not down from above. This revealed a tantalizing glimpse to those outside. Always groups of the pleasure bound could be seen standing on tip toe trying to look over the shades and see if there was anything tempting within—no use spending pennies if there was not. The clever ones carried books under their arms to stand on so that they might better see over the shades and spot their prey. The hoi-polloi dubbed them the intellectuals.

The café was the gathering place of all the high-grade kept women, wild society women, dissipated men, ladies of the night, fairies, pimps and its of that generation, probably the teachers of today's crop of gay youth that seems to have assimilated everything at a tender age.

In those days, even the women of the demimonde, and their male analogues, comported themselves in public as well as today's so-called respectable young men and women.

By twelve the fun had become fast and furious. Miss Savoy and the famous Mr. (and Miss) Painter were there and laid a wager as to which one could entice the most good-looking people to drink with the party. Finally they became so reckless that they commissioned some of their companions to go out on Broadway with the order, "Drag in anything nice you see."

Never was there such another evening at the place. It marked the high tide of the Café Martin.

22

FAY WAS LUCKY. A turn in the market made her independent. She resigned her position and matriculated at one of the universities to finish the pre-medical course which she had previously outlined. It left her much free time, and it is to be feared that some of it she did not use as judiciously as she should have done.

More money of course made her more popular. It always does! She met many handsome young men at college, who, as she said, "needed to be brought out," or "needed to make their bow to society." She treated them well—Saturday luncheons at the prominent hotels; theatre parties; dances afterwards, wherever the most enjoyable music could be had. She was somewhat older than these boys, but looked young. She had the advantage of experience for which they admired her quite as much as her physical attributes.

Now, college boys are always much sought after by the society buds. One of Fay's chief amusements of a Saturday afternoon and evening was to pit her wiles against the social position of the young set that always crowds about such places as are on the lists approved by the "Matrons." The boys would desert any of the buds at any time to do Fay's bidding, that is, so long as she was interested in them.

Many a society marriage quickly followed a jilting by Fay, the "sweet young things," catching the youths on the rebound, as it were. It is often that way—far more often than women generally imagine.

In college Fay was as successful socially as she had been with the Broadway set, though it required a change of method.

"Do something for Alma Mater," was the slogan. She responded nobly and did everything in sight, and if it was not in sight she ferreted it out.

One of the biologists, commenting on her, said, "She certainly lives up to her name. She's quite the queerest thing I've ever had in my classes. Learn? She absorbs subjects; but she never asks me a question that is not connected with reproduction. I half believe she does it to embarrass me. She has some theory of her own about glands, too. Her own interpretation of sexual variation from the normal is that it is conditioned by functional disturbances of various endocrine glands. At that, she may be right."

What Fay learned about him was even more amusing than what he suspected about her.

He was still a half-way Presbyterian, despite his education, and still had many of the inhibitions of that good Christian sect. He liked to draw, and would hire a model, ostensibly to pose for him; he would sit in one corner of the room, watch her take the pose, sigh spasmodically, then say, "That's all, you can robe yourself." And these women he did not secure through the usual agencies; instead he would sally out on Broadway late at night and pick them up. Yet he was wont to boast that he had never been immoral.

The French professor told Fay what the biologist had said about her, and the philosophy professor told Fay what a Broadway woman had said to him about the biologist. The criticism of the biologist was the nearest Fay ever came to scandal at that college. Of course Fay played the part of the leading lady in the college show of that year, and she lived the part. No wonder! Also she made the polo team, the basketball team and the baseball team. The football team she left for others. She had not time to do everything.

Withal, Fay had a gay life that year. She was making the most of it to fortify herself against the four years of medical school, with its nerve-racking, soul-torturing duties.

❧ 23

As soon as the college examinations were finished, Fay and Henri Voyeur and another friend, Percy Chichi, set out on a summer tour to include the Pacific Coast and as much as possible of that which lay between it and New York.

"My grand cruise," Fay styled it.

They visited Atlantic City in time to attend the famous Iceman's Ball, noted far and wide for the fashionable drags displayed. Now, in Atlantic City, the icemen are all colored and quite as likely to be ladies as men. Nevertheless, all the famous ones of Philadelphia, and many of those from New York, white, lily-white indeed, attend the function, which is more or less of a panic, of course.

Then they stopped at Philadelphia and Vine-streeted to their heart's content.

They had an evening in Baltimore before going on to assault the social battalions of Washington, and Fay pointed out the hallowed spot where she had been led astray.

At the capital they spent the greater part of a romantic moonlight night in the ever beautiful Lafayette Park. Five different times Fay took a drive, and never walked back.

In Chicago they did the famous bathing resorts. But they tarried only a little while, for they were anxious, as Henri, said, "to get out to the wide open spaces," and to this Percy Chichi added, "Where men are men and women are double breasted."

A Scarlet Pansy

In Colorado they stopped at a cattle ranch and were guests at the bunkhouse. Here Fay could be useful and, as always, pitched right in and did everything possible while Henri became amorous with the cook, and Percy Chichi, who was good at plain sewing, fussed with the cowboys' clothes.

One cowboy Fay found well nigh irresistible. She led him on till he was so madly in love with her that he threatened to shoot anyone else who even tried to borrow her for an evening, let alone take her completely away from him. Of course Fay would become bored with such a usual situation. She wished to go on to 'Frisco, to the gayer life there.

The cowboy, tall, tanned, handsome, strong and virile, was so infatuated that he could not endure the thought of separation from her. Over and over when they were alone he would say, "I wish it was possible for us to marry. God! Wouldn't that be great?"

"That would be just too great for anything," Fay assured him. "It would lead to the murder of two people at least, that of myself and of the first man other than you that I looked at."

"But you wouldn't want to look at any other man!"

"No, not till you had worn yourself out; which wouldn't be long at your present rate. Then I'd be looking for something more peppy while you were sleeping, and afterwards you'd swing the gun. We'd better thank God that marriage is entirely out of the question."

"Well, love is not," sighed Cowboy. "Crawl right up into my arms, honey, and love me some more." They were off again.

Fay loved the passion of this man of the cattle ranges, but her experience had taught her that satisfaction only could result in a nervous exhaustion that would be displayed by irritability, and the end would be dispute, jealousy, recrimination and eventual hatred. She wished to preserve a happy memory of this cowboy, and also she wished him to remember her as tenderly. She must leave him while she still longed for his vigorous embraces. But in his present frame of mind he could not let her go.

Now, when she would steal up behind him, put her arms around him and kiss him on the neck, he still became wildly excited and amorous—such a contrast to the affair with one lover who, toward the last, had so often blurted out venomously, "For God's sake, can't you ever leave me alone? I want to do some work once in a while. How can I think with you pawing me and smearing yourself all over me all the time?"

Better to break Cowboy's heart, and the little that was left of her own, than to spoil their remembrance of each other by eventual hatred.

Besides, she knew she could not be constant. Nor, she realized when she thought it over calmly, did she wish to be. Had it been possible she would have chosen to love Cowboy till she was tired of him, and then come back to him when she was tired of somebody else—a lovely arrangement, for her. Well, she knew that once Cowboy's insistence began to wane, she would be seeking stolen sweets elsewhere. What had been an ideal must remain an ideal!

The last night of her stay they rode far out on the desert. He tethered their horses. They had brought supper with them. After eating, Cowboy piled one saddle atop the other and spread a blanket on the ground. He lay with his back against the saddles, Fay cuddled in his arms. Together they watched the glory of the sunset fade. As the twilight deepened, Fay snuggled closer. She loosened the collar of his shirt and ran her hand softly over his warm chest and felt the steady beating of his heart. She kissed his hands, his brow, his cheek, his lips, his eyelids, over and over she kissed him everywhere.

They returned to the bunkhouse. Cowboy hastily retired for the night. He would not kiss Fay before the others. He was quite exhausted; but not Fay! She was still aquiver, wild with an excitement that would kindle any man, no matter what his pretentions to virtue.

Had Cowboy seen what she did he would have killed her. There were other young men working at the Bar Star Ranch, some almost as vigorous and attractive as Cowboy. Fay lingered at the bunkhouse door. She forgot her intention to preserve an ideal. To use Fay's own words in telling of "the greatest night of her life," "What I did is just nobody's business." Sufficient to say, whatever it was, she did it.

She and Henri and Percy Chichi left the next day, and if the sendoff was a hearty one, 'twas because Fay had given the impression to each of her separate dozen lovers that he was the favorite. To them her visit had been a welcome relief giving interlude.

Fay wrote to Cowboy often for a time; then gradually her letters were less frequent and far less lengthy, and finally she put in an artistic touch of despair as her wanderings took her further away: "Cowboy, dear sweetheart, it seems that Fate is determined to keep us separated. My memories of you will always remain the sweetest of my life." That was after a silence of a month. She never wrote to him again.

He missed her so. In desperation he married the pretty daughter of a saloon-keeper, and probably that marriage was happier than it otherwise would have been. The wife was accepted as a makeshift, as are so many wives—and husbands too—and as such she was judged and her limitations easily tolerated; after all, toleration is a fairly good basis for a successful marriage.

24

IN SAN FRANCISCO THE TRIO, Fay, Henri Voyeur and Percy Chichi, were the guests of the famous Beach-Bütsches.

The Beach-Bütsch family had settled in California so long ago as to be eligible for all of the wonderful societies which there exist for the annihilation of the inferiority complex. Coming from Europe, the family had originally settled in Fay's natal village, Kuntzville, Pa. Then the name was invariably spelled Bütsch. Eventually, the family being prolific, and procreation then being held to be naught but a virtue, had increased to such an extent that expansion became necessary. Thus one branch settled here, another there. So they had spread and intermarried till they were allied to all of the "best" families of America.

With attempted Anglicization of the name, some had changed it to Beach; some had retained the original spelling, but some, as if to take the curse off the name, modified the patronymic by combining it beautifully by means of the aristocratic hyphen, with the name of the maternal grandparent, or even with any nice name which they fancied. Some Frenchified the name, making it La Bütsch.

There was an elegant Miss Drexel-Bütsch of Philadelphia; also there were the Brown-Bütsches of New Rochelle (very classy indeed), and a whole Bütsch-Fuchs family in New York. But no matter what variations they made of the name, they still all belonged to the same family and retained the dominant family characteristic.

The California branch had long been represented by the Beach-Bütsch family; the Chicago branch by the Bütsch-Beach family, the St. Louis branch by the Bütsch-Bütsch family, the New Orleans offshoot by the La Bütsch family, and New York by every possible combination of the name; there were even Levy, Cohen and other Yiddish Bütsches. In California, the elegant and very accomplished Old Aunty Beach-Bütsch was the head. She and the rest of her kin were (and quite properly) in no sense ashamed of the name and clung to it tenaciously.

In more recent years, with great wealth, the family tree has begun to die out at the top, as is usual in all families that are too far removed from the necessity of working and, incidentally, living regularly. Nevertheless, some one of the Bütsches, hyphenated or otherwise, occasionally gets married and proceeds to multiply, that the breed may not be lost to the world; anyway, there is always someone left to live worthily up to the name.

Old Aunty Beach-Bütsch, a very understanding sort of person, laid out a program for the entertainment of her guests, such as she knew they would like.

First she arranged with Reggie Beach-Bütsch, her nephew, to take her guests on a slumming tour, always the chief objective of visitors from the East. So they explored the Barbary Coast and visited the Bull Pen and the Log Cabin, places which Miss Savoy, in her infinite wisdom, had recommended to them as being especially entertaining.

Then they visited Chinatown. A very rich merchant, seeing Fay, became enamored of her at once. Certainly he appealed to Fay. With time something might have come of it, after her fears had been allayed. She accepted his jade, but not his love; she was afraid of leprosy.

Perhaps one of the most amusing episodes of their visit to California was an evening spent at a party across the Bay. Here were gathered together, at some sort of old home party, all of the famous Bütsches of California. Among those present were Freddie Bütsch and his brothers, Percy and Clarence, each renowned for some special accomplishment. Then too there were some of the O'Neill-Bütsches, Riley-Bütsches, Jones-Bütsches, and other Bütsches without number. Also there were Junior Beach and Marjorie Beach and Sissy Beach, who had dropped what to them had seemed the undesirable part of their hyphenated name. They had been taken severely to task for this by Old Aunty Beach-Bütsch, who never lost an opportunity to castigate them for this action and went roaring about, "You dirty whelps, you ought to be ashamed to face the rest of us. I'm proud of being just what I am, a Beach and a Bütsch."

There had just been one of those so-called scandals when someone in San Francisco had done as he or she pleased, had been publicly "exposed," hounded and possibly incarcerated in a dungeon for doing what God (if there is one) had given the impulse to do. Everybody was excited by the injustice.

Sissy Beach spoke in a high-pitched voice: "I wish to Gawd there was some place in these U.S.A., where a temp'ramental person could lead an untrammeled life and be and act natural. As it is, the rich can get away with anything, but the poor must live by laws which should never have been perpetrated. Conduct! What right has any individual to be interested in my conduct, be that what it may, so long as I do no harm to him and do not interfere with another's right to life, liberty and the pursuit of happiness?"

She thrust between her lips a cigarette holder of exaggerated length (anything Sissy had to do with would be exaggerated), and pulled it back and forth as if to stimulate her imagination.

"What's the matter with Palm Beach?" asked a pretty young thing who had not been out long.

Sissy whooped excitedly: "For the rich, the very rich only, not for the likes of you and me."

"Try Butte, Montana," suggested the ever practical old, fat and most sophisticated Bütsch present, indeed none other than Old Aunty Beach-Bütsch.

"And why should one retire to the desert?"

Fay answered that "I just came from the so-called desert, and the most thrilling episode of my life."

"You tell 'em dearie," commanded Old Aunty Beach-Bütsch in her affected high-pitched campy voice, and then she added, "I've been for long stretches of time in Paris and Berlin, where freedom is a thing that is lived, not talked about, and I'd stay there were it not that I crave the American type. And so do the Europeans, let me tell you. Why, the greatest thrills of my life have been in the desert mining camps and out on the cattle ranges."

So followed Fay's story of herself and Cowboy. All listened openmouthed and yearned. When she had finished, one of the younger, more imaginative and still idealistic Beach-Bütsches, Miss Kitty, began a wish-fulfillment day dream—

"Wouldn't it be grand if there were an island or something—"

"Or something," contemptuously uttered one of the aunties, then sniffed; "Now, don't get all mixed up with Homer and Tennyson and the Island of Lesbos too. Go on!"

"Let me see," the other continued pensively, "where was I? Oh, yes, wouldn't it be grand, wouldn't it be just perfectly, marvelously gorgeous, if there were an island, or some place, an Island of Bliss—"

"You are sure you mean bliss?"

"Yes, an island or some place where we could all live or go to easily whenever we pleased and do all the things we wish to do without thought of the narrow-mindedness of others."

"You are asking too much. Oh, for the Isle of Crete! You are wishing a return to the good old Pagan times when all honor was paid even to prostitutes."

"No, not asking too much, just asking for natural morality, a thing which varies with each bird, beast and human and for which due allowance is not made in lawmaking. Do people, for instance, indulge in 'love' for the express purpose of procreation, or do they enjoy the love and incidentally have a child? Until they do the former (which has never been and never will be), they have no right to criticize those who indulge in love for love's sweet sake, and by love, you know what I mean—no matter how a person may love."

"Are you talking of sexual aberration now?" queried Old Aunt Minnie.

"Well, I'd not call anything by such a lewd-sounding name. I'm elegant, I am (she went through the dainty motion of replacing a stray back curl), I only defecate, micturate, deflate, and indulge in emesis and tussion as occasion may require. Now look those things up in the dictionary, dearie, and you'll at least know how to express them if not to do them, elegantly in public."

"Oh, you slay me!" ejaculated Old Aunt Minnie.

Marjorie Bütsch then contributed her bit to the conversation—"Pish, tush and shush! She's getting refined!"

"Getting refined! I've always been. I was born that way."

"Born that way! You were put into a dirty hole the same as the rest of us and came out the same way we did, in a cabbage patch. Much, quite too much of your assumed elegance is purest affectation. Says the bard: 'A rose by any other name would smell as sweet.' Without going into too much detail, dearie, let me assure you (she pronounced this so meticulously that it suggested another word), let me assure you that a smell by any other name would be just as bad. You can defecate and micturate all you wish, but that won't indicate that your intestinal peristalsis and your kidney functions are any more normal than mine, or any less offensive, e'en though I describe them in older and far plainer English. So there!" She gave a defiant toss to her head.

"Are you razzing me?"

"Suit yourself. And as for being born elegant, you'd be the one to hold that you were born of an immaculate conception."

"Well, I was!"

"There she goes. What did I tell you, girls?"

In her precise, prissy way, Miss Beach-Bütsch explicated: "Not only I, but every other person, dog, fish, bird, animal being that is not reproduced by"—here she swallowed hard—"parthenogenesis, is the result of an immaculate conception. No matter how gross, how accidental, or how brutal the sexual congress may be, any volitional act of the participants certainly ends with the freeing of the spermatozoöns. From then on the fate of the male and female parts of the future embryo depends on an act of God, entirely. Spermatozoöns swim like eels. If God choose to bring the ovum and the spermatozoön together, he does so, and then, and then only does actual conception take place." Again she tossed her head grandly. "Far be it from me to criticize any act of God and hold it is not immaculate. Quite the reverse!"

"How profound you can be, Kitty. I wonder if everybody understands you. You've been taking up with someone learned, I see! Go right on! You'll soon have us all edified, if not educated."

So Miss Kitty Beach-Bütsch continued. "On our island, wouldn't it be gorgeous to have the men, the real he-men, wear uniforms?"

She had struck a responsive note. With that they all became enthusiastic, as their kind will about anything useless and impractical, and first one and then another made a suggestion.

Ella Bütsch, who was legal-minded, said, "The only sins will be theft, blackmail, cheating at cards and murder."

Marjorie, who loved wild episodes, stipulated, "There will be no breach of promise suits permitted, for anyone of any sense knows that when one is all pashed up, he, she or it is not really responsible and therefore any promise secured at such a time should not be binding."

Minnie La Bütsch, who loved gaiety, catalogued the amusements—costume balls, drags, dance halls where one might dance as and with whom one pleased regardless of sex or the brand of perfumery used. Jazz orchestras made up of men or women who really knew how to.

"I like polo-players," piped up Maude La Bütsch. "Have some polo players. I like to see their bare arms and their bare necks and chests."

"Chauffeurs and army officers for me," piped up Sissy Beach. "Puttees are my fetish."

Then Old Aunty Beach-Bütsch, the fat, gray sophisticate, added her preference: "Don't forget the men in blue overalls and blue shirts, the plumbers and steamfitters and such. I like 'em rough and strong and sturdy, you know."

"Oh, Aunty Beach-Bütsch, don't! Rough trade, after you're through with it, is such a bore!"

A Miss Jackson-Browning, who had not been present at the beginning of the conversation, asked, "Are you talking of a Turkish heaven?"

"No," Miss Kitty explained, "just talking of freedom as it should be practiced in these U.S., or any other place professing to be a republic. We are planning an island to be peopled with men who are wise and tolerant, women who are understanding, a place where everyone would do as he pleased so long as he did not injure others in doing it; a place where each one's own brand of morals would be respected, conditioned as they so often are by prenatal developments."

Soft-voiced Old Aunt Minnie was the next to state a preference. Aunt Minnie, who loved reciprocity, stipulated, "Don't forget to have some of those luvvly, graceful chorus boys live on your island too."

"Why, Minnie," shrieked one, "I didn't know you loved chorus molls. I'll have to get my panties pleated and begin my daily exercises with a lipstick and an eyebrow pencil."

"Now, Kitty, please go on with your enchanting island," Fay besought her.

So Miss Beach-Bütsch continued: "We'd have ladies of the day and ladies of the evening and ladies who are not ladies and gentlemen who are not gentlemen, and a house of all nations where girls from every clime could dwell and appear in our free and easy society in their native costumes, or lack of costumes. We'd have gambling with cards and wheels and numbers and we'd have swimming pools and athletic stadiums and all sorts of sports, including all the famous indoor sports. And we'd have—"

"Now, Kitty, who would finance such an enterprise?"

"Well, the jewelers would be with us and most of the lawyers and doctors, and in fact most of the professional men and women in all walks of life. You don't know your geography if you don't know that. There'd be just millions for it—millions of people, I mean, if you could get them to tell the truth."

"How do you calculate? Some more bitch arithmetic!"

"And now have you finished with all your gorgeously marvelous wishing?"

"I think so," Kitty lisped.

"Well, you left one thing out. How about having a few good fairies on your dream isle to wave their magic wands and give you everything you want?"

The party broke up. The Eastern visitors received numerous invitations. Everyone said, "You must come over." Miss Ella added, "Just let me know when you're coming and I'll bake a cake"; Marjorie lilted, "Do come whenever you can"; Kitty, "Bring your knitting and your plain sewing and I'll teach you a few fancy stitches and some embroidery—California stuff."

Followed a delightful week of California.

The Percival Beach-Bütsches gave a drag the next night under the protection of people higher up. Henri, Fay and Percy Chichi were invited. Fay decided to be brilliant and go as a queen. She had with her a drag—"Something gorgeous, simply devastating," Percy Chichi called it. Henri and Percy had the fun of helping her with her elaborate makeup. Fay gave one final glimpse into a full-length mirror and exclaimed, "I'm sure I don't know myself. No wonder I'm a misunderstood person with little dabs of paint making my ladylike features look like what they ain't."

Arrived at the party, Fay made a triumphant entry. Everywhere she was greeted with exclamations of approval or surprise: "Gorgeous! Marvelous! You slay me! You slay me completely." Fay was a long way from the hayfields of Pennsylvania. She had lived up to the prophecies of one of her former doting school teachers: "My dear, you will go far."

A member of congress wished to make love to her. So did a lieutenant of police, even though she explained her real status to them. The male man, the real virile he-man, could not fail to become amorous on seeing Fay disguised as a queen.

"Where is your king?" someone queried.

"I'm a Virgin Queen, like the kind you read about in history," camped Fay.

Two of the younger Beach-Bütsches were there, dressed as gamins, sucking on huge peppermint-flavored candy sticks. When Fay stepped out of character long enough to grab one and pretend she was going to take a suck, the merriment was hilarious.

So spontaneous was she.

Only one who has camped in the Far West would know how to appreciate and enjoy such a party to the full.

Dozens of high-grade prostitutes and kept women of the town were at the drag, all determined to honor the Eastern visitors and make the occasion a memorable one. Some lovely women from the Bull Pen had been invited, one of them, the most beautiful of all, a three-way woman who had been educated in Paris and spoke French, Spanish and English.

The prestige of the Bulls and the Dikes was shed over the affair, and these people, along with the Bütsches, prominent as they were, could carry any social function to a glorious success.

Fay and Henri and Percy Chichi must have attended half a dozen balls while there, and then—after the balls!

Always Fay went in her royal disguise. This acting did not fail to stamp her character. Forever after her gestures were queenly; she learned not only to play the part but to live the part.

Among the crowd that Fay met was one of the Dikes who went by the nickname of "Bobby," though her real name was Marjorie. "Bobby" was wild about baseball and played it like a man. Fay was wild about men and liked to watch them move when playing ball. She and "Bobby" became great pals, for one could pass along to the other the good things that the other did not care to accommodate.

"Bobby" was clever; had to be. Her family was rich, but thought to reform "Bobby" by cutting her allowance. "Bobby" reacted characteristically and, like so many of her kind, lived off of other women, trading on the admiration which she was able to inspire. At that time she was featuring Miss Fish, the very rich and powerful. One afternoon she insisted that Fay lay aside her regal role long enough to call with her on Miss Fish.

Miss Fish was in the mood to be entertaining, in her way.

She showed them the recently acquired old paintings and told the price paid: she showed them the wonderful new swimming pool and priced that; "the Fish family bathtub," "Bobby" dubbed it. She showed them her wonderful organ, which had cost her so much. Everything Miss Fish possessed was either "wonderful" or "quite wonderful."

Miss Fish could never see enough of "Bobby," who, of course, was always bored, but had to endure, if she wished to borrow money. Really she had brought Fay along as buffer. It was "Bobby, dear, come here, dear and let me fix your tie, dear" (Bobby of course wore severely tailored clothes, like any other collar-and-tie woman). "Bobby dear," went there. "Now, Bobby, dear, take my hand while I mount the steps. There, dear" (she released "Bobby" and gave her a pat on the shoulder). "I don't know what I'd do without you, dear. You are such a help, dear." "Bobby" rolled her eyes mischievously at Fay, and Fay smiled and nodded her head in understanding.

In commenting on Miss Fish afterwards, Fay said, "Despite all her wealth, she's quite the most ignorant woman I've ever met. Why she does not know enough to shave the hair from her axillae and use deodorants, to say nothing of such gentle arts as eye-brow plucking and the use of perfumes. Where and what kind of an education has she picked up? For Gawd's sake, somebody give her a dictionary, and tell her to look up the useful words and the anatomical names of the more discussed parts of the human body. The way she described things they sound revolting, whereas if she used high-sounding euphemisms, they'd perhaps sound artistic, if not appealing." Miss Fish had reached that stage of life where she enjoyed reminiscing rather than performance and was given to telling in the utmost detail all about her various escapades and peculiar adulteries; of how she was first seduced, and how many in turn she herself had brought out.

Fay and Bobby on their way home dropped into the tearoom which the Bütsches patronized at that time and where some of their number could be found every afternoon. Here they would linger and rant and rave about their Johns, "parties" with this one and "parties" with that one, and almost invariably when pressed to give details, would draw in their lips tightly and say, "My lips are sealed."

"Yes, now!" camped Fay.

There they ran into Sissy Beach, and nothing would do but that they should promise to go across the Bay again that night to attend another party. Before going they went back after Miss Fish, who would not miss anything for the world, especially as the famous Bulls and Dikes were to be there too, and, lucky stroke, they also picked up Henri Voyeur and Percy Chichi, for the party which started out to be a grand dinner ended in a panic. However, the first part of the evening passed off gaily enough.

Among those present were Miss Ella Bütsch and several of her sisters, all of whom were obsessed with the desire to look like Oscar Wilde. It's more than possible that they did, for physiological and psychological peculiarities seem to be reflected in the visage. For instance, the goitrous, the hydrocephalic, the acromegalic, the kiphotic, each bears a resemblance to its own kind. Miss Ella used to carry in her pocket a photograph of the great poet. She wore her hair cut in the same fashion. She was fond of decking herself out à la Wilde and reading "Reading Gaol," for the benefit of anyone who had the patience to listen. Usually auditors were scarce, for each desired to strut his own stuff and be the centre of amazement, if not of amusement. Miss Bütsch's recitations were quite likely to be interrupted by "Oh! Shut your trap, Ella! I want to show the new queen's walk," or "You Wilde woman, don't you ever get tired of your own voice?"

To these and like comments Miss Bütsch would invariably reply, "You have no Art," and the answer usually was, "You don't know the half of it dearie; just try me and see."

In the midst of a little spat between the Bütsch sisters, the hostess announced dinner. She did not call it dinner, but coming into the drawing room performed a curtsey in the manner of a queen's lady in waiting and intoned, "The feast is spread," then led the way into the dining hall. Pridefully she explained, "I have not only a feast for the eye, but something substantial to satisfy the taste of any and every one."

She displayed a heterogeneous mixture: "Fish, all kinds of seafood, meat, chicken, cheese, tomatoes, fruit, bananas, nuts, anything you want," she camped, "and if you don't see what you want, ask for it, or go out and drag it in. Now, don't go away and say that you didn't have a good time."

And there were things to drink too—and *eau de vie.*

Some tough sailors whom some gay thing had cruised and dragged into the party, a semi-pro pinch-hitter and a local pug, of course, drank too much, seeing the drinks were free, and preliminary to passing into coma reached that stage of self-importance that could only be gratified by being disagreeable, overbearing and destructive. They made openly sneering remarks about their lovely hostess and her boy and girl friends. The pug wished to put the gloves on with "Bobby" Dike, who was angry enough to accept the challenge, but specified that the bout should be without gloves and that Queensbury rules should be ignored; that the bout should end only with a knockout and that any implement within arm's reach might be used; and she added, "You can forget I am a woman, or even anything remotely resembling a woman."

At his point Miss Fish screamed, "Oh! I'm so nervous! I'm so nervous I must leave at once. I cannot afford notoriety. I have so much to lose."

"Yes," said one Bütsch, "you've millions to lose, by the time you die, and you're always afraid of having to pay hush money!"

Henri and Fay saved the situation; they "knew their stuff," knew how to handle rough trade when it became too rough.

Henri took Bobby by the arm and persuaded her to walk out on the verandah with him, where he had something to tell her.

Fay stepped over to the "tough guys" and guffawed, "She's funny! Why it makes me laugh to think of her tackling anybody as big as you. It would be like a kitten trying to claw a lion." (Just in time she had thought to change dog to lion). "Now, let's have some more drinks. Aunty Beach-Bütsch, break out some more liquor."

Fay poured out a stiff one for each of the men and suggested bottoms up, and then another and another. She pretended to drink too. One passed out at once. The other became less noisy and more fish-eyed. In fifteen minutes the toughs were all in a state of coma.

Then the dirty work began, the Bütsches' revenge.

Fay obtained assurance that these men did not know their way to the houseboat. Then one by one the inebriates were carried bodily further down the dock and laid on an old scow, but first the belongings of one set was transferred to the pockets of the sailors. Then the scow was towed out a little way from the dock and set afloat.

The court records the next day told the story, and the newspaper headlines announced, "Drunken Sailors Battle Drunken Civilians After Robbing Them and Stealing a Scow."

When it was all over, Old Aunty Beach-Bütsch lapsed into very uncouth vernacular and exclaimed, "Well, I've had my bellyful of rough trade."

Sissy Beach could not refrain from being cattish: "I'll say you have!"

"Oh, you slay me! You traduce me," wailed hoary-headed old Aunty Beach-Bütsch.

25

THEY HAD A WONDERFUL TIME IN CALIFORNIA. Fay's last vacation was finished. Ahead of her lay four years of hard work in the medical school, with summers spent clerking in hospitals, and all that to be followed by the grind of two years of internship. She enrolled in one of the very excellent Philadelphia medical schools.

Her work began in mid-September. She was fascinated by the subjects. Each day satisfied her craving to know some of the secrets of life. Her very effeminacy was an asset in the work. She could cut, snip and dissect more deftly than her more masculine fellow students. She studied in a different way from the others. They memorized. She correlated, if need be, using drawings and writing as an aid to memory. Almost incessantly she was at work, not diverted by sports or social climbing. Of course her fellow students despised her—at first.

One thing Fay permitted herself: Saturday night outings. These she would often spend either in Philadelphia's Chinatown or at the famous Baden-Baden in Vine Street. Occasionally she attended the weekend costume balls, where she usually walked off with the prize. At intervals she would flit to Washington or New York, but the rewards in pleasure did not seem to be commensurate with the expense and trouble of such extensive travelling. Philadelphia has more than plenty!

Of course Christmas week in New York was different; but even ever-fascinating New York was discarded by her on New Year's Day for Philadelphia's great offering, the Mummers Parade. In this Fay always made it a point to take part, appearing as a queen, the role she played so well. And how regal she could be! Completely so. The word "queen" is old Ango-Saxon for woman. Certainly it should be as easy for one woman as another to play the part. After all, there's much truth in the saying that the Colonel's lady and Jule O'Grady are sisters between—no, under their skins. Fay loved to flirt with the real he-men who lined the route, to return quip for quip and gibe for gibe.

In those days Prohibition was not. There were drinking places everywhere, ranging from sawdusty saloons to gilded hotel bars, and though Fay did not care much for drinking, she did like the flattering attention of men in general and especially of men in particular, those she selected from the crowds who paid her court. Then the place to find men, real he-men, was in the drinking places. Now they are widely scattered throughout the country on drunken fishing and hunting parties, willing as ever but so much more difficult to locate.

Men viewed the Mummers Parade with the very object of paying court. For one of a flirtatious disposition, as Fay had become, this was a gala occasion. There was trade everywhere. Of course there was always the usual sprinkling of dirt, but the clever ones, with their sharpened sensibilities, their so-called intuition, were almost mind-readers.

And the trade, both rough and otherwise, adored Fay, for she could always amuse them—make them laugh, man's great craving. Indeed, some of the rough trade was not so rough after all, and could be very gentle between the sheets. Fay was of the type they all liked to cuddle and she enjoyed all the petting they were able to bestow, if their bodies and mouths were clean and they had a clean body odor. She averred that a real healthy, clean he-man of like race has a definite sex odor that is agreeable. Certainly she'd had experience enough to know, if anyone would. So, using her eyes, ears, olfactory senses and judgment, Fay picked and chose. She was showered with needless gifts. Men were forever wishing to give her this, that and the other thing.

Once, when Miss Jacqueline Bütsch, then a novice, complained to her that men were so expensive, Fay laughed and told her, "One piece of trade," as she dubbed a lover, "should be good for luncheon, another for tickets to the matinee, another for dinner, and still another for theatre in the evening." Certainly Philadelphia always offered entertainment when Fay wanted it.

So passed the first year, made up of much hard work alternated with a few spots of high play.

The medical class discussed her much. Of course most of them continued to despise her. To begin with, she was above them in native intelligence, and also too good in her studies; then too, she was not "one of them," and they did not understand her, and true to human nature what they did not quite understand they either feared or hated. The truth is each was secretly willing to try for her favors. Always they were imagining the very exquisiteness of sensation which might be enjoyed. Their imaginations disturbed them and made them uncomfortable. So, in fighting their desires, they also fought Fay. The conventional are ever intolerant of those who live as they please. Jealousy of a freedom of spirit which they cannot attain drives them on to seek to destroy such a freedom. So, after talking the subject over in a secret meeting of those who thought it their duty "to uphold the honor of the school," one of their number was delegated to lead Fay on, to seduce her and compromise her.

One called Hemans had been selected. Night after night he called on her, ostensibly to study with her. In truth she taught him much. The man did not appeal to her. Her intuitions guided her aright, for one evening, a chap named Mason Linberg, a very handsome fellow who ran with the crowd, dropped into Fay's room. They were alone. That the walls might not hear he spoke almost in a whisper—"Fay you know I admire some of your characteristics very much, especially your scholarship. I have had a more liberal environment than the majority of these poor students. Therefore, I do not judge you, or others. Whatever your private life may be is no concern of mine. I'm here to warn you. The other fellows are trying to frame you, and I think that bumptious Hemans has been chosen to lead you on. Just be careful."

"Thanks, Linberg," said Fay, "and since you are liberal minded, let me give you the reward you deserve." She stepped over to him, put her arms about him and looked into his lovely blue eyes. . . . She kissed him—very gently.

Hemans continued his visits. When he thought friendship had progressed to such a stage that it might be diverted into passion, he put his arms about Fay. "Don't do that, it makes me uncomfortable," said Fay. A few minutes later he tried again, at the same time trying to pull her head down against him. "Don't do that!" "Please don't do that!" She spoke more sharply!

"Don't you like me, Fay?"

"Yes, at a distance, but to me you smell like fish." He did not comprehend that.

"I smell the same as you do, like the dissecting room."

"That was a figure of speech," explained Fay.

But he would not be repulsed and began again trying to force her—to pet.

"What are you after, you son-of-a-bitch?" yelled Fay.

In those pre-war days son-of-a-bitch had not become the term of endearment and praise it now is and was considered a deadly insult.

Hemans muttered, "I'll never speak to you again."

"Don't! I'll be satisfied," Fay assured him.

In revenge, Hemans lied to his fellow students and told them he had proven that Fay was all they had suspected.

She was called before one of those sanctimonious gatherings so dear to the collegiate, "a student committee."

"We do not consider you desirable," they told her gloatingly.

Fay arose in her wrath and borrowed language which she had heard some of her rough trade use with good effect. For at least once in her life her voice took on an almost masculine tone: "See here, I don't give a damn what you or your associates and friends think of me. I have the number of every one of you—you kettleful of stinking fish. But you haven't so much as that on me!" (She touched the tip of her little finger.)

"Hemans says otherwise," the "chairman" announced like a judge giving sentence.

"Is Shemans here to face me? Bring it here and let it say to my face the lies it has told you," demanded Fay.

So the uncomfortable Hemans was brought in. Fay flew to the attack, not waiting for any of the procedure so beloved of men "sitting in session," the ritual which the class of 1912 wished to follow.

"You damned son-of-a-bitch, what have you been telling these people?" she shouted furiously. "Now admit that you haven't a thing on me; admit that you lied. If you don't, I'll choke the truth out of you."

Hemans flushed painfully. Finally he spoke: "I told you fellows what I thought was the best thing to tell you to get rid of this person."

"And it was a lie!" screamed Fay. "Tell them!"

"Well, it was not quite exactly the truth," he admitted.

"There's your answer," sneered Fay. "Some day I'll prove to you that I have more guts than any of you self-styled men." She wiggled her hips (or was it dragged her fanny) out of the room.

Little Fay cared. She realized full well that back of their hatred, fostered by those who had reared them, was jealousy of her freedom from the responsibility that cumbers their own lives, the responsibility that they wish on themselves, the upkeep of a home, the protection of children and all the problems of marriage and family life. If she had only married, and played less openly, they might have forgiven her; but she knew well the futility of marrying to reform, to change one's nature.

That ended the chief collegiate episode of her first year in medicine.

26

THE SECOND YEAR OF FAY'S MEDICAL COURSE HAD BEGUN.

Came a Saturday night in late September, balmy and pleasant as the Philadelphia fall days are apt to be. Fay was downtown and stepped into a tearoom adjacent to the City Hall. The place was crowded with rather rough-looking stuff, but over in one corner she spied her good friend, Linberg. She motioned to him and at the door said, "Come on! Let's beat it from this place. It's simply full of dirt."

Out onto Market Street they sauntered. Fay recognized a subtle change in Mason Linberg. "What has happened to you, Mason?" she asked. "You impress me as being more matured, more experienced, different from what you were a year ago."

"I am different," he replied. "I spent the whole summer at Atlantic City; had a good job in a hotel." Then he went into details of all the opportunities that such a position offers in the way of enlightenment and social development and ended, "I've been brought out socially, as it were!"

"Oh! You haven't yet been brought out," Fay told him, laughing.

"Well, I'm here to learn. I put myself in your hands."

"Be sure you stay there," Fay warned him. Then she continued, "It is Saturday night and we shall celebrate. I have more pennies this year, lucky in some deals which my old banking friend in New York saw to. First, we'll pick up a body guard, preferably one soldier and one marine, or one sailor. They are easier to manage than if we take two of the same kind—not well enough acquainted to connive."

A passerby spoke to Fay, who did not return the salutation. Mason called her attention to the fact. Fay explained, "I never speak to tearoom or t.b. acquaintances on the street! Neither does anyone else who is socially experienced."

They continued to cruise Market Street. Down near the Reading Terminal, Fay saw Whitey, fireman first-class, a tall, broad-shouldered blond with flaxen hair, a chap with whom she had been out on former occasions. "Isn't he marvellous?" she asked Linberg. "Do you wish to take him on?" Mason did not object.

Whitey had been standing at the corner of 12th and Market gloating at the "skirts" as they passed by. Pay day was still in the offing. Therefore, free amusement for the evening appealed to him.

A little further on a lone Marine was standing. "That looks good to me," said Fay. "I'm going to cruise it. Do you know him, Whitey?"

"Not very well," answered Whitey. "But I guess he's O.K. If he ain't, well, it's just too bad, for I'm here, little one, ain't I?"

As they approached, Fay looked directly at the Marine and smiled slightly. He brightened and grinned broadly.

"Want to join our party, soldier-of-the-sea?" queried Fay.

"Sure! Whither away?"

"Willow Grove, first. After that, any place you say, but we're going to end at Baden-Baden, in Vine Street. That satisfactory?"

"O.K. with me! All set? Let's shove off. Can't get goin' too soon to suit me. Got anything to drink with you?"

"No, but we have the wherewithal."

They settled themselves in a Willow Grove car, and as Fay paid the fare (for 'tis ever the woman who pays and pays and pays), she peeled off two five-dollar bills from her roll, with, "Here, sailor-boy, here's your spending money," and "Here's yours, Gorgeous," to the Marine.

"Thanks," the Marine had the grace to answer. "You're good."

"You don't know the half of it, dearie," camped Fay. "I know how to spend money like a drunken sailor. Whitey taught me, didn't you, Whitey?"

136

"Taught you! That's to make the porpoises laugh. Little anybody can teach you. I think you were born wise. Say, Fay, did I tell you about the last ship's dance? One of your sisters, Little Egypt, the couchee-couchee who follows the fairs, well, Little Egypt come over in a drag all gold and pearls and diamonds. What a wow! Prettiest thing there. She got too many drinks under her belt. She said she lost her self-control. I'll say she did. About a dozen kids got her back of the coal bunkers and started to use her somethin' fierce. I happened along in my dungarees, and she threw herself at me. There was a pretty mixup of grease paint and machine grease and she says, 'Fer God's sake, save me, Whitey!' So I says to them guys, 'Hey, youse, this is my kid. Beat it!' And say, did they beat it? I guess yes. The only thing Little Egypt lost was her wig."

"Mason, you have nothing to fear from this boy," Fay assured her friends, "He's a square shooter. Aren't you, Whitey?"

"Ah, live and let live is my motto. Little Egypt is all right—in her way. Maybe it ain't my way; maybe it ain't your way; but she don't harm nobody. If you don't like her ways, keep away from her. If you want to go with her, that's your business, and if she wants to go with you, that's her business."

At Willow Grove they dined and listened to the music, tried all the feats of strength and tests of skill, won a lot of dolls and blankets and canes which they did not want and gave to some boys at the gate. It was about ten when they left and returned to Philadelphia to a small imitation of Atlantic City, a colored cabaret in Susquehanna Street. One of the entertainers, a slim, pretty mulatto girl, sang, then went from group to group repeating her chorus, writhing her body suggestively, the spotlight accompanying her on her rounds of silver gathering.

Arrived at Fay's table, she acted more amorously than ever, even bringing a chair back into play, rubbing certain parts of her body against it. As the yellow girl moved on, Fay leaned over, pretending to smell the contaminated portion of the chair, then straightened up with a wrinkled nose and a wry expression as if the odor was vile, and shook her head in unfavorable judgment. Her pantomime was greeted with howls of delight. Of course, the action was not refined, but there was no need for refinement in that place, and Fay was adaptable. Besides, she wished to make everybody laugh.

Fay danced with Whitey; she danced with the Marine; she danced with every strange good-looking thing in the place, moving with them in their sensuous swayings, back and forth, up and down, twisting and driving movements, becoming more and more amorous as the night went on, for everyone who knows anything is aware that the dance is just a form of uncompleted sexual indulgence, just as hugging, kissing or any other petting, though the dance, bringing into play the senses of hearing and of rhythm, in addition to sight, touch and smell, is the most potent combination of sex stimulation that exists, outside of certain drugs.

Finally Whitey, always outspoken and to the point, said, "Come on, Fay, let's get out of this. I want action."

So they left, Fay walking close in the embrace of the adorable Whitey, Linberg and the Marine following.

Whitey was eager. They took the shortest route possible to Baden-Baden.

Sunday morning Fay awoke to the pleasant sound of church bells ringing. She felt gloriously happy. She ran downstairs to the bath. At the door she stopped. She heard the Marine and then Whitey's great booming voice. The Marine spoke in a high-pitched Southern cracker drawl: "Five dollahs! That Fay's got mo' money. They both got good watches too. Let's roll 'em. They're nothin' but a pair of damn—"

"You dirty pimp," Whitey broke out. "An' I thought you was a decent he-man. Fay's my friend. She's treated us swell. I've a notion to crack your Goddam skull. Now you beat it out of here and don't you even look back. If I so much as hear another peep out of you, I'll be a dentist to your pretty teeth, and I won't use forceps, neither. Now beat it." He did.

As Whitey came out in the hall, Fay asked with an innocent air, "Where's the Marine? Isn't he going to have breakfast with us?"

"He ain't goin' to have breakfast with us, now, nor never! He's dirt! If you ever hear of him tryin' to make trouble anywheres, let me know and if you even so much as see him standin' still on the street, tell me. I'll see he keeps movin' fast."

Thus grew up the tradition, perhaps wrongly, that "Marines is dirt."

Despite the Marine's defection, they made a merry breakfast party, such as can so often be seen of a Sunday morning in that older part of Philadelphia.

A Scarlet Pansy

There were Fay and Whitey and Linberg and four or five more gay young things that fluttered as they walked along.

The party passed the Tenth Street Fire House and gave their friends there a friendly wave of the hand and were good-naturedly razzed in return. One chubby-faced fat fireman put his hands on his hips, wiggled and let out a "Whoops-my-dear!" Another called, "Ella, you're losing your hair pins," and still another, "Kitty, you should wear your veil when you're on the streets."

"Come on and have breakfast with us," Fay invited generously.

"We cahn't, doncher knaow. Duty b'foaw pleasure," the tallest one, Gripes, spoke mockingly.

Fay tossed him two dollars with a gay, "Go get yourselves a can of beer then. That'll shut your traps."

They passed on to howls of, "You must come over! Oh, you must come over."

All of Fay's set knew these firemen. In warm weather the fellows usually sat on benches in front of the firehouse and camped madly with any one who, as one of the Beaches expressed it, "was too obvious." A swaying, short-stepped walk, or clothing that was especially indicative, would call forth comment interspersed with all the familiar war cries designed to put the poor things *hors de combat*.

That morning Fay's crowd was in the luck. The firebell rang, and soon the truck, loaded with men, swung into the street. As they passed the gay girls screamed, "Fireman, save my child, yours and mine."

Fay and her party continued on their way to the vicinage of Camac Street, where they broke fast at a cellar which caters especially to the "temp'ramentals," a place presided over by one of the more humble members of the Dike family, a place where one almost needs to learn a new language to understand and take part in the conversation. This Dike, unlike the usually lugubrious members of that large and conspicuous family, sometimes described as notorious, sometimes as famous, sometimes as infamous, this Dike was very gay, jolly and happy-go-lucky. "Billee" Dike did not make a great amount of money, but she made a living and was at all times surrounded by congenial companions of all sexes. The typical attitude of most of the members of the Dike family is that they are nature's tragedy; that of Fay and her friends that they are nature's joke and that it is their duty to turn life into a roaring farce. Now, who is right?

As Fay and her satellites entered, one girl was weeping on Billee's shoulder, telling how she was heartbroken because "Bobby" had stood her up and given to that "awful thing" that seal ring which Norma had given to Carter, and Carter had given to her, and she had given to "Bobby," and it wasn't fair because "Bobby" had promised never to take the ring off her finger.

The lady, Miss Bull, continued telling Miss Dike the story and at the end repeated, "I simply can't be happy again till I've been stewed."

"Well, don't get stewed here," cautioned Miss Dike. "I don't want the place to get a bad name. Remember, a good name is more to be desired than great riches."

"By whom?" screamed someone in Fay's party. "Not by me. I'll take the pennies every time."

"You would," said Miss Dike witheringly. "You're that kind. And after you got the pennies, you'd spend them foolishly on some grand thing that didn't give a damn for you. I know you. You're like our old friend Aunty Bütsch-O'Brien, the original Aunty Bütsch-O'Brien, who, it is said, went through the family fortune and spent her declining days (tho' Gawd knows she never declined anything) in the poor house."

"Oh, Billee, hurry up and put on the teapot and the waffle iron," begged Fay. "I'm hungry."

"Didn't you get anything to eat last night, dearie?" lilted Miss Dike. "Where'd you go? What did you get?"

"Ask Whitey," replied Fay. "He was with me. He can tell."

Appealed to, White answered oracularly, "Bygones is bygones. I never tell nothin'."

"That's why I trust him and love him so," said Fay.

"Love him how?"

"Love him so—" she made a movement as if to demonstrate.

"Well, don't love him so, or love him so-so here. This is a respectable house."

"Who said so? Oh, yes, I remember the alderman told that to the judge the last time you were arrested for—"

"Never mind what I was arrested for. Just remember that charges were not proven," defended Miss Dike. "You must recall that people were very excited at that time and were going to make us all pure—by law."

A Scarlet Pansy

"Pure?" someone yelled. "Gawd knows my name is pure. You're completely pure too, ain't you, Billee?"

"Yes, but I'd like to be otherwise, if I only knew how. They say you have to be double jointed, and I simply can't qualify."

All this while Miss Dike was boiling coffee, bringing out dishes, stirring batter, ably helped by everyone in the place. In one corner of the dining room someone was crooning the Habanera from Carmen, while "Gypsy," a somewhat nondescript sort of person who had "moments," was strutting her stuff—a Spanish dance, "garbaged" with two rings of onion over her ears for earrings, a stalk of celery between her teeth for a rose, and a red tablecloth for a Spanish shawl. One "gifted" person drummed softly with table cutlery, spoons and dishes, and another used two potlids for cymbals.

The cop on the beat passed by. Then attracted by the sounds of merriment, came back and stepped in. (They are always getting in where there's anything good.) He was a handsome young person who had worked his way up in life, having started as an elevator boy, then become a local lightweight boxer, later a successful beach patrol, and finally he was a cop. Later on he won a beauty contest and went to Hollywood and became internationally famous—a lovely rise!

Everybody was delighted to have him present, and before he left the very best of them laid themselves out to give him a good time.

"How you're cutting up," he greeted them. "That's right; we're only young once."

"Young?" gurgled an old aunty who happened to be present. "You flatter me! Just for that I'm going to entertain you. I'm going to recite." She suited action to word, hopped nimbly up on a bench and began:

"The West, the West, I love the West.
Next to the East, I love it best.
The hoptoads hop, the birds do sing,
And I'm too glad for anything.
I shot a prairie dog today.
Oh, mercy me! Hooray! Hooray!"

There was sufficient applause to hearten her. She announced in her grand queenly manner, "The next time you come I'll recite 'The Bastard King of England.' That's a long one. You'll all like that! Mine is the unexpurgated edition. It tells exactly how he did what to her and she did which to him." Then she called to the cop, "Now you can come sit on my lap and make love to me."

"Later on," he answered.

"How much later?"

"When the wife goes to Atlantic City."

"And that will be?"

"In two weeks, and you must come over. Got to make a pull now."

They loaded him with gifts. One thrust a package of cigarettes into his hand; another put half a dozen cigars in his cap; another gave him a box of candy for the privilege of touching his club; and still another gave him a package of cravats for having been permitted the honor of holding his gun.

Fay handed him the inevitable two dollars, "just for being a good fellow," and he went away—happy.

One had been thrilled; another stunned; another frightened by proximity to the law; another had been "recognized"; and the old aunty had been completely overjoyed.

There were about thirty people in the basement. The number was augmented by the arrival of a dozen university freshmen who were getting their first taste of freedom and the wisdom of the ages. They were pretty young boys, evidently from very good families, and they showed great adaptability in fitting themselves into the fun and frolic. It was anything for a laugh!

One, taking off his coat, said, "I'm so hot I could fry an egg."

The subject of eggs having been broached, one boy demonstrated how big his mouth was by closing it on an egg without breakage. Then there broke out a perfect orgy of mouth measuring, each one trying to demonstrate how much he could get into his mouth—if necessary. The quarter of a waffle was set as a standard.

"I bet on Sissy Beach," one of them wagered.

"My Gawd! Is there a Sissy Beach here in Philadelphia too?" someone asked.

"Wait till you see," was the answer.

One boy, who evidently knew Miss Dike well, had disappeared upstairs. At the moment of the question he returned, but he had undergone a transformation. His suit had been exchanged for a street costume of Miss Dike's.

A Scarlet Pansy

His face had been made up, and he wore a huge picture hat, the vogue at the time. Truth to tell, women's garb suited him better than men's, and he was destined later to win stellar honors as the leading "lady" of the Varsity show; that almost goes without saying. In repose his mouth was not so large; in fact it was beautifully formed and curved and would have been a suitable adornment for almost any feminine face. But the most unusual feature of that most unusual mouth was its extensibility. Wagers were laid. Fay bet for him, for she had seen him perform some place or other. With a sense of artistic balance, Miss Dike insisted that Sissy should be the final to demonstrate.

The first contestant tried and choked as the point of the waffle touched his pharynx. The second one, to mark his record, bit down hard and included not only the waffle but one of Miss Bull's fingers in his bite. "Oh, he's a biter," she shouted. Of course the old aunty fluttered over to administer first aid.

The contest went on. Another one made the mistake of holding his breath. A crumb slipped down his throat and he exploded, the waffle hitting the old aunty on the nose. In queenly manner she rose to the occasion: "At my age, any attention is a compliment. Thanks." Then the field was open to Sissy.

He sat on the edge of a table, one foot crossed over the other, one hand lying palm upward in the other relaxed on his lap. He smiled a superb, growing elastic smile as the accomplished Dike slipped the entire waffle into his mouth and withdrew it still dry.

There was a hubbub the like of which only such a crowd could make. Loud were the cries, "Sissy! Sissy! Sissy!" followed by a typical freshman yell:

> "Rah! Rah! Rah!
> Don't tell Pa.
> Sissy beat 'em.
> Ha! Ha! Ha!
> Sissy! Sissy! Sissy!"

followed by "Speech! Speech! Speech!" Then Sissy lisped, "This is my debut in Philadelphia society, and I thank you for the very hearty welcome you have accorded me. If I have made you happy, I am very pleased to have made you happy. And in the future, if I can do anything else to make you happy, I shall be very pleased to do any and everything to make you happy.

And let us remember on this calm Sabbath morn, that where two or three happy ones are gathered together, there also shall others be made happy, and if we continue to do everything, and promote happiness, after a while there will be so much doing—to make people happy, that perfect happiness will be diffused throughout the whole world and at last everybody will be made happy. Ladies, gentlemen, and others, I thank you." He then ran nimbly up the stairway.

Whitey spoke feelingly, "That kid can have just anything I got just any old time."

Then the very Russian Miss Stupintek made her grand entry, in gorgeous Sunday morning drag. She was fond of declaiming that she had been the favorite of a Grand Duke when just turned seventeen, but the Duchess had found out about the affair and created such a scandal that the Stupintek had to choose between flight and Siberia.

"Zhoos t'ink," she would grieve. "Almos' vas I de same like a Dooshess."

So in the free and easy and generous society of Philadelphia's best, she was accorded the honors, which she had earned, and was dubbed, "La Duchesse Stupintek." She knew too how to carry herself with an air that was even more than queenly. She too was possessed of the imperious psychic urge!

In Philadelphia, Miss Stupintek trimmed hats for a living and complained bitterly whenever a needle pricked her flesh—"'Ere I vork. In Rooshye, I do odder t'ings."

Pressed for further explanation she would shrug her shoulders, roll her eyes, and with pouting lips murmur, "Oh, odder t'ings." Then, as if enlightening sufficiently, "T'ings I lof to do."

To hear her say "lof" would almost set the imagination running wild. To see her say it certainly would, and also would give an adequate understanding of the thorough training which that Russian tongue had undergone. When she sounded the "l," the under side of her tongue caressed the inner border of her too crimson upper lip, and as she finished the word "love," the tip of her tongue darted out of her mouth as if in invitation.

She said little; but she did much!

When La Stupintek did deign to speak, everyone listened, for the few words she spoke were always pregnant with meaning. She created either a riot or a panic wherever she went. Evenings she never appeared except in grand drag a la duchesse, with yards and yards of costly lace or velvet trailing along behind her.

It was La Stupintek who, in later years, when war was declared against Germany, announced bravely, "Now I go to Shairmannee. I fight at ze Shairman. I swear I kill die Krone Prints; but eet weel take mahnts and mahnts and mahnts." After that she was called Dee Kroneprintsessen.

This was Fay's opportunity. Long she had wished to know "La Duchesse" and study her.

The feast was over. Nothing more remained to be done but to go to church. There was a flutter of departure and the usual little squabble as to who should pay.

"Here, let me pay," spoke up Whitey. "I got some dough. I had all kinds of a good time. Now lemme do my share." Nobly he broke out the five dollars which Fay had given him the night before and settled the bill for their portion of the crowd.

Then the Catholics went their way to "worship" at St. Sappho's and the Protestants to "worship" at St. Messalina's.

Fay was not in the least religious. She had dismissed all that years ago as "just so much superstition."

"Going to church?" asked Linberg.

"Why, certainly," she answered. "It's the only safe place to kneel nowadays."

So she attended with her crowd at St. Messalina's and went through the motions.

Linberg asked her afterwards, "And what did you pray for, Fay, you old infidel?"

She pursed her lips, assumed an old-maidish look and answered, "I prayed the same as I always pray. 'Dear Gawd, send me a nice piece of trade; and when I die, let me die in the arms of a lover.'" Little she reckoned that her prayer would be answered.

The rest of that year was made up of hard work, mostly, interspersed with an occasional repetition of a Saturday night such as their first one. More and more of her fellow students were "stepping out," some spending freely the money which their parents sent them, and some, the poorer ones, profiting financially by their excursions into the downtown night life.

Linberg and Fay and a few of the others would now dish the dirt at times, exchanging bits of current new slang, repeating brilliant remarks they had heard, telling the gossip of the very amusing social set in which they moved.

27

June came. Fay and Linberg worked through the vacation as substitute interns in one of the better New York hospitals, "a perfectly grand place."

Of course it was a joy to Fay to have the privilege of initiating Linberg into the pleasures of New York night life—that city whose chief charm is its vastness and the opportunity such size offers for promiscuity. Normal home lovers flee its contaminations and hurry to the suburbs as fast as overcrowded conveyances will take them. This daily efflux speaks much for the innate chastity of the poor wage slaves who daily are obliged to invade Manhattan to earn their sustenance. One could moralize indefinitely on this—if one were so inclined.

First Fay introduced Linberg to Riverside Drive, after dusk, naturally. The Drive was crowded with gobs.

"Oh, the fleet's in, the fleet's in," joyously caroled Fay, as what girl wouldn't who'd had Whitey? "Whitey's a C.P.O. now. I wonder what he brought me from Panama? I wonder! I wonder! I wonder!" she lilted.

"Just stop wondering," a voice sounded in her ear. She turned quickly, looking up into glorious deep blue, black-fringed eyes.

"Who are you?" she asked, and then added, "I don't know you!"

"Well, there's no harm getting acquainted, is there?" the handsome sailor asked.

"There!" Fay turned quickly to Linberg, "didn't I tell you I always make friends wherever I go? Come on, sailor man, speak your little piece. You're lonesome; you're unacquainted; you have no friends in New York; you don't know where to go; you want a cigarette; you want a light; you have only a nickel to get back to the Yard. Now, you tell the rest."

"You told the most of it, except I got a six months' roll and you're the person I've picked to help spend it. I like you, kid! Get me? I like you! Were you ever in the Navy?"

"Quite the contrary," camped Fay.

Fay did look very young that night. Before coming out she had rouged and touched up her sensuous lips, oh, so carefully.

"But my friend here," she said. "I can't leave him; he's new to New York."

"Oh, he can come along as ballast!"

They started. The sailor spent his money freely—theatre, supper, cabs, and afterwards—well, it was Fay's night off, so what was the difference? She whispered to Linberg before they parted, "I believe I'm in love again. If I'm murdered you'll know where to look for me."

Before he parted from her the next morning, the gob took Fay's address, promising to call her up again at night. He thrust gifts upon her—a beautiful jade ring which he had picked up in Panama; bottles of expensive perfume; silk pajamas; embroidered handkerchiefs; all the pretty things which sailors bring back to their sweethearts. But she never saw him again.

A few days later she said to Mason with a sigh, "Something must have happened to him," and ever afterwards she spoke of him as her "royal lover," for he had told her over and over again as he caressed her intimately (and she caressed right back again), "You are some queen! You are some queen!"

Parted from her sailor, she hurried back to the hospital. She and Linberg made the urinalyses, and the work had to be done quickly. Later in the day they took histories, which they loved to do as it gave them an opportunity to probe into the lives of others and learn much, very much, that was amusing. And how they did probe!

Both were trying to make a good impression on the chief of their service in the hope of getting appointments as interns after their college courses were finished. Before a week rolled around, Linberg jokingly announced to Fay, "The chief has his eye on you, and I think his regard is favorable. I think he's trying to make you!"

"My Gawd! So soon? What must an innocent girl do under such circumstances?" camped Fay. "And I thought I had been behaving discreetly."

Linberg was right. A few days later Fay was invited by the chief to dine at the Plaza. She was not one to turn a friend down and quickly answered, "I would be delighted to join you, doctor, but I have promised Mason Linberg, the friend who came up here with me, to go out with him tonight. He does not know the town yet."

"Can't you bring him along?"

"That would be splendid. You will find Mason very entertaining. He plays piano well and sings enchantingly and," she added significantly, "he's just as broadminded as I am." She thought, "I'll let that sink in."

Then the good doctor went on to explain, needlessly, that his wife and family were away and that he became very lonesome of evenings; that his usual club friends were out of town and that Fay and Mason would be conferring a great favor on him; anyway, he went on with a lot of useless explaining.

The truth was that he was one of those people who had learned too late in life what was the matter with him and that marriage could never hold him. He was glad to be rid of his family, secretly wished he had none.

The invitation meant much to Linberg, as he had little spending money. Fay, as usual, had plenty. So they had their "little hunk of supper" at the Plaza. And afterwards there was a roof garden show and nice drinks at an exclusive café. Then the ride home in the chief's automobile—more or less of a novelty.

That evening was but the beginning of a pleasant summer for them with the chief's extra car and a chauffeur at their disposal all the time. The chief ceased to be lonesome and assured them that their youth (though Fay's was somewhat spurious) and enthusiasm had given him a new outlook on life, a "rejuvenation," he called it.

The chief was very, very wealthy and could offer them all that was best in New York. These treats impressed Mason. They were "old stuff" to Fay, though she enjoyed flitting about.

So the happy summer passed. They promised the chief they would be especially attentive to the course in obstetrics and venereal diseases, and he in turn promised that they should "intern" under him.

One day when the chief and Fay were alone and she was cuddling in his arms, he said, "I'm so glad I've found you."

"I'm so glad you've found yourself," was Fay's rejoinder.

When it was time to return to Philadelphia, he drove them over in his car, stopping at Princeton, en route, to visit an old college chum (and exhibit his charming young friends too, probably). The friend talked long and broadly on psychology. Physically he was a repulsive specimen, but he had compensated for that by cultivating his mind. Fay summed him up exactly: "He's a very wise person."

Late in the afternoon they continued on their way, detouring through the pleasant pastoral parts of Pennsylvania. They even had the good doctor camp along the wayside.

The chief, not having had to earn his money, was generous with it. Before leaving Philadelphia, he took an outline of their courses, then equipped them with the very expensive books necessary for their next year's work, bought each of them a microscope, gave them season tickets for concerts and theatrical amusement, paid Mason's tuition and room rent for the year and insisted on giving both of them charge accounts at tailors' and department stores. That man was grateful for his happiness.

All of these gifts were a great help to Mason. Of course Fay was not rich, but she had plenty of money. She demurred at accepting such favors from the chief, but in the end accepted, as it seemed to make the old dear so happy.

Fay, in speaking of the dear doctor, later said to Mason, "There is no person more to be pitied than the one who finds out what he really wants too late in life; that is, after marriage."

28

THE THIRD YEAR OF FAY'S MEDICAL WORK STARTED WITH A RUSH. There were new subjects to learn and old ones to review. Good student that she was, yet she found the work taxing. Sometimes she found herself becoming irritable. Then she would whisper to Mason, "Virtue has its own reward. Watch me be good for a while," and her Saturday night sprees would be limited to the theatre, the opera or a concert. Mason plugged away with equal assiduity. Now they could only spare a part of Christmas week or part of a night before a holiday for gadding. Of course, the chief came over on an average of once a month, and they taught him how to cruise. Usually he brought his family with him, but as Fay was in medicine and always Mason came along too, the surgeon could "get away with things" under the very nose of his wife.

The high spot of that year was probably the course of lectures in psychiatry and the course in neurology, taught by the same professor. Psychiatry of itself did not attract them so much, for they had more or less of a fatalistic feeling toward the patients, believing that the treatment of mental disease is a thankless task and should have started with the ancestors, but they enjoyed the lectures by reason of the antics which the professor indulged in when demonstrating the symptoms of various types of disease. His powers of mimicry could hardly be excelled. Tremors, palsies, twitches, limps, deformities, all of these he could simulate so convincingly as to make them recognizable when seen in a patient. The lecture he seemed most to enjoy giving was on certain phases of psychopathia. He loved to talk of the androgynous.

He knew his subject well; that part of it Fay said he knew all too well. She verified all of his statements when she visited Berlin just before the World War began. Then she wrote to Mason, after visiting the corner of Unter den Linden and Friedrichstrasse at night, that if indeed there is a third sex, there it could be found and that Professor Jimmie Stay had not exaggerated.

The professor would describe all sorts of aberrant types, their prominent, wild eyes, their too thick or too narrow chests or hips and their too thin or too heavy leg muscles; he would illustrate the swagger of the feminine type and the mincing short-stepped swaying gait of the masculine, the fluttering, so-called; he would tell of their nocturnal amusements and occupations, and when he had finished he had so enthused his entire class that they were ready to go down town and start a laboratory course at once. In speaking of his Berlin experiences he always ended his remarks, "But they never approached me. They seemed to sense in some way that I was not one of them." And here Fay whispered to Mason, "Poof! Poof! Some more of that protective coloration!"

After the course was over Fay confided to Mason, "If there's one thing I despise it is a person who pretends he is something he is not. Imagine that one posing as a real he-man."

"Posing is the only way to be respected and disreputable at the same time," answered Mason.

29

THE THIRD SUMMER VACATION FAY AND MASON SPENT "JERKING BABIES." By preference they went out together. They were sent to poor families all over New York City, mostly to Italian and Negro families, occasionally to an Irish, German or Jewish family.

Marjorie Bull Dike, in from California, was taking something in summer school at the same time. She was reconciled to her family again and had money; besides, she'd come into an inheritance. She possessed a new car, and she insisted on using it for their benefit. Marjorie preferred to go about town with men. She whistled, smoked and drank like a man. She was that kind. At the wheel, in her sport togs, she passed for one. When she went with Fay and Mason on their cases, she stood by, ready to help, pretending to be a nurse. She had at one time started a nursing course, but like everything else on which Marjorie embarked, it was never finished.

But Marjorie liked to regard the drama. Papa, mamma, grandma and at least two children usually filled the two ill-ventilated rooms. Mamma probably would be found rolling about on the soiled bed groaning, "Mama, mia! Mama, mia!" or "Howly Mary! Howly Mary!" or "Lawdy, Lawdy, Lawdy!" or simply, "Oi, Oi, Oi!" depending on the nationality. The women would all yell in their respective tongues, "Never again, Never again!" Papa would be scared speechless. The children would cry. Grandma would joke and jest with the patient, telling her it was nothing; that she had had her fun and that as soon as this was over she would forget the pain and be ready to start all over again, for "'tis a pain that's soon forgotten." And it looks as if Grandma is right.

Sometimes it would be an "unwed mother"; this always moved Fay to camp to Mason her own version of that dear old nursery rhyme: "There was an old woman who lived in a shoe who had so many children because she didn't know what to do."

On their return to New York they had seen the chief, of course, but he was not so attentive as the previous summer. Absence had not made the heart grow fonder, but had provided opportunity for interest to wander to a younger and newer acquaintance.

30

THEIR FOURTH YEAR IN THE MEDICAL SCHOOL FLEW BY AS IF ON WINGS. They now did practically everything that a regular practitioner of medicine would do, though they lacked much of the assurance that the successful practitioner cultivates.

Of course the nurses in the hospital connected with the medical school tried to marry the handsome Mason, and of course they detested Fay for her very obvious influence over him.

Now, as often as not, Mason and Fay were joined by the other members of their class when they went downtown for their gay Saturday nights. At last these boys away from home had discovered that the world is not the sexless, friendless place they had been taught it was, and before the end of that year most of them had been had. The broadening influence of city life had "wised them up," and at least they had become pleasantly tolerant of others, all except the one who was destined to become a medical missionary, incidentally quite the poorest student in the class and also quite the most gullible. Even some of the professors were, to speak poetically, "occasionally lifting the veil." One day when Fay asked one of them if he would kindly spray her tonsils for her, he camped gaily about the subject.

They were graduated. Mason and Fay, now joint possessors of a Ford car, hurried away to New York and to their hospital appointments. They were interns and as such had to live in the hospital. But they had their own lives to live too and to that end began looking for a flat.

They decided that the flat must be in a part of town where they could do much as they pleased; that it must not be in too refined a locality or their speed might be cramped.

Finally they found a "walkup flat" on the third floor of an old-fashioned building which housed three other apartments. Above them were four students. Well and good! Below them were two very elegant-looking young ladies, who became friendly with them at once, even before they had leased their flat. Later they found that these good girls were kept by several rich men (though each man thought that he was the sole lover of the girl he was interested in) and that, being practical and wishing to put something away for old age, they chose a cheap apartment instead of having an expensive place. Besides, their lovers preferred to visit in a part of the city where there was no chance of recognition. On the ground floor lived what the kept women called "the only respectable person in the place," a Mrs. Backhaus, a woman of probably fifty years. "So long as you don't make a noise and let her get anything on you, it's all right," one of the kept women assured Mason and Fay. Said the other, "She's always trying to catch the students when they rush dames upstairs. We help them circumvent her by having the girls call on us first. Nothing like a little cooperation! I hope we will be friends, if you decide to take the flat." Kept women anywhere are always more or less lonely and long for friendships founded on something else than necessity. So long as their own shortcomings are overlooked, they are usually quite willing to overlook the shortcomings of others, though there are some who, hoping to pose as respectable women, criticize every and anything they can in others. Often kept women are amusing company, as Fay and Mason found out.

31

MISS PAINTER WAS GIVING A RECEPTION, AN AFTERNOON DRAG. Mason and Fay had been invited. Old Aunty Beach-Bütsch, of San Francisco, was visiting New York, and the reception was in her honor. Fay had been asked to be on the receiving line. That required an entirely new and elegant drag. Her place was to be next to Miss Savoy, the impersonator, noted for her low comedy, sometimes too low. Fay was indeed glad, for this promised great fun. She was familiar with the story of Miss Savoy's defense of her personal reputation. Miss Savoy had been variously described, and one dramatic critic had told her to her face what he did not dare to write as a columnist—"Miss Savoy, you are a dirty-mouthed slut!" To this Miss Savoy had calmly answered, "The very idea! Why how you slay me! A dirty thing never came out of my mouth. My language is perfectly pure, innocent. What others make of it— well, if someone choose to distort the innocent into evil, such a one is evil himself—evil incarnate, incarnate, mind you." She swallowed obviously as if she had rid herself of the statement with an effort.

Socially, Miss Savoy had more good connections than any woman in New York. She was the offspring of excruciating Helen McH———t, the celebrated beauty. Helen McH———t had in turn been unfaithful to both of her commonlaw husbands and all of their male friends too. She was noted for her wit and could make anybody laugh at anything, everything, or nothing. Miss Savoy kept up the family traditions. Through the beautiful Helen, Miss Savoy was related to the Bulls, the Dikes, the Godowns, the Pickups, the Mawgans, the Carters, the Munros and other famous people. She was indeed original. She was college-bred but only allowed that to be perceptible at times. Still, she had an education and was a person of parts. At college, when asked to fill out one of those intimate, too intimate questionnaires, when she came to the question, "What sports are you interested in," answered, "I am a sexual athlete. Naturally, I am interested in all indoor sports." Only association with Miss Savoy could give an adequate idea of her complex personality. She created a stir wherever she went, and more, she kept it going.

Miss Savoy's speaking voice was a marvel. Formerly she had sung, and once when taking the high note of a love song which she sang to the tune of Gounod's Ave Maria (properly, she insisted), her voice broke, and ever after she spoke in a foghorn contralto; she said it was change of life.

Then too, among the important guests was to be Senorita Chienne y de las Perras, of South America, and the world in general, a brilliant adventuress who could have been a queen in her own right, if she had chosen to assume the title. She was both French and Spanish, but elected to be known as La Senorita. Her movements were the poetry of motion, and where her American sisters fluttered, she undulated, rather than walked. She was renowned for her beauty and her savoir faire. When someone mentioned her manners to Miss Savoy, that whimsical person gave utterance to some gossip: "They do say her bedroom manners are marvelous." But Miss Savoy was likely to say anything, anywhere, either in private or on the stage. It was this which made her a theatrical star and also caused her to be sought after by all "society." Her social leadership was undisputed. When she had toured South America and Spain she had made it a point to become acquainted with all of the Perras, representing as they do the epitome of culture in both of the Spanish portions of the world. She was wont to pay them tribute thus: "Why, till I learned Spanish ways, I didn't know a thing, dearie."

The promised presence of both the Senorita and Miss Savoy added to Fay's and Mason's eagerness to attend the reception.

Thus, they were looking forward to an amusing afternoon. Before they attended the affair, Fay advised Mason, "Be sure to stand near, and you'll hear more than an earful when Miss Savoy begins to spout. So far you've only met her when she was on her good behavior."

A Scarlet Pansy

It was a brilliant occasion in East 69th Street. None outshone Mason and Fay. Mason's tall figure was one to enhance the value of the finest New York tailoring. Fay wore a blond wig, just suited to her natural coloring, and a blue velvet drag from Louise Brown & Co., with a picture hat which framed her beautiful face and accentuated her loveliness. Her ermine-bordered coat gave the necessary regal touch. With the bearing of a queen she swept through the corridors of the fashionable apartment house, while all society looked on and gasped in surprised envy.

As at all such receptions, there was much twittering conversation. One overhearing the greetings accorded would have decided that the crowd was made up of New York's most punctilious and polite. It was always Miss This and Miss That. Occasionally an "Ella" or a "Kitty" would slip out, but that did not necessarily mean that was the proper baptismal name of the person addressed, or even that the person was of the sex that the name connoted; rather it was oftenest used in good-humored derision; thus they often used "Miss" also. Not only real girls but men that were not real he-men were often referred to as "Miss So-and-so." A necktie of peculiar flaming hue worn by any man would bring forth comment: "See! Miss So-and-so is all dressed up in drag this morning." A man with a boutonniere would be described, "Miss So-and-so is wearing a corsage bouquet."

As for their surnames, many of them preferred to travel incognito and assume names which seemed best to suit their personalities, or even to hide their identities, as is so common in good New York society. A chance resemblance to any famous woman, especially an actress, often provided the requisite *nom de guerre*.

Some gave free vent to their fancy, and half the time the name chosen might even be that of the opposite sex, indicating probably the temperament and inclinations of the person, if not the actual sex, which after all, may have been more or less problematical. So at this reception the titles applied more to disposition than to sex.

The other side of their personality, the less conventional, they were wont to speak of as a different person—for instance, Miss Savoy commonly spoke of herself as "Your mother"; Miss Kitty of herself as "Your sister"; Miss Beach of herself as "Your Aunt Ella." This Miss Beach had been born Vasilacopoulos, but when she went into society she changed it to the good English name of Beach.

At these receptions the camping was always brilliant.

Fay took her position in the receiving line beside Miss Savoy, who graciously whispered, "My Gawd, you are queenly. Nobody would suspect you of being what you are."

Then the other guests began to arrive. Robert, the butler, announced in his voice, which had first been trained at a railway station:

"Miss Kitty Fuchs!"

"Indeed! Miss Kitty! But how delightful! I've been longing to see you," almost shrieked Miss Savoy.

"I'm so glad you approve," minced Miss Kitty.

"Well, it's nobody's business but your own, and besides, the butler should not tell," chirruped Miss Savoy.

"That's the lady's name," explained Mason, who was standing near.

"Well, she shouldn't have such a puzzling name," defended Miss Savoy. "My mistake," she went on, stifling her laughter with her lacy handkerchief; then, regaining some degree of self-control, she continued, "I beseech you, Miss Kitty, I beseech you to exonerate me." If Miss Savoy committed any social lapse, and 'tis to be feared she committed many, she would hasten to seek exoneration. To ask pardon or excuse she held was common, and Miss Savoy would not be common, no, not for the world.

"Miss Kuntz!" bellowed the butler.

"Plural! Oh, you marvelous woman," burst forth Miss Savoy. "I've heard so much about you and your wonderful ways. I've been hoping to meet you, too."

"Miss Tom and Mr. Tom."

"I am perplexed. Which is mister and which is miss?" asked Miss Savoy. "I can't tell which from t' other."

"Mr. and Miss Fish!"

"Again, I am bothered," said Miss Savoy. "Noun or verb?"

"Verb, of course, stupid," explained Fay.

"Active or passive?" chortled Miss Savoy.

"Mr. and Mrs. Morrison Godown!"

"Both?" almost shrieked Miss Savoy. "Mrs. Godown, are you anomalous? No offense. Please exonerate me. That's a new word I've just learned, and I'm using it for practice."

"Miss Stepp."

"My Gawd! What a tragedy," giggled Miss Savoy, and everybody else.

"Miss Fall—of Idaho!"

Miss Savoy could not resist—"Well, dearie, don't fall too low; you may regret it. I'm always careful about that myself—a certain degree of discretion."

"Miss Ella Fitzhugh!"

"Hugh only?" questioned Miss Savoy, and then added, "I don't believe it."

"Miss Billee Browning!"

"What? Billee too? Oh, my Gawd!" Then turning to her hostess, Miss Savoy suggested, "Dearie, you'll only have to give the society reporter a list of the names of those present to let the public know just what kind of a party it was."

Then there was a collation, and a lovely "co-ed" (a typical homo-mollis) from Springfield College sang a lovely song in one of those lovely sissy tenors which in recent years someone has kindly dignified as crooning.

This was followed by gay music and gayer dancing and much intense loving, and finally conversation, and the subject was man, the real he-man.

It began with Old Aunty Beach-Bütsch, who opined, "There are no real men, any more, no real he-men."

"Before we can discuss that properly," said Miss Savoy in her most erudite manner, "we must define the term. Just what is meant by a he-man?"

Miss Minnie Beach, who had been described as so romantic she could idealize a sewer, closed her eyes as if entranced and murmured poetically, "A real he-man is Gawd's most glorious work."

"That's not complete enough," said Miss Fuchs, dipping her oar into the conversational flow. "I suppose after all a real he-man is a male who can propagate."

"There's more to it than that," corrected Miss Savoy.

"Let's solve it by elimination," ventured Miss Browning, who had a degree from a famous Massachusetts university.

"That's mathematics," shrilled Miss Savoy. "Leave out all bitch arithmetic."

"Miss" Astor made some useful suggestions in her high-pitched voice, rippling along at a furious rate: "A real he-man does not care to juggle a frying pan, whether at home or camping in the woods. He does not teach school, either, and he does not name his son Junior as if it takes two of 'em in the same family to make one good whole man." She cast her eyes towards heaven, then continued rapidly as if she had found the inspiration which she had been seeking, "No honest-to-God man is a minister, a nurse, a physician, a musician, a painter, a poet, any kind of an author, a chef, a butler, a house servant, a waiter, a tutor, an actor, a stage dancer, a college professor, a shopkeeper, a hair-dresser, a barber—"

"You can't run on like that forever," broke in Miss Savoy. "Give somebody else a chance to express an opinion. But are there any other occupations to which he has an aversion?"

"Dozens of them," added the well-informed Miss Astor. "Millinery, dressmaking, all the occupations in which women and Frenchmen delight, also bookkeeping, clerking in shops of all sorts, especially jewelry stores, all the refined occupation, hundreds of the jobs which city life has brought into being."

"There seems to be an abundance of intermediates to fill them," said Miss Savoy as if weighing the evidence. Then she turned to Mason: "Now, doctor dear, speaking as a professional man, tell us something about real he-men."

"A real he-man never needs to be circumcised. Also a real he-man can always leak without turning on the water faucet," said Mason, who had had one drink too many and hence lapsed into vulgarity.

That set off old Aunty Beach-Bütsch, who rocked back and forth in glee as she added her bit: "A real he-man can fill out his pants properly."

Then Mason added some more: "Even with age a real he-man does not take on fat and look like an old woman in the face."

Quoth Miss Browning, "Up our way they think hair makes the man; but I have seen bearded ladies."

Fay offered as her contribution, "I have observed that a real he-man has no inhibitions."

"A real he-man never becomes bald!"

"A real he-man is never knock-kneed!"

"A real he-man is never a smarty!" in chorus piped up Miss Browning and Miss Fish and Miss Godown, each trying to be heard above the other.

"No real he-man is ever rich," said Miss Hoover, "and I ought to know something about it. Only those who possess the woman's instinct of greed save and seek to acquire unnecessary wealth. That's the reason so many rich men's sons are—well, what they are, the its that you see them. Poor things, they inherit the parental taint in an intensified form. No rich man should ever take the chance of being a parent, with all the disappointment that inevitably follows. If a he-man has anything he spends it all liberally. But that doesn't mean that a liberal spender is necessarily a he-man; there may be other motives, conscious or unconscious."

"You have given us food for thought, Miss Hoover," spoke up the hostess. "Now somebody else give us some useful information."

Miss Stepp started to sing, "Remember, this year's trade is next year's—" but someone interrupted, "Oh! Shut up! Don't destroy all illusions!"

Miss Fall, who was always raving about odors, pleasant or otherwise, and who always put one perfume on her tongue, another behind each ear, another on the back of her neck and in her hair and still another on her breasts, her hands, her knees or any other places where she thought they might be most useful, then contributed a very important observation: "He likes to be clean and not smell bad, but he does not care anything about style so long as he's not conspicuous."

"You can put me down as holding that real he-men always have long fingers and long noses," said Miss Pickup.

Miss Godown broke forth: "He can be told by the way he speaks. He talks briefly and to the point. He is not argumentative like lawyers. He never soliloquizes. He never hems and haws and precedes his remarks with useless exclamations of well and now, and he never stutters." She paused a moment, gave a careless wave of her hand and added, "Et cetera."

"What are the signs of lost manhood?" asked almost-innocent Miss Stepp.

"Are you sure you mean signs of its having been lost, or indications of its never having been possessed?"

Miss Stepp did not answer, but continued to question: "Don't you think you can tell real he-men by the way they run after women all the time?"

"My Gawd, dearie, no! Half of that running after women is an attempt to reinforce their very imperfect feeling of mannishness." It was Miss Savoy speaking again with the voice of authority. "No real he-man ever runs after anything. But whatever comes his way, he's ready for it, (I said whatever!) and then forgets it after it's all over. A real he-man will take all the petting you will give, and enjoy the sensation, but he won't bother to pet back again. Why, a real he-man would never even bother to get married if some woman did not keep on pestering him and making a nuisance of herself until he did it. And believe me, no real he-man can ever remain faithful to one woman, unless that one woman keeps all the others herded away from him." It was easy to see which way Miss Savoy's mind ran—in a rut.

The Dikes, the Bulls and Miss Bull-Mawgan, who had strolled in late, looked bored. Nevertheless, La Bull-Mawgan, who knew men (and women), if she knew anything at all, gave her definition: "A real he-man, is a human male who never gets nervous." She paused as if for thought, but seemed to be unable to get her wits together sufficiently to continue further (Marjorie Bull Dike had come into the room).

Here the ever elegant Mrs. Slatterly, who seemed to know a thing or two, broke into the conversation. "But why all this furor about a real he-man? I think they're nicer if they are a bit effeminate; then they can be induced to do things that a real he-man could never be persuaded to attempt."

"Well, you're the one who ought to know!" said Miss Savoy.

Miss Browning, who detested silence, broke forth again: "Once I thought I had a real he-man. I found out he was fish. It makes me sick to think of him."

"Control yourself, dearie," Miss Hoyt hastened to warn. "Too late now!"

"Mason has an idea that the hormones are responsible for real he-men," volunteered Fay.

"Oh, the hormones! The hormones!" camped Miss Savoy with delight. "Go on, Mason, and talk about the hormones and the adorable glands. You always sound so convincing. I love to hear you."

"Reserving all my ideas for publication," said Mason, who did not wish to be bothered further. He was over in a corner swapping spit with something nice he had a crush on. They had no time for anything but sex stunts.

Fay held a spoonful of sugar over her cup of tea. It was an opportunity for the ever-observing Miss Savoy, who called out to her, "Fay, is that invert sugar?"

Fay turned the spoon upside down, dumping the sugar into the tea, stirred vigorously, sipped it and replied, "It is now, dearie! But why question the fact?"

Then Fay contributed some of her personal observations: "Real he-men do not have big fat buttocks, or big breasts, or fat arms or big thick calves; those things belong to the female or the male intermediate. To tell the truth, dearies, the real honest-to-Gawd grand glorious he-man is just about as common as his opposite."

"And what do you mean by that?" asked Miss Godown, who feigned ignorance.

"Now, Kitty, don't you know what a fairy is, a real live fairy, not the story-book kind?" asked Miss Savoy.

"Whoops, my dear, I should say I do."

"Then, speaking plainly," said Fay, "what I wished to impress upon you is that the real he-men are just about as common in the population as fairies are."

"Well, then, how do women ever get—along?"

"They put up with the makeshifts, grab the best thing they can get, not the thing they really want."

"But how can they produce a breed of real he-men if they can't breed with real he-men?"

"The truth is, they don't, dearie."

"You make me wonder about my father."

"Yes, and your grandfather too!"

"I should think women would love real he-men so!"

"Well, with all the drivel that has been written about love throughout the ages, have you ever heard of a fair damsel or a fine dame falling in love with a eunuch? I ask you?"

Miss Savoy, who had been listening attentively, then said, "To put it succinctly, a real he-man must be possessed of marvelous sexual attributes."

Then Mrs. Slatterly, who wished to justify her yen for flossy gentlemen, became profound and declared, "The basis of civilization is founded on the gradual repression of the too-masculine type. Why if every male of the species were a real he-man there would be a personal war just as soon as two of them met. They'd kill each other off. It is good for them to have some attraction for each other instead of too much repulsion."

"Is Reggie over there a real he-man?" asked Miss Godown in her most innocent manner and just as if she didn't know.

Reggie spoke up in a high-pitched voice: "If I had been brought up differently, I might not be as I am. Please leave me out of the discussion."

Then Oswald broke forth bitterly: "Huh! Look at me. I was brought up right, exactly as the doctors and psychologists specified. I was a he-man once. Yet look what happened. After having grip, complicated by pneumonia, and then meningitis, I was a different person; there was some inner change. What in hell has so-called morals to do with my life anyway?"

"But you are digressing, Oswald!" said the hostess. "Have a sense of humor. Remember, Gawd must have his little jokes on the human species."

"I feel bitter, bitter against the half-men who make our laws. Come on, let's legislate against the tides too."

"Be practical," suggested Miss Bull-Mawgan. "The only recourse is to see that every ecclesiastical student is properly seduced, and thus liberalized. The pulpit, after all, makes the laws of this country."

A chap from Philadelphia named Queen spoke up: "Well, dearie, I was a seminarian once and I'm here to tell you that the theological schools are not without their liberalizing propagandists. That's where I was brought out pretty. What do you think, Mary Savoy, is it the bringing up that makes us as we are?"

"No, indeed!" answered the almost omniscient Miss Savoy. "Oswald is right; the outward is but the expression of the inward. I think we've exhausted the subject, all but the laboratory course. Now that we know what a real he-man is like, let's all go out and look for some."

People began leaving. There was the usual laughter and shrill callings back and forth, the exchange of "brilliant" remarks as the party broke up.

The reception, which started with such elegance, ended in a typical panic, as so often affairs in society do.

Arrived home, Fay said to Mason, "Now you can feel that you've made your bow to 'society.'"

Said Mason, "Our hostess is most elegant and seems to try to be important socially. Does she succeed?"

"I'll say she does," answered Fay, "and so do all of our crowd."

32

At Christmas, Mason and Fay "threw a party," a grand affair. They sent out cards to all of their friends in New York and Philadelphia—La Duchesse Stupintek, "Tillie-the-Toiler," Miss Savoy, "Bertha the Sewing Machine Girl," Miss Mae Bull, Miss Elsie Dike, La Bull-Mawgan, Miss Kuntz, the Beaches and the Fishes, the usual gay crowd; also to dear Old Aunty Beach-Bütsch from California, who had continued to remain in New York after the horse show and other of the major social events. Among those invited were many stage people and many supposed doubles of famous actresses who assumed the names of the stars they imitated or, more likely, caricatured: "Carter," "Miss Anna Held," "Lillian Russell," not to mention a few of the notables who were impersonated.

There was a Christmas tree.

The Beaches appeared, dragging their usual gorgeous laces and velvets regally behind them. The "noted actresses" came in all the borrowed finery which they could command.

Fay was gayer than ever, the reaction to a difficult life-saving emergency operation which she had performed on a tenement house brat during the afternoon. She said to Mason at dinner, "It was glorious to see that purple-faced little child come back to life. And I don't mind telling you that after it was all over and the mother was weeping, I broke down and shed tears, too. Now they look on me as a tender-hearted angel. Well, I suppose I am to them. I left them a fifty-dollar bill. I couldn't bear their misery."

The weather was cold and snowy, conducive to that elevation of spirit which comes when one steps from the inclement out-of-doors to a festive interior. The tree was borne down by gifts, and for every guest there was a present of at least one cake of soap of a much-advertised floating brand, wholly suited to the personalities of the recipients,—just in case they did not have one in their homes. Then they provided Dutch Cleanser "to brighten up their prospects," lovely rubber goods appropriate to the sex of the individual, gorgeously colored douche-bags and beautiful pessaries; medicaments with specific directions for their use for specific diseases; atomizers for throat spraying; half a dozen diapers for a lady who, it was rumored, would need them unless she got out of her predicament (which she did later on unless the whole thing was a fabrication); canned tomatoes; tinned fish; and other things with directions to make use of them when they could not get anything else. Too, there were other presents of a more expensive type—a beautiful prayer book for "Bertha the Sewing Machine Girl," who, though she was known to be a clandestine prostitute, was, nevertheless, very religious (she had been one of the petits-jesus); a splendid necklace for "Tillie the Toiler" (so dubbed because she worked so hard—at anything she did); exquisite perfumes for those who were ladies, or at least thought they were ladies; handkerchiefs for everybody, with the price tag left on—just under 70 cents—but Fay insisted she was too busy to take the tags off. "Besides," she said, "I'll leave them on so they'll know I'm not cheating."

The two kept women who lived on the floor below were bidden, and when one of the college boys stuck his head out to hear what all the pow-wow was about, he and his crowd too were invited, and accepted alacritously.

The first arrivals came quietly immediately after theatre, but as the night advanced there was more and more hilarity and noise. By two o'clock the three establishments were thrown into one. They were all keeping open house, traipsing back and forth, clattering up and downstairs, whooping, singing, shouting and making a jolly noise just suited to such an occasion and to that type of people.

About half past two, the respectable Mrs. Backhaus, who lived on the ground floor, came out into the lower hall in wrapper, bedroom slippers and curlpapers, and shouted angrily up the stairs: "I want to know what this noise is about! Don't you know that this is a respectable house and that respectable people should be in bed and asleep?"

Mason, liquored up a bit, called down, "Oh, we're willing to go to bed, come along!"

At that Mrs. Backhaus screamed, "I warn you, one and all, I warn you, that if these carryings-on do not stop, I shall call the police."

By that time Fay was in the lower hall. The only respectable woman in the house looked her up and down, at first not recognizing her under her wig and drag, but when she did, broke forth, "You, you dissolute people; you are responsible for this. I'll find out all about you before this is over. I'll look up your employers and tell them just what kind of people you are."

"Oh, go on and tell them, you old blatherskite," retorted Fay. "And when you've finished, remember that to the pure all things are pure, and that includes us. Besides, I know a few things about you, too," she continued, making up her story as she went along. "You're the woman whose first child does not belong to her husband, though he thinks it does. I've heard all about you!"

"I'll have you arrested!"

"Me? Arrested! And you want me to tell in court all I have heard about you?"

Now, no woman who has lived all of her life in New York City is so stainless that there is not some weak place in the armor of her respectability, and this woman was no exception. She feared what Fay might really know. But she was the kind who wished to have the last word.

"I wish my husband was here!"

"I wish he were, too," carrolled Fay. "I'd take him right away from you. You know I could!"

"You're a bold, bad person." Mrs. Backhaus, the respectable, turned towards her door.

"You don't know the half of it," laughed Fay.

"And I don't want to, either!"

"You wouldn't understand it if you did!" Then Fay had an inspiration. Up the stairway she flew. To the Christmas tree she hurried, telling them all, "I'm going to take a Christmas present to dear Mrs. Backhaus." She selected the largest douche-bag remaining, then quickly slid down the banisters to the ground floor, knocked at the lady's door and, as Mrs. Backhaus opened it, said, "Merry Christmas. Here's a pretty douche-bag for you," then pranced away towards the stairway, narrowly avoiding the douche-bag which dear Mrs. Backhaus hurled after her.

"Now I'm going to call the police," the irate woman declared.

"I hope they'll send the reserves. They'll be fresh. We can use them," Fay gave back answer.

They had not long to wait. Soon a big, good-looking officer arrived. Fay came down to meet him. Mrs. Backhaus, her door ajar, was peeking out to see all that could be seen. As soon as the officer came in from the street she began: "Officer, arrest that person and all of that crowd upstairs. Not only are they disturbing the peace but I have every reason to believe they are grossly immoral people." And to Fay she said, "You ought to be ashamed of yourself acting this way on Christmas Eve."

"Officer," said Fay, "she ought to be ashamed of herself. I gave her a Christmas present, a perfectly lovely douche-bag, and she threw it at me. Now, is that a Christian spirit?"

"What kind of place is this you're runnin'?" asked the officer like a magistrate hearing the evidence.

"Come right on upstairs and I'll show you," said Fay as she took his arm. At the landing she turned and stuck out her tongue at Mrs. Backhaus.

On the second floor Fay explained to the officer: "Now, these ladies in this apartment really have reason to feel aggrieved. We woke them up out of their beauty sleep. You know it was their beauty sleep. See how beautiful they are! Well, they are not complaining about the rumpus, but have joined in the festivities as becomes good Christians. It's Christmas, and we should all celebrate. Don't you think so, officer? Now come up to my apartment." The officer was ushered in and looked about in admiration.

"My, what a swell place you got," he said, "and this is what yuh call home?"

"Yes, and you must make yourself at home, too, thoroughly so. See our tree! Just take anything off it you wish. There's some queer soap, always useful, even though amusing. Did you get any presents yet? No? Oh, you poor thing! Mason! Go get twenty-five dollars out of my gold mesh bag and bring it here to the officer." (Fay had no gold mesh bag, but she did have the twenty-five dollars.) "Officer, do have some champagne. Cigars? Cigarettes? Help yourself."

"Thanks, don't care if I do," said the officer politely as he stuffed his pockets full of all they would hold, then downed a glass of champagne as if it were so much water.

Fay knew her stuff. "Have some more champagne, officer?"

"Thanks, don't care if I do." He drank as most people would drink when possessed of a terrible thirst. And so she plied him with the delightful and deceptive liquid.

"Now, officer, I want you to meet all the celebrities, since you'll have to give a report on us and our guest. This is 'Bertha the Sewing Machine Girl.' Bertha, do your fancy curtsey. This is 'Tilly the Toiler.' This is Aunty Beach-Bütsch all the way from California. And these are all the stage celebrities, or at least they pretend they are. Most of them are chorus molls, but, oh! so talented and accomplished." Fay rolled her eyes expressively, then continued. "Mason, fix up a nice box for the officer and put in a bottle of champagne, too, for evidence that we were giving a respectable party. And somebody open another bottle now. Have some more champagne, officer?"

"Not so fast! Not so fast! I'm almost full up now. Where's the—" he whispered to Fay.

"Third door down the hall, officer. But you need not be afraid to speak right out loud here. We call things by their right names, don't we girls—a spade's a spade." She appealed to those surrounding them.

The modest officer retired but soon returned.

"Come here, dear," Fay called to him, and then to some of the girls and chorus molls standing about. "Now show the officer what you can do."

Beach, the one from Philadelphia nick-named "Sissy," was there that season doing an impersonation of Eric-Erica, the museum wonder, one half of whose body was feminine, and the other half masculine. "Sissy's" left side had been shaved of all hair. A false but very real-looking mammary gland had been attached to the left side of her chest. The makeup of the left side was of delicate pink and white; that of the right of deep tan and red. The left eyebrow had been replaced by a delicate penciled line. Bracelets and rings adorned the left hand and arm. The left foot was encased in a dainty silk slipper. On the right foot, "Sissy" wore an athletic shoe; on the right hand a boxing glove.

Like a good showman, Mason made the introduction:

"Ladies and gentlemen, we have before us Eric-Erica, the most renowned and most marvelous anatomical puzzle known to modern medicine." He slipped a Spanish shawl from the left shoulder. "As you will see, one side is feminine." Here "Sissy" assumed the attitude of a Venus the Milo. "On the other side"—he removed half of a coat, "we have a masculine form." "Eric-Erica will now tell you of her or his peculiar nature, one half feminine, the other half masculine." "And the midline neuter," Miss Kitty Beach volunteered. There were titters. Then the supposed Eric-Erica recited a little piece, turning the feminine side first to the audience and speaking in a feminine treble out of the left corner of the mouth:

"Ladies and gentlemen, I was born as you see me—part male, part female. Shortly after my birth, the most distinguished savants of the world were called in to observe me and decide to which sex I belong. One doctor held to one thing; another to another. The advisability of operative procedures was carefully considered, pro and con, and there was much learned discussion as to whether, by the excision of certain projecting parts, one set of organs could be caused to atrophy and the other set, thus set free, to develop independently. But my mother, a deeply religious woman, said, 'What Gawd hath joined together, let no man put asunder.' In reality, I am twins in one body. In the embryo we choose our sex, and I, well I just chose to be something different. Now, some of you might consider this a great disadvantage. The truth is that it gives me a wonderful choice—of interests. I am a person of one head and one heart and one body, but also a person of two sexes. I can marry either a man or a woman. Were I so to choose, I could gratify either sex. Modesty, strongly reinforced by the prejudices of the general public, prevent me from exposing the more intimate parts of my body. But if there is a physician in the audience, or any body of scientific men present who wish to verify all of my claims, for the very small consideration of five dollars I will submit to an intimate medical examination—this only in the interests of science, however.

"In one phase of the moon, I have a predilection for the feminine role; in another phase a desire to act the opposite part. For those who may be especially interested, I may state that in the full of the moon I am entirely feminine in my reactions and at that time undergo the usual ordeal that any normal female is subject to; I refer to the physiological hemorrhage. As you will see, the left side is feminine. Were a person of the opposite sex to touch this exquisite dainty skin, I would shiver with delight. The officer may touch me." He swatted the rounded buttock.

"See!" exclaimed "Sissy," shimmying deliciously, then went on with the rigmarole: "You will observe the wonderful development of my left breast. From this I lactate. Officer, when your wife gives birth to twins the next time, I know it will be twins, you're such a strong rugged man, I'll let you use this side for a wet nurse. You will observe the delicate turning of the shapely lower limb. With this I can do ballet steps and coincidently execute an Irish jig with the masculine right foot. With my dainty left hand I do not only plain sewing but most delicate embroidery and also play the scale on the flute, my favorite instrument."

Then "Sissy" turned and continued in a hoarse husky masculine voice: "This side is that of a he-man. I box! I fight! I play baseball! I chop wood like Theodore Roosevelt. Look at that chest! There's no tit there. Look at that leg! See that muscle! That's kicked many a ball to a goal. An' I'm here to take on any man for a bout, provided he'll strap one arm to his side. I'll do the same. I couldn't trust my ladylike partner on the left not to scratch or gouge an eye. Ladies and gentlemen, we thank you, myself, and the little sister that is in me."

The officer stood up. "The rest of yuh can stay free, but that's the one I'm goin' to take back to the station house for me arrest."

All the ladies and near-ladies spoke up: "Sissy, you have all the luck. What a gorgeous time you'll have." And when the time came, Sissy went willingly enough with the officer and had the time of his young life, and returned the next day—unscathed.

The party went gaily on. "Tillie the Toiler" did her couch dance, shaking her grass skirt right in the face of the policeman.

Wells, the triple-voiced, sang in base, contralto and soprano—"I need thee every hour," completely mystifying the officer as to her actual personality. Sometimes Wells was a little bit mystified herself about that too, as who wouldn't be, under the circumstances.

Then everyone urged Fay to give her imitation of a tenement-house woman having a baby, but she refused to bother to take off her elaborate drag and perform.

After that everybody danced, each one claiming the right to break and have one turn with the officer. Finally he and Fay retired to one of the rooms to talk things over in a friendly way. After sufficient time, he left, declaring to Fay that he'd never had such a good time in his life.

He was loaded with gifts under one arm and little "Sissy" Beach under the other, loudly asseverating, "It took me four years to graduate from college. How long will it take me to graduate from jail, officer?"

"We'll keep you there always," he answered jocosely.

"Oh, goody, goody, goody, what loads and loads of nice reckless people I'll meet," shrilled "Sissy."

At the foot of the stairs, Virtue, as typified by the not-too-tarnished Mrs. Backhaus, was waiting.

The officer assured her, "Lady, I give 'em all hell. I beat up the sassy one and I give a black eye to the big fresh one that goes round wishin' douche-bags on her respectable neighbors. This one under me arm is the ringleader, and this one goes to the Island, just to put the fear of God into people who don't know how to be respectable." Mrs. Backhaus retired to her apartment and shut and locked the door. The officer turned to the gay crowd on the stairway, gave them a solemn wink and went his way.

But the party was not yet over. There was a loud noise in the hall below, many shrieks and much masculine guffawing. The ebullient Miss Savoy had arrived! Arrived, indeed, accompanied by what she styled the guardians of her moral rectitude, four handsome young men, one a rich man's chauffeur, another a light-weight boxer, a third a member of the beach patrol and the fourth a metal construction worker. So much hubbub could not fail to arouse the inquiring instinct of respectable Mrs. Backhaus, who, in curl papers and flannel wrapper, again sped into the hall. Fay and Miss Kitty Fuchs hurried down to meet them.

Miss Savoy made a picture, indeed; tall, slender, garbed in richest black, her red wig topped by a picture hat, her slender waist corseted till there was room only for her backbone and one lone intestine to pass through the narrowest part of the garment, a picture indeed as she advanced with both arms outstretched, exclaiming, "Fay's mother, I am sure. Merry Christmas, mother, how are you and all the brood?"

The only real refined lady in the house glared, sweeping Miss Savoy in contemptuous judgment. "Your place is upstairs, but it ought to be on the streets," she announced severely.

"Oh, me! A woman of the streets," camped Miss Savoy in her voice which suggested any and every old thing, "You flatter me! I've never done it yet, but now that you encourage me I shall go right out and try as soon as I have attended the party. Come on, sweethearts, do you want to go upstairs?" Her inflection suggested more than her mere words.

Then she raised her skirts unnecessarily high, revealing thin legs, much lace-trimmed white petticoat and bright green silk drawers, as she said, "to bring out the color of my red hair." Percy Bütsch suggested, "You must be a contortionist."

"You don't know the half of it, dearie," answered Miss Savoy.

Then Miss Fuchs accused Miss Savoy: "You are stealing my thunder; you have borrowed my idea, Miss Savoy, you who pride yourself on being so original. You know well that I have long gone about bragging that I always have my sweetheart wear blue socks to match the color of my eyes. You can't work over my originality and get away with it."

At the second landing Miss Savoy almost stumbled over fat old Aunty Beach-Bütsch, who, seeing indistinctly, in her alcoholized mood fumbled about as they passed and groped wildly.

"What are you trying to do, dearie?" chirruped Miss Savoy.

"I'm trying to get up—"

"Up what? Oh, stay where you are and be comfortable!"

As Miss Savoy's head appeared above the top of the second balustrade, someone caroled joyfully, "Oh, the fairy godmother has come, bringing beautiful gifts with her!"

Miss Savoy advanced, distributing kisses impartially. Almost out of breath, she gasped to Fay, "Dearie, look what I brought to your party. Yes, I knew you would be pleased."

And Miss Etrange, not to be outdone, urged the others, "Now, girls, make these good-looking young men feel welcome. Mason, will you show them where to put their things?" And Mason did.

Miss Savoy raved over the gifts she received, especially the handkerchiefs, which she insisted were "Lovely! And just the size of pleasure towels."

Fay made the rounds, introducing the actress as the accomplished and notorious Miss Savoy, "a success, of whom you've all seen much and I hope will see more." Then she urged, "Now, Mary, just show them your green drawers." Then Miss Savoy performed the famous curtsey which she had learned in one of the cribs of New Orleans—a writhing, a brief whirl which threw her skirts high above her head and allowed a glimpse of the green silk drawers before the skirts had settled about her body again.

Miss Savoy was in her element. She strutted her stuff gaily, knowing well that every innuendo, every double meaning would be appreciated at full worth. "Bertha the Sewing Machine Girl" passed. Bertha had long resisted the temptations of New York and had only recently been brought out. Miss Savoy knew the story and gargled, in an attempt at gurgling, "Oh, Miss Bertha, how is your virtue?"

"Alas! It bothered me so much I had to get rid of it," gushed that one.

Fay and Mason had not been the least snobbish. Their invitations had been sent out without regard to the social or financial standing of their acquaintances, "brilliance" being the sole criterion for entrance into the charmed circle. Each had at least one entertaining accomplishment. Some sang; some danced exquisitely; some acted; some played various instruments. Their music ran to sentimental love songs or to the gayest of dance rhythms.

Miss Savoy was versatile. She could talk man-talk, woman-talk, boy-talk, girl-talk, baby-talk and even fairy-talk.

To them and their crowd life was one hilarious riot, as it can be in a city the size of New York.

The party had been a success. True, Mason and Fay were dispossessed the day after Christmas, but then, they cared not. There were other places.

33

Fay and Mason had almost finished their internships. Fay had become more serious looking. She still possessed the same betraying voice which challenged the interest of all men and caused them to try to lead her on, incidentally leading themselves farther than they did her. If there was any choosing to be done, Fay did it!

Mason, with maturity, had fulfilled his early promise. He was now handsomer than ever, and added to that had assimilated all the arts of love.

The chief, though he had been indifferent to Fay and Mason for some time, now that separation loomed had, perversely enough, resumed his interest in the pair.

Of course, Fay now had her own growing fortune. Good spender that she was, yet she was careful never to go beyond half of her income. Her one grief had been that her mother had passed away, the mother for whom she was now in a position to do so much.

With growing means, and with advancement in her profession, Fay's opportunities were enlarged. She could now have afforded a baby, had she wished one—an adopted one, of course, that almost goes without saying, for Fay believed that no one was justified in reproducing a victim for the diseases, troubles, disappointments and unhappiness that are the lot of the average person.

What Mason lacked in personal fortune, the chief made up. It was he, the chief, who decided that Fay and Mason should postgraduate in Berlin and Vienna.

So it was arranged that they would be abroad for two full years and at the end of that time return to New York, where Mason would relieve the chief of all gonorrheal and syphilitic patients and Fay take over obstetrical cases.

Fay was tired. The crop of bastard babies that spring had been "something fierce." In those days the men were only a little less virtuous than the women. While Fay was "jerking" little bastard babies, Mason was disinfecting diseased males.

Fay was eagerly looking forward to seeing Europe again. With the banker, years before, she had learned the art of travel. Now she was to enjoy it all again, with the avid Mason.

Their plans were made. The eve of departure arrived. Fay was waiting up for Mason's return. She was sitting alone in half reverie, thinking of him and his comradeship that meant so much more than love. The sharp ring of the telephone ended her reverie.

It was Mason speaking: "Fay, dear, I have a great surprise for you. I'm married!"

"For God's sake, Mason, when and why and to whom?"

"Married half an hour ago to Marjorie Bull Dike. Now you understand— a marriage of convenience. Life will be safer for both of us and, as we have a perfect understanding of each other, far more complete than the average couple possesses, we shall be able to do much to add to each other's happiness. Now, what I want of you is this! Get all the Bulls and the Dikes and the Beaches and the Beach-Bütsches and the Bütsch-Beaches and the other members of the family together and come down to the ship. We've arranged to have our reception there—orchestra, dancing and collation, in fact, a typical Bohemian impromptu."

Mason married! Yes, it was better. The outward appearance of the conventions would be preserved—the inward, oh, well! the less said the better. It was the politic thing for everyone in their set to do. It would not change Fay's relationship to Mason. Besides, Marjorie Bull Dike needed protection. Already she had taken part in several escapades which narrowly avoided gross scandal. Mason, despite all his many and very varied love affairs, had been discreet enough to keep always within the bounds of his own social set. But not Marjorie! It was characteristic of Mason to play safe. Even in 1914 blackmail, though not a tenth as common as in these degenerate days, was something to be reckoned with. Now, blackmail is the first concern of too many of the present-day sons and daughters of the foreign-born. They are not seduced by love, as Fay had been, but are seduced by the desire, which their parents have inculcated, to prey on others.

Mason well knew how to deal with anything sinister. Yes, Fay was glad. Marjorie Bull Dike, now Mrs. Linberg, had always been a good pal. Fay remembered with amusement how they had cruised together when she visited San Francisco, each lending cooperation in landing trade for the other, often exchanging favors. The trip would be more interesting with her. Marjorie was unlike the average run of Dikes—she was always gay, never afflicted with the familial morosity.

Fay spent a good hour telephoning and then went to the ship.

After Fay, Miss Savoy was the next to arrive. She had rushed from the theatre without change and was, of course, wearing a remarkable drag. Her greeting to the newlywed couple was characteristic:

"Oh, my dears, let me kiss you—anywhere you wish. And let me wish you joy, or is it give you joy. I'm a woman of experience. If there's anything in the home life you don't know how to do, just tell 'your mother.' I'll show you how to do it. I offer you my felicitations. I wish somebody would marry me— over and over again. I'd like to be married every day of the week." Turning to Marjorie—"And Mason dear is going to shelter and provide for you! Some people have all the luck. I don't know which one to congratulate and which one to wish happiness to; the rule I believe is to congratulate the man and wish happiness to the woman—but I'm all confused. Please exonerate me." Then she turned to Mason and gushed on, "Where's the cabin boy? I must have the cabin boy at once. Call the cabin boy." A steward appeared. Miss Savoy, assuming a vacant idiotic expression, broke forth as she looked him over. "Are you the chambermaid? I've never been on a boat before. At least not when I was sober. I didn't know they had he-chambermaids aboard ship. I suppose you serve both the gentlemen and the ladies? Oh, how gorgeous! I envy you your lot. But I did not summon you here to jest. I just can't keep my back hair from falling down. Will you get me some hairpins?"

The other guests arrived and behaved more or less discreetly when in the brightly lighted saloon, but what they did in the stateroom, well, as Miss Savoy said afterwards, "That's just nobody's business."

Each arrival had something suggestive to offer in the way of a wedding gift. At that time of night it was well nigh impossible to buy gifts, but they all rose to the occasion, stopping at the all-night drugstores picking up what they could, as Ella expressed to Kitty, "more for the camp of the thing than anything else." And then she continued, "Knowing them as I do I would not put it past them to have had ante-nuptial experience, nor have I any narrow-minded ideas that they won't indulge in extramarital relationships. The things they won't do—well, ain't Nature grand!"

"Do you think the marriage will take?" asked Kitty.

"What do you mean take?"

"Will they have children? Of course, Marjorie Bull Dike could give birth if she wished to, but the question is, will she wish to."

"Well, I doubt if she ever could give birth even if she wished to. You know as well as I do that she's as queerly constructed in her physical makeup as she is in her—well, in her mental. Look at her too narrow hips. Could a child slip between them? Look at her flat breasts, her mantee walk. If that thing can grow a child, they can be made in a test tube."

"What about the handsome Mason?"

"He's adaptable—I think. But after all, it's a sensible marriage, what all of us in our set should do, to play safe." Miss Kitty Beach believed in finishing a subject. Rushing up to the couple, she asked, "Are you going to use birth-control, or are you going to have children?"

"If there are any children, Mason will have to give birth to them," Mrs. Linberg, née Dike, announced. "If there's one thing I object to it is getting all mussed up giving birth. I've been on several baby-jerking expeditions with Fay and Mason. There's simply got to be a new way invented, for I won't stoop to such vulgarity."

"Vulgarity? Remember some things, dear, are all in the point of view."

Miss Savoy proceeded to uphold Mrs. Linberg's point of view: "I don't want to be a parent. One of my friends had a little boy and when he was five years old he died of diabetes; another had a little girl with epileptic fits; and my mother had ME! Every family has something the matter with it. No, indeed! No children for me!"

About that time Old Aunty Beach-Bütsch came aboard and made her sweet remarks in her usual frank and outspoken way: "Marjorie, I envy you.

I've always had an unholy yen for Mason myself. And what will all the Bütsches and the chief do now that you are dragging him away to Europe? Over there they'll probably seduce him in some new way we don't know anything about yet, and he'll never come back to us."

"And what might that be," suggested Miss Savoy, but for once no one listened, for Marjorie, the unblushing bride, was speaking. "Aunty-Beach-Bütsch, control yourself! I shall lend him out to friends and near relations. We are coming back in two years."

"And I shall have drunk myself to death by that time," wailed old Aunty Beach-Bütsch. "But Mason, we shall be friends to the end."

Another opportunity for Miss Savoy. "Which end? I didn't know you loved Mason so much, Aunty Beach-Bütsch!"

"Love him? I love every inch of him, from the ends of the hairs of his head to the tips of his toenails. Why I love his very guts!"

"That's a very vulgar but adequate description of the depths of your passion, Aunty Beach-Bütsch!"

The crowd came thicker and faster, and there was less opportunity for extended banter. Dancing commenced. Mason and one of the Beaches disappeared into one of the staterooms and were gone—a long time. When somebody commented on the fact, Miss Savoy, in regal manner, rose to the defense of the queen's favorite child: "Well, what are staterooms for?"

The dancers romped, wriggled, squirmed, bounced, jolted, bustled, strutted, glided, bumped and pistoned back and forth for at least two hours. Then there was a lull for food and drinks. Near morning the reception broke up.

Of course, Miss Savoy was the last to leave, and as she put her foot on the gangplank struck a dramatic attitude, calling to those aboard: "Pause one moment! Has everyone on the boat been seduced? Well, if they haven't, it's not my fault. I did my part. I gave them a chance." As she passed along the pier she confided to Miss Kitty Fuchs, "We've given them a ready-made reputation aboard that ship. Everybody will be waiting to meet them; they'll know who and what they are!"

Fay returned to the flat, attended to gathering the odds and ends together, bundled everything into a cab and came back to the ship to await the send-off. By eleven, those in society were there by the dozens to wish them bon voyage—Miss Fuchs, Miss Kuntz, Miss Godown, Miss Fitzhugh, Miss Hoover, Miss Astor and all the prominent ones, the "flagrant ones," some envious Beach called them. They swarmed all over the ship, making the most of the opportunity to see strange things.

A bell sounded and then the cry, "All off who are going off." The ship began to slip from the dock. There was a mixed sound of clanging bells and whistles and shouts of goodbye from the pier and decks. Those on the pier seemed more anxious to attract attention to themselves than to pay heed to their friends aboard ship. There was an hysterical quality to the gaiety—so characteristic of New York.

Followed loud shouts of bon voyage. Most of them gave it an English pronunciation, but not Miss Savoy, who shouted bon voyage and other French messages through a megaphone, some of the messages more discreetly expressed in the foreign tongue than in the native New York idiom. She explained to one of the waiting Beaches, "I want everybody to know I can speak it, too."

A bystander (from Boston, of course) was heard to ask, "Who is that vivacious one so fully endowed with vim, vigor and vitality?"

Her companion answered, "That's Miss Savoy, the notorious impersonator."

"Whom is she seeing off?"

"See that queer-looking woman in the mannish clothes and the very handsome young man and well, I don't know what the other one is, whether it's a man or a woman. Let me have your glasses a moment."

34

Hardly was the ship beyond Sandy Hook than Marjorie, née Dike, came running to Mason and Fay, who had been pacing the decks, making campy remarks about such of the other passengers as exhibited any least idiosyncrasy. "Now, Marjorie, we are cruising in every sense of the word," Mason greeted her.

"Yes, and someone else is, too. What do you think! La Bull-Mawgan and that damned bitch, Elsie Dike, are aboard ship, sneaking over to Paris again!"

"Well, what of it? That's their right!"

"But you don't understand! Don't you remember how La Bull-Mawgan rushed me at Fish's party? I'm going to watch them, and I'm going to take some of the self-conceit out of La Bull-Mawgan before I get through with her. They've seats at the captain's table, and I'm going to get one there too."

"The captain," camped Fay, "I'd love to kiss the captain to find out if it's true that these brave men of the sea have that salty flavor people are always telling about."

Of course, the wealth of Marjorie Linberg, née Dike, procured seats at the captain's table. Marjorie would not have given a tinker's dam to sit there had it not been that Miss Bull-Mawgan and her dear friend were to sit there, too, and Marjorie was determined to make it uncomfortable for them both. She could!

At that time, La Bull-Mawgan was at the zenith of her attractiveness, and her following was—a multitude. Certainly she was the high priestess of her cult—the woman cult. Wherever she went she was followed by a coterie of ecstatic feminine admirers. She was popularly reported to have initiated more young girls than all the other women in New York together. But that was stretching the truth. Some enemy must have started such a rumor. Afterward, Marjorie, in describing the lady, said, "She has nothing on me except brazenness. I can flaunt myself in some places, but not quite in every place as she does. Well, she gets her thrills, and I get mine."

There was not much of importance which happened aboard ship. While Mason and Fay enjoyed cruising, Marjorie, true to her instincts, took part in all the sports, the rougher the better, interspersing her games with—oh, well, as La Duchesse Stupintek would say, "odder t'ings." Of course she had little annoying spats with Elsie Dike, and of course when Elsie was not about Marjorie paid court to Miss Bull-Mawgan.

At the end of the trip, Miss Bull-Mawgan gave a pressing, a very pressing invitation to Marjorie: "My dear, I shall be charmed if you will visit me in Paris."

"And does that include my boy friend?" asked Marjorie.

"Why, certainly, if you insist."

"And I suppose you will offer me the usual string of pearls, the grand imitation French kind you are so fond of distributing?" said Marjorie, who had grown jealous during the trip.

Miss Bull-Mawgan looked disturbed. "I don't know what you mean; but, if you wish to have a string of pearls, yes!"

"Thanks," said Marjorie with mock politeness, and then, "You can go to hell, Miss Bull-Mawgan. I don't want to have anything to do with you. Oh! I'm not such a virtuous kind of person that I think myself any better than you, but—you smell like a disease to me."

La Bull-Mawgan controlled herself with difficulty. Marjorie continued, "When I look at you, I think that at birth your mother made a mistake and threw away the baby and raised the placenta." She had given the crowning insult of society. Thus Marjorie had revenge on La Bull-Mawgan for a fancied slight. But that is like women. Marjorie had a nasty tongue when she wished to use it.

That Amazonian Miss Bull-Mawgan looked venomous, then gave Marjorie a resounding slap in the face. She should not have done that, except to a woman of her own size. Thus was started the famous feud, which was to be patched up and break forth again and again at intervals through the years and, for that matter, is still going.

It was in such crises that Mason was invaluable. His sense of humor never failed him. As Marjorie rushed away, Mason hurried to Miss Bull-Mawgan, who, of course, made the story much worse than it really was and even gave a specific name to the disease which she said Marjorie had accused her of harboring. "How I sympathize with you, Dr. Linberg," she said cooingly. "But just the same, tell that damned wife of yours if she ever comes to Paris, I'll have the Apaches garrote her."

Mason and Fay had not been idle aboard ship. They had indulged in delightful midnight flirtations and done pretty much what and how they pleased.

35

The voyage was over. Mason and Fay were congratulating each other on the number of delightful affairs they had consummated aboard ship. Marjorie, née Dike, was lamenting, "Oh, you two show so little discrimination that it's easy for you to have a good time wherever you go."

"We must be common," suggested Mason.

Marjorie lifted her eyebrows and smiled, then voiced her own hope: "I'm waiting for Paris. There I shall be happy—many, many times. I'll stay there while you and Fay do your work in Vienna."

They debarked at Boulogne-sur-Mer, Mason and Marjorie to hasten to Paris and Fay to Berlin, which she planned to visit for a while before going on to the postgraduate schools in Vienna.

Fay's early Pennsylvania life now proved of use to her. There she had as a child picked up "Pennsylvania Dutch." At college she had learned German grammar and literature and her ear was "formed," so she had no difficulty in conversing with the Germans.

Once settled in the Adlon, she hastened to possess herself of a copy of "Freundschaft" (Friendship) and also bought a copy of "The Isle" to mail to Marjorie. She had a few letters of introduction but also planned to make some informal acquaintances—"by intuition," as she called it.

The local slang amused her much—"warmer bruder, süsse frucht, tante," etc.

Part of her first evening Fay spent in a small resort in Fuchtwangerstrasse. Later she went to Picadilly and still later, past midnight, to the corner of Unter den Linden and Friedrichstrasse to observe the type of night life there offered. Professor Jimmie Stay's description was correct. Here she saw Berlin's night wanderers in all their variety—men that looked like women; women that looked like men; and men and women who sold themselves to anybody and everybody. She wrote Mason fully and added, "By comparison with what I see in Berlin, Mason, you are worth 10,000 marks a night. Just for the camp of the thing, I have taken out a special license. At last I have a legal status befitting my station in life. One could quite well copy German methods in many things. Certainly Berlin is one of the most tolerant cities in the world. I like it better than Paris. Why can't so-called Christian American cities emulate her? Miss Savoy's conclusion gives the reason: 'Americans do so love to manage everybody's business but their own. Religious people won't permit anybody to be happy if they can help it. To them anything that is enjoyable is a sin. Not content with being miserable themselves, they wish to make everybody else miserable, too.'"

Fay thought she had never seen such beautiful blond young men, but their youth made no physical appeal, for her fetish was for men of 28 to 35. She found that the German, once he had passed 19, was likely to become fat, gross and physically repugnant. There were exceptions, of course, and one of these she met quite casually while visiting Potsdam. He was a man of title, tall, slender, blond, even more handsome than Mason Linberg. And he had never had a love affair!

"I am Count Karl von G——," he said simply.

"And I am Fay Etrange, an American visiting Europe for medical study."

He was very frank. "I did not know Americans could be so fascinating," he told her. "I do not know why I am following you, a person of whom I know absolutely nothing, but to whom I am drawn by some unknown power. We know nothing of each other, yet I trust you."

"For being fascinated, I kiss you," said Fay, "and for trusting me, I kiss you, more and more and more" (suiting action to word). She had to teach him everything about love, most delightful of all instruction, but, what was more difficult, she had to make him believe that he was teaching her.

Their friendship ripened rapidly. Together they visited theatres, museums, cabarets, and at the end of a week Fay became a guest at his castle. The Count's father was dead, but his mother, a very beautiful woman of middle age, still lived at the castle. Like so many Americans of mixed ancestry, Fay found herself much more at home with these Germans than she had ever been able to feel with the English or with any other Europeans except the Russians.

Many guests were present at the castle that weekend. One and all seemed to make an intensive study of Fay. Her quite open love affair with the young count caused no adverse comment; in fact, it was taken as a matter of course.

A like situation in America would have led to much gossip and condemnation, if not actual interference. What did surprise the Germans was that Fay appeared to be well educated. Fay was not much of a pianist, but the castle had an excellent organ, and the technique of playing that instrument seemed natural to her. In more recent years she had made a practice of reading music daily. Thus she was able to help entertain these music-loving people. Then too, her horsemanship was good and she could hunt with them, though she cared neither for riding nor for hunting, unless Karl was with her. Her ease in conversing with them also pleased, an accomplishment so unusual in English-speaking people. Too, she was able to discuss all of the newer psychology—a subject then beginning to be popularized.

True, Fay was unusual, but not more unusual than are many young Americans. Her former life, that is, the part that had to do with her personal advancement, seemed to these Europeans a story of fascinating adventure rather than the account of hard work, which it really had been.

They pressed her with questions respecting her ambitions for the future. Knowing that these sincere and broad-minded people would not be shocked, she told them that she wished to do research work in venereal disease and, if possible, to find a cure for gonorrhea, that so-called "social disease," which has been fastened on mankind as a penalty for enjoying love. She told them of the work she had already done and of the theories which she had formulated. This was fortunate, for the count knew well a physician in Berlin who would be glad to put a corner of his laboratory at her disposal.

Fay decided to defer her visit to Vienna when the countess pressed her to remain another week.

Each morning, Fay and handsome Karl rode through the woodland paths of the estate. Sometimes they broke fast in the woods; other times they would go out on the great lake and fish all day. Everywhere they went, there was excuse for love-making. A beautiful scene would require that they stand arm in arm and view its beauties till they were so saturated with it that a new desire for love was aroused within them. Then they would embrace joyfully and kiss tenderly, the while murmuring sweet words of devotion, seeking to draw nearer and nearer to each other, to become one. So the lovely summer days passed.

Evenings, after dinner, there were the usual gatherings of all the guests in the huge reception hall. Acting was natural to Fay. The most finished actors are not those who appear on the stage, but those who must play perfectly several uncongenial roles in real life. Sometimes Fay would amuse them with impersonations, always with the help of Karl—fashion fantastic drags from material usually reserved for other purposes: bedsheets, pillow cases and bath slippers turned her into a "white sister," regretful of having left "the world" before she knew what it was all about; lace curtains and a bouquet turned her into a bride who had experienced love before she had met her husband and was concocting schemes for further deceiving him. She was in turn a Negro girl nursing her half-white child; a New York society woman attempting an English accent, than which there is nothing funnier; a krankenschwester (nurse) in despair because the doctor she had loved too well was to marry an heiress, and the unborn child had not been disposed of; most amusing to them of all was she as a Pennsylvania Dutch girl stamping through the mud to feed the chickens and pigs and, incidentally to be loved by a yokel behind a haystack.

Near the end of the week a new guest arrived, the middle-aged and very distinguished Count von M——, a man accustomed to having his way in most things, and especially in love.

Fay had been amusing the guests with her impersonations. When the Count von M—— saw her he experienced one of those sudden flare-ups of ardor for which he was noted. She had heard much of the man, who had an international reputation, and though she did not reciprocate his feeling in the least, yet it was pleasant to receive the attentions of such a renowned person; she encouraged him. For the time being she forgot Karl. Dancing began.

She danced thrice with the Count von M———. As her partner was about to engage her for the fourth time, a servant stepped up announcing that Count Karl wished to see her at once in his apartments. Fay excused herself and hurried after the servant, whom she dismissed at the door of Count Karl's sitting room. She knocked, calling, "Karl, may I enter?" "Yes," he answered in a strange harsh voice.

He was standing, gazing into the fire, his back to the door, but as she stepped within he wheeled about, a pistol in his hand. His face was flushed and wild-looking. He shouted, "How can you torture me so. You do not love me. I am going to kill myself here, now."

"Not love you? What can I do to prove to you that I love you, Karl?" she asked appealingly.

He let the pistol fall to the floor and stretched out his arms: "Oh, come to me, Liebchen, come to me and tell me you love me." She went to his arms and smoothed his hair and patted his cheeks; tenderly she gave him her lips again and again. "That is my answer, naughty boy. Now, don't be jealous any more. The Count von M——— is such a noted man that I thought it an honor to you as well as to me to dance with him. I do not love him. I do not even admire him."

"But he wins everyone," Count Karl continued. "He would ruin you."

"No, Karl, he could not ruin me. I am the only person who could do that. But I promise you here and now, Karl, that I shall be all yours, as long as you want me."

"And you will stay in Germany with me. You will give up America?" he asked.

Fay believed more in caresses than in words, the teaching of Miss Savoy. She remembered that whimsical person's advice—"Kiss their sensitive nerve endings"—and kissed him a long, lingering satisfying kiss. Then she explained gently, "Dear Karl, I have my work to do and you have duties of your own, too. My immediate course in life has been arranged. After two or three years I shall be free. I must remain in Vienna for two years. But our separation shall be only temporary. I shall come to you and you shall come to me. So long as you want me, remember, I am entirely yours."

Then she kissed him again and again.

They reciprocated!

"Ah, Karl dear," she murmured, "you satisfy me so completely. But the past has taught me that nothing so sweet can ever last. I warn you, dear, not to believe that Fate will make an exception of us. But I shall never be to blame again for hurting you. Now, if you wish to die, let me die with you, happy!"

He laughed hysterically. "Die? Now? No, we shall live—for each other—just you and I, for each other," he repeated over and over, fondling her, kissing her lips, her cheeks, her eyelids.

They were very happy. Sometimes Fay thought of the cowboy and of others. All had something in common physically; all were tall, muscular, blond, vibrant with health. But Karl had all the things which the others lacked, the social and mental attributes of the educated and well-bred. At last Fay had found that which she had sought, unconsciously, so long.

36

THE FOLLOWING MONDAY, Fay and Karl returned to Berlin, the former to plunge at once into some research work for which she found better opportunity there than elsewhere, the latter to prepare for the army manoeuvres.

Karl's apartment was, of course, at her disposal, and so she left the Adlon. Evenings they dined at various of the famous restaurants and then sought out places where they could dance together.

Fay was doing exceptionally fine work. She found she could hire excellent technicians to assist her. This made progress more rapid, for she was thus able to devote all her time to direction and interpretation. Her happy frame of mind made easy her many hours of work.

Count Karl had but recently purchased a new automobile, at that time beginning to be a practical success. They would roll luxuriously about the city in the evening or drive to suburban inns that were renowned for the splendor of their entertainment.

Often as Fay reclined in his arms he would speak softly and gently: "Beloved, this is heaven if there is such a thing as heaven." And she would assure him, "Karl, my very dear Karl, our love is the sweetest thing in the world. Give me your lips again, dear."

They carried their devotion to the utmost limits. Even when dining they would sip their wine from one glass and share their food, morsel by morsel.

"I had never dreamed there could be such happiness as ours," Karl often said. Then she would kiss him in answer.

Not a day passed but they would exchange gifts. Count Karl's were of course magnificent, for he was extremely wealthy. He gave her many beautiful pieces of jewelry, and Fay gave lavishly to him too.

Fay wrote to Mason, then in Vienna, telling of her happiness, and Mason, congratulating her, told of a wonderful new love affair of similar intensity which was taking his attention, and also of another one which the amorous and insatiable Marjorie had begun in Paris.

So events went on week by week.

Near the end of July, Count Karl returned from Potsdam one evening in a highly excited frame of mind. His regiment was to go to Metz for the manoeuvres. There was rumor of activity on the French border. It was even thought that war might ensue. The French were reported to be planning with their allies to attack Germany. To Karl, war-trained as he had been, this contingency seemed an occasion for rejoicing. To Fay, trained to think in terms of peace, the horrors of such an eventuality brought naught but dread. Of course, she had not thought of her own country being so unwise as to become embroiled in a squabble over European jealousies. Then too, she dreaded what Fate might have in store for Karl and for herself, too. But she did not refer to her formerly expressed fear that such perfect love could not last.

Karl insisted: "It will soon be over. If France retires from her arrogant position, I shall be with you—soon. If she does not recede, it will take less than a month to humble her. And I hope that she does not yield. Then we shall conquer her and occupy Paris in a month, and you and I will live there."

37

Together the Countess von G—— and Fay went to see Karl depart. He kissed his mother dutifully. Fay he held a long time in his arms as he passionately kissed her cold lips. She was as one stricken with illness. Horror of the possibilities of the future had marked her face. She could not speak; only tears welled from her eyes, in answer to his words.

When the train had departed there was a brief farewell to the Countess; then Fay hastened to her laboratories to try by hard work to submerge her dread.

Less than a week passed and the war broke out!

There were too brief letters from Karl filled with words of love, telling of success and predicting further successes. Then nothing more from him. Anxiously, Fay journeyed to the castle now occupied solely by the Countess von G——. She found that noble lady grieving, but her sorrow assuaged by pride in a son who had given his life for the Fatherland. The report told briefly that Karl had been killed when a French mine exploded.

Fay condoled as best she could, but already the countess was beginning to feel the distrust which permeated all of Germany, the distrust of those who spoke English.

Fay returned sadly to Berlin.

During her absence her laboratories had been dismantled to make room for governmental activities, the preparation of immune serums and various vaccines. Her copious notes, mostly in abbreviated shorthand, entirely meaningless to anyone else, had been confiscated. At that time what could not be understood was suspected. Fay volunteered to help them in their work. After all, they knew nothing about her, and then, too, their own feeling of self-sufficiency precluded the acceptance of favors from outlanders.

Mason had written from Vienna that he too was *persona non grata*.

Fay acted quickly. She journeyed to neutral territory at once—Switzerland. But she was bored, without occupation. She had to shake off the frightful depression which the death of Karl had caused. The newspapers gave brief war news. She was saved the pseudo-patriotic piffle which cumbered the American periodicals during the war. The Swiss papers spoke of the work of the Red Cross. Fay decided to go to Paris and offer her services. Perhaps in helping to assuage the sufferings of others she would forget her own heartache.

38

FAY WAS PUT TO WORK AT ONCE, of course in a subservient position. Europeans are slow to grant an American the recognition due to merit. She was put in the medical and surgical wards. Her obstetrical training was of little use, for soldiers do not have babies, at least the usual run of them do not, though she did come across one which had the delusion that he had given birth to a dead, rotten, foul-smelling baby, composed of feces. She did not have to psychoanalyze that one to find out what was on his mind.

Fay found the young medical men of her own age to be much less well trained than herself. Theories they knew, and they loved to waste time discussing Professor X's view or Professor Y's perhaps opposing conclusion. But for the work in hand they were not so well fitted. Men who would never be skilled, even in minor surgery, were visualizing themselves as masters of neuro-surgery.

Fay could speak French after a fashion and of course could read and write it fairly well. However, there were always enough English-speaking patients to take up more than her time, and she was assigned to them. She was at first delegated to do dressings, work that could have been attended to by a well-trained nurse. Fay took delight in showing the French how much more quick, thorough and effective were the methods which she used. Despite the horrors of war, the French still found time to be very jealous of anybody and everything, no matter how trivial. Perhaps that is their dominant trait. Jealousy! Singers, artists of any sort, even the artists of free spending, can enlighten one. Perhaps that is the reason there is always a war looming up in that part of Europe.

One morning Fay was hurrying down the receiving ward to which she was attached. A trainload of patients had been brought in during the night. The ward nurse called, "Monsieur, le docteur, venez ici, s'il vous plaît."

"In a moment," answered Fay. No sooner had she finished speaking than the air was rent with the cry in German, "Liebchen, where are you?" Fay stopped. Did she hear aright? The pained cry continued, "Liebchen, here am I. I heard you. Come to me."

"Who is calling?" cried Fay in a startled voice. She turned toward the sound.

"Here, here, Liebchen!"

The voice was unmistakable—the voice of Karl. She went to the cot and bent over. A helpless, motionless creature lay there, the whole head bound, little of the face showing but distorted lips. A staggering odor of carrion, combined with a horrible fecal smell, came up from the still human mass—her beloved Karl. By an effort of the will she overcame her nausea, stooped and gently kissed the swollen lips. She murmured words of love, closing her eyes that she might not see, compelling her imagination to recreate the beloved Karl of the past. She listened to his voice; that alone was unchanged. With eyes closed she could recall him as he had been. He was able solely to move his arms. As she stood over him whispering the words he loved to hear, he drew her close to his pain-wracked, befouled body.

His wounds had been left undressed too long. Two missiles had struck him; one had lacerated his face and blinded him; another had passed through the abdomen and out through the back, not only paralyzing him but leaving a defiling fistula from which half-liquid fecal matter constantly oozed. The only reason he had not been left to die on the field was that his uniform had been practically stripped from him. When the litter bearers came up, calling out in French, he had answered them in their own tongue with an accent which suggested only the Parisian haut monde.

Fay obtained the necessary permission to dress his wounds. Poor victim! His pain was agonizing at all times, and the apportioned supply of opiates was inadequate to ease his sufferings materially. Intensifying the loathsome situation, there were not dressings to spare to keep him decently clean. Fay at times succeeded in begging or purloining morphine, or, likelier, the more plentiful heroin, but with the least abatement of the effects of the drug, poor Karl would cry out in agony—heart-rending shrieks that horrified all who could hear.

Three dreadful days he lingered. The last night Fay, already worn out from loss of sleep, remained with him, listening to repeated requests to tell him that his vision would return and that operations would cure and restore him to her; listening to vain plans for a life after the war; promising him, not in vain, that she would remain with him.

The effect of the drugs would begin to wear off, and finally he would scream, blood-curdling screams of torture till Fay could beg just a little more sedative. Suddenly he became ominously quiet. She realized that his sufferings were almost at an end. He remained conscious till long after midnight, at intervals murmuring words of love for her. Before the break of day he lapsed into unconsciousness, breathing more and more slowly. At the end of a half hour he went out.

Fay kissed the cold blue lips, then gave vent to an anguished cry, perhaps a prayer: "God! Stop it!"

But God did not stop it; none of the Gods stopped it; neither the French God, the German God, the English God, the Protestant God, the Catholic God, nor even the Yiddish God (who was the precursor of them all) stopped the slaughter. Perhaps those who uttered the prayers left some whimsical dido unperformed, such as crossing their fingers, or touching the lips with the left hind foot of a rabbit when they prayed. There were millions praying to the French, German, English, Protestant and Catholic Gods, and hundreds of thousands praying to the Yiddish God, yet it did not avail.

Poor Fay collapsed. When she came to she was in bed. A moment she regarded her surroundings, then fell into a deep sleep, from which she did not awaken for many hours.

She was well, but tired. Her first thought was of her duties and of attending to Karl. Then she remembered. Hurriedly she dressed and returned to the ward. Her first inquiry was with regard to the disposal of Karl's body. It was too late! Too much had happened in between. She could learn nothing.

Fay debated whether to try to write to the Countess von G——, but finally concluded that no matter how innocently she might word her letter, it would probably be misconstrued, never be sent and cause the ever jealous French to vent their wrath on her. She did nothing except try to forget, applying herself harder than ever to work.

Fortunately, she was transferred to another ward and given added responsibilities. The rapid movement of events caused the recent incidents to appear far distant in perspective. Karl's death seemed as part of an ugly dream. At the end of a month, quite worn out physically, she was ordered to take a week's leave.

Paris was a dull dark place at that time. Fay found a room in a small hotel in the "Quartier" and went to bed, where she remained the greater part of three days.

39

ABOUT THREE O'CLOCK OF THE THIRD AFTERNOON Fay dressed with great care and went out. As she entered rue de l'Odeon, she saw a young English officer standing, looking about rather helplessly. He approached her. "Pardon! I say, you look as if you can speak English. You can, can't you?"

Fay smiled and answered, "Sorry, I only speak Americanese. Will that do?"

"Jolly well. You are a good sort, I see that. Do you happen to speak French, too?"

"I understand it and speak well enough for all practical purposes, though my accent leaves much to be desired."

"Then do you mind helping me a bit?"

"Certainly, I'll help you if I can." She went with him to a nearby pharmacy and assisted him in making his purchases, watching carefully to see that he was not cheated. Meanwhile they chatted as if old friends. The buying attended to, the Englishman asked, "Would you care to dine with me tonight?" "Do you know of an interesting place, something unusual? Perhaps we can see a bit of the town together."

Fay did not bother to consider. Nothing made any difference anymore. She assented without enthusiasm, and this very lack of eagerness impressed the Englishman as evidence of sterling worth.

Fay suggested Page's. Someone had told her it was gay. They found it was more than that—almost as wild as the "Jungle." Madame wished to kiss them both in welcome, but Fay drew back, laughing, and inquired, "How much extra does that cost?" Madame smiled and waved them forward. They were seated against the wall at a long table with many others. There they could see everything of interest that happened. Much cheap wine, some brandy, and an occasional bottle of champagne were in evidence. A polyglot babble dinned the eardrums. For Page's was the gathering place of all the temperamental set, native, Parisian or visiting.

The Englishman drank quite too much brandy and became proportionately gay; it takes alcohol to make them forget their inhibitions. Suddenly Fay became possessed of a wild mood, in reaction from all the dreary horror she had been through. She shouted and sang and camped quite as madly and effectively as Miss Savoy at her best. Deliberately she made all the common mistakes which English-speaking people fall into when attempting to learn French. The others present pointed her out as *une belle*, the same expression which is used so much in Baltimore and New Orleans.

About eleven they left. Her Englishman was handsome; unlike so many of them, he had a lovely clean mouth, beautiful even, healthy white teeth which shone invitingly behind blood red lips. He was acceptable.

The next morning she left him after breakfast, promising to meet him in the evening.

40

Now the old urge had been thoroughly aroused. To forget one, Fay enjoyed another. But that was not so easy in Paris at that time, for she was, above all things, fastidious about her "type of man." There must be a certain build, a certain personality, a certain verve. The short, ill-formed typical Frenchman made no appeal to her. She did not admire the type Parisien, with his short neck, exaggerated nose, badly formed body, made more repulsive by lack of proper, and what to Americans are ordinary hygienic practices—his vile breath laden with odors of garlic pyorrhea and putrescent food.

Often the English would attract, until they opened their mouths to speak; then she would look away, and go away, for an Englishman has to be exceptionally well reared before he can be induced to put a brush to his teeth, no matter how well cared for he may otherwise appear.

But Paris was beginning to present many of diverse nationalities. Thus, usually when Fay craved a new love affair, she had it. All of these men, new to Paris, sought variety too, sought it recklessly. Doomed as they were to a chance at the front, they felt that they must crowd what remained of their lives with every experience possible.

Fay returned to hard work, and during her brief leisure played harder than ever.

Even air raids she learned to take with the same calm she had felt for American thunderstorms.

The days sped, and often as not the nights sped more rapidly.

One evening Fay was dining at le Chalet. Miss Bull-Mawgan was in the crowd. She and Elsie Dike were still in Paris, "Doing their bit," they said, piously, but others said they were doing more than that. Certainly they did whatever spectacular war work would yield them the most publicity. Elizabeth Thorndyke, the other of their trio, nicknamed "Clittie" for obvious reasons, had remained in America, using her masculine-like voice to harangue others in drives for this, that and the other thing.

There was talk of the United States entering the war. "How foolish!" exclaimed Fay. "We are neutral and shall remain neutral. Why should we become involved in this quarrel and send our own good men to hell?"

Miss Bull-Mawgan, who tried to be really more French than American, thrust out her long jaw and puckered her mouth decisively. "You'll see!" she said. "The big interests want it. America must come in to protect American capital. I know whereof I speak. Besides," she went on sentimentally, "America owes France a debt of gratitude for aid in Colonial days." Miss Bull-Mawgan may have been right. God knows the debt's been more than paid now!

"I hate to think of the useless sacrifice of America's young men," Fay said pensively. "What is anyone gaining?"

Miss Bull-Mawgan, propagandist that she was, then became accusatory: "You are pro-German, Fay! Everybody knows you had a love affair with a Boche officer—and what a love affair! You are just as pro-German as you dare to be. All of you Pennsylvania Dutch are!"

"No, kitty-cat," answered Fay, smiling, "I am not pro-German. If I'm pro-anything, I am pro-peace. As for being Pennsylvania Dutch, I happen to have not one drop of Dutch blood in my veins. My ancestors were French, English, Scotch and Irish and of the four the French is the least dilute. Being born in Pennsylvania does not make one Pennsylvania Dutch, any more than being born in Africa makes a white person a Negro, or being born in Hartford makes one an aristocrat, or, for that matter a woman!"

"What do you mean, you bitch?" angrily spoke Miss Bull-Mawgan, always spoiling for a fight with someone.

"You understand me well enough, Kitty. You are being so flattered by the French, because of your money, and for purposes of their own, that you're allowing your usual good judgment to be set awry. They'll be wishing some sort of a decoration on you the next thing, and you'll be so grand you won't want us to call you by your first name."

"Now, stop being petty, Fay," urged Elsie Dike, who always sided with Miss Bull-Mawgan, possibly because of a real admiration for her, more likely because of the very substantial financial returns which accrued from her studied kow-tow.

"Well, Kitty, let's set them all an example of neutrality. Let's stop international politics and be ourselves for a while. Come on and dance with me and make Elsie jealous," suggested Fay gaily.

"You'll have to let me lead," grumbled La Bull-Mawgan in her heavy rather masculine voice, that voice which expressed her inner urge. She would have been far happier if she had been born a man.

"I am adaptable. I can do either," answered Fay.

So they were off, Fay determined to be gay in spite of war and air raids.

41

ANOTHER YEAR PASSED. La Bull-Mawgan's prophecy became fact. Fay's reaction was one of stupefaction. Her first utterance, knowing her country's politicians and rich men well, was, "Now the graft will begin!" There has been ample time to prove whether she was right or wrong.

The old Catholic Beaches were doing work with Casey, the Protestant Beaches were working with the Y and even one of the Beach-Bütsches of Philadelphia was with the "Army," for the religionists were bound to make the most of this war and vied with each other, quite jealously, in trying to gain publicity—and funds. After all, it's a business, so why shouldn't they?

Soon American troops began to arrive in France. The first detachments were moved about and exhibited everywhere, as much to hearten the discouraged French and English and to "give them morale" as to strike terror to the Germans and "break their morale." Such useful phrases they used during that war of slogans!

Handsome, tall, blond Western and Southern men began to swarm about Paris. Fay compared them with the other men available. They were enchanting, quite as thrilling to her as they seemed to be to the French girls.

American misses too began to appear. La Bull-Mawgan and her coterie, whom Fay often saw, of course, were overjoyed. Their hopes certainly, and their achievements possibly were high.

Fay was far happier serving these, her handsome countrymen, than she had been at any time since the death of Count Karl von G———.

A Scarlet Pansy

Tall Oregon and Washington and other Northwestern boys, alert, easy to look at, clean of skin, with shining clean teeth flashing their enchanting smiles! Those were men!

Fay yielded herself eagerly to their embraces, always feeling that any pleasure she might bestow would perhaps be the last the lovely lads would have opportunity to enjoy. Truly she loved them. That she forgot one in the moment of loving another did not mean that her love was any less sincere. Rather, it indicated that she was capable, again and again, of arousing within herself that necessary park of infatuation, temporary though it might be, to make a new and strange contact a thing of agonizing joy.

One day Fay ran across two of the younger Bütsches from California. They laughed uproariously as they "dished the dirt," quoting all of Miss Savoy's wisecracks which they had heard at an entertainment in Brest. They sang Miss Savoy's campy chorus—

"Whoops! Whoops! Whoops, my dear!

Can you tell me if she's queer?

Would she learn to do the crawl?

Would she go to balls and all?

Would she dance the can-can-can

these two, even these two had been capable of

For her great big strong he-man?"

With all their frivolous attitude toward life, their moments of sacrifice and heroism. They told how they had run into each other on the front after a battle. Said Percy, "We stood there talking so philosophically to each other, and then we began to camp, right out on the battlefield—"

"Ex-battlefield," amended Clarence. "You know well enough where you'd have been if there was any shelling going on, probably sheltered in the captain's arms in a dugout."

"Yes, and you'd crawl into a hole somewhere."

"A hole, of course!"

Then they told Fay how they had volunteered from their little California town, how one of them, partially inspired by the other, had written an article for the hometown paper, heading it, "Two Bütsches Go to War." Percy explained, "Of course the wise guys about town intentionally mispronounced our name. We were the first there to volunteer, and we made it appear that we were two patriots worthy of emulation."

Clarence added, "And they'll have to be some gifted emulators if they keep pace with us. Going to war has been simply gorgeous. We had leave in New York and looked up Aunty Beach-Bütsch. She is doing canteen work and doing everything else that comes her way. We had delicious shivers all the way across to Brest—isn't that a lovely appropriate French name? And since we've been in France we've had a delirious time. Already Percy and I have misbehaved in every way possible we have learned about, neo-French included. Here there are so many delightful ways of getting into mischief. Don't you think so, Fay?"

"My lips are sealed!"

"Now! But wait till the shades of night—"

"Say, Fay, have you met the Prince, yet?"

"No, I haven't met the Prince yet and don't want to. I am only interested in men, real he-men. The Prince! The Prince of Bitches I should say. Puts on drag and carries on to the limit—to the limit, I said."

"Well, what is this Miss Bull-Mawgan like, the one we hear so much about now?" queried Percy.

"I'd hate to describe her. I might be sued for libel, you know. Besides, we are supposed to be friends—now. She can be very charming and gracious."

"And what is Mason's wife like? I hear she always signs her name 'née Dike!' just as if everybody wouldn't know without being told."

"Well, she's slender as a lath and boyish in appearance, and having the blood of both the Bulls and the Dikes in her, she of course runs true to form. When she puts on a uniform she looks more like a man than a woman. That makes her happy. She's an ambulance driver now. I've even seen her stick a tiny false moustache to her upper lip—affecting the English near-man. She's very elated at present; been wounded. Now she goes about shouting that she's proven herself just as good as any man. She's a panic! Evidently she forgets the physical limitations, or chooses to ignore them, or even overcomes them; she's quite ingenious enough to do it if there is a way. She speaks French like a native and often takes Mason and me to task for our lack of interest in perfecting a French accent. We retaliate by telling her we'd be quite as proud of speaking perfect negroid-English, bastard-English, as we would be of speaking perfect French, bastard-Latin. You'll probably meet her and like her. In one way she is different from the rest of the Bulls and Dikes; she is gay, not morose, not a gloom shedder."

Here Clarence broke forth: "Did we tell you about Sissy Beach? When the war broke out, that one was all spilling over with patriotic fervor and rushed to join the Navy. The doctors examined Sissy and found him physically fit, but a mean old pharmacist's mate who had heard Sissy talk gave the doctors the wink and suggested that Sissy had a speech defect. As you know, that one's voice is all defect. The board demanded that Sissy tell why he wished to join the Navy. He started off in his high-pitched coo of 'college leading lady,' telling of his burning patriotism, his eagerness to drown for his county, the duties of all true red-blooded Americans. They let him rant of ten whole minutes. He used every bit of patriotic hokum that the one-, two-, three- and four-minute speakers ever invented. Then they turned him down with, 'Young man, this man's Navy is no place for you. Why you wouldn't even make a first-class yeomanette.' Sissy broke down and wept—'hot scalding tears,' he described them, and said, 'I think you are the meanest old things! So there! You deliberately discourage the efforts of a loyal patriot.' Then Sissy floated away—you know that walk—declaiming, 'Well, no one can say that I am not willing to immolate myself on the altar of my country.'"

"What's Sissy doing now?"

"He's become an entertainer; goes to the camps and the Navy Yard and sings and dances and pirouettes and amuses everybody and tells all friends, 'I'm doing my bitterest bit.'"

Said Percy, "Did I tell you that at Brest, Miss Savoy and I got together to dish the dirt?"

"Yes, and she wrote to Mason and me all about it. She still refers to herself as 'Your Aunt Mary' or 'Your mother.' Listen to this!" Fay took a letter from her pocket. "Honest, Your Aunt Mary thought she was pregnant by two Frenchmen, impossible as that may seem, but over here, after visiting Lourdes one comes to believe almost anything possible, especially after seeing two Frenchmen osculate each other. Honest-to-Gawd, dearie, the way they kiss is just nobody's business. Your Aunt Mary is too busy these days to do aught but plain sewing."

Marjorie, née Dike, came along with her newest sweetheart. Fay introduced them and whispered to Percy, "Talk about the scar on her cheek. She loves that. She thinks it's noble."

Marjorie was wearing a new very mannish uniform, quite fitted to her mantee figure, with trousers and puttees like a chauffeur's.

"Why, Mrs. Linberg, I didn't know you were a woman at first," exclaimed Percy Bütsch. "I mistook you for some fancy sort of Frenchman. That pleases you, I know, for I hear you always wanted to be a man instead of a girl. And that scar! Is that a scar of battle?"

"Yes, sustained in the Argonne. I've done my bit. Let's not talk of it. Give me a cigarette, somebody. I thought some of you Bütsches would be over soon. When the German men see you, they'll throw down their arms and—"

"Surrender themselves to us, I know you mean that."

"You don't have to go to the front right away, do you?"

"We leave in two days."

"I'll give Mason permission to take you to any hole in Paris you wish to visit."

"Oh, joy! The holes of Paris! What may they not be?"

"He'd do it anyway without my permission. But then you know ours is one of those happy marriages of convenience—absolutely no jealousy; he does as he pleases and I do what I please, and we are loyal and protect each other. If you wish, you may come along with me to La Bull-Mawgan's. She's my friend again, now that we are in war work. There'll be a gay crowd there—everybody, anybody, everything, anything. Since the war, we all hobnob together, demimondes, haut monde, actors, dancers and Americans. Believe me, we raise hell having a good time, for we don't know how long we are going to stay here or where we go after we leave here. Be candid! Which do you like, femmes, or the others? I'll arrange anything you want."

They talked in low tones for a while, then as Marjorie née Dike marched off with the two, Fay camped, "Don't forget your rubber coats, dearies, it may rain—or something!"

Fay had to go back to the hospital to do some thoracotomies.

Percy and Clarence did not come back. Later on she met Clarence just back of the lines.

42

WITH AMERICAN BOYS AT THE FRONT, Fay could not feel at peace in Paris. If they must suffer, she must suffer too! She resigned from the Red Cross and became a war correspondent, but as there was not much permitted in the way of writing she of course filled in when possible in any hospital work at hand. A few days and she was transferred to work near the front. She had hated to say goodbye to Mason and Marjorie. She embraced them, kissing first Marjorie and then Mason, and with Mason she put a warmth into her caress such as she was not accustomed to bestow upon him. Marjorie turned the situation into the farce beloved of their crowd by half growling, "Fay, you damned bitch, I believe you're getting a yen for my husband!"

With gay laughter they waved goodbye to her at the Gare du Nord.

The first few days in the town near the front were comparatively easy for Fay, really a rest. And when Fay recuperated it meant one thing—she began to look for further excitement, a love affair or, for that matter, probably several love affairs. And there were wonderful men in that town of all nations, men engaged in various enterprises.

When Fay looked at a man, the probing scrutiny she gave him never failed to arouse his interest. He might wonder, "What's the matter with me? Why did she look at me in that critical manner?" Anyways, men always followed her, adroitly engaged her in conversation, and tried to please her and merit her good opinion. At least that's the way it worked out.

Fay was now at the height of her beauty—thirty-three years of age and looking ten years younger, as so many of her kind do for some queer reason.

Conquests were easy; she had in turn, and lost, either through their orders to new duty or by her own discard, three captains, ten lieutenants, twenty-five sergeants and a sprinkling of privates that were unusually handsome. One day Fay observed a group of young officers during their off moments reading a book by Krafft-Ebing, which they dubbed their "Bible." Surreptitiously they were seeking sophistication. She suggested, "Now add Havelock Ellis to that and you'll learn something." They all blushed like schoolboys. After all, they were hardly more than that, though classed as "men."

Fay of course spent much of her spare time in an estaminet, at that time the crude centre of the social life of the town. Here she would sit and sip champagne, treating liberally in a quite un-French style. One evening as she was about to step into the pleasant haunt she was restrained by a firm grasp from behind and someone commanded, "Guess!"

"Whoops, my dear, I know that voice—Clarence Bütsch!" As he released her, she turned and asked, "What are you doing here?"

"I'm not doing it, only hoping to do it, Fay. And how's 'your mother'?"

"Me? I'm fit for anything, overworked though I have been. Come on in and dish with me—and flirt, too, if you wish. In this place there's plenty doing, as usual."

They entered, arm in arm, firing questions at each other with the speed of machine guns: "Have you heard from dear Old Aunty Beach-Bütsch? Where's Miss Savoy?" and inquiries about the Miss Fitzhugh, Kuntz, Fuchs, Katz and Sissy Beach.

Poor Miss Fuchs, who had the misfortune to be born in Germany, when her parents were making a visit to the Fatherland, was being shadowed all about New York as an enemy alien. She was famished for love. She did not dare to speak to a single enticing stranger. She had been threatened with deportation after the war ended. Her speed was seriously crippled. Thus she was miserable indeed.

This that and the other member of the Bütsch family had joined the Navy, for it is a peculiarity of their family to drift to the coast towns and not dwell inland. They seem attracted to the sea in all its aspects. One or two

A Scarlet Pansy

of the Bütsches were known to have achieved appointments in aviation, with startling results, socially.

Miss Savoy was still in Brest, camping with the soldiers, singing her droll songs, stepping her crazy dances, delivering her patter in her usual mezzo-soprano foghorn voice.

Fay and Clarence took their seats on a bench against the wall—a vantage point. They drew themselves closer together as a femme pushed in beside Clarence and tried "to make him." The "Frenchie" displayed her wares, opening her mouth wide, revealing her pink tongue, rolling her eyes, then she pinched his cheeks and said, "You come wiz me? Hein?" On the other side of Fay a young French officer squeezed in and tried to interest her in an evening's entertainment: "I see you, I love you." Fay nudged Clarence and proceeded to mystify both of the strangers with gibberish—

"Atwhay allshay eway oday ithway ethay itchbay anday eerquay renchmanfay?"

"Ivegay emthay ethay airay!"

"You not American?" asked the "frog."

"Nitchky," answered Fay, shaking her head.

"Eenglish?"

"Nitchky, nit nitchky!"

"Russe?"

"Nitchky, nit nitchky," they answered in duo.

Then Fay drew rapidly a small map of the mainland of Alaska and Asia with the Aleutian Island between and pointed to them.

"Some Aleuts?" asked the Frenchie.

They both nodded their heads a vigorous yes.

The femme proceeded to maul Clarence, and the frog tried to kiss Fay. As neither appealed, it was boresome. They pushed them away vigorously.

Suddenly Clarence whispered to Fay, "Look! How is that for a specimen of American-made pulchritude?"

Fay looked toward the doorway, then in a low voice said to Clarence, "My God! I'm lost again. He's so handsome that to regard him gives me a delicious pain. I almost lose my breath. Clarence, I've got to have that. Now cooperate."

212

The newcomer was a young officer, at least seventy-four inches tall, with a noble head, athletic shoulders and body that tapered downward like a perfect Greek statue. His hair was thick, dark and wavy. His eyes large, darkest blue, luminous, and their expression piercing; his nose was properly aquiline; his lips full, bowed, not too small, and the corners of his mouth had a slight upward trend; his chin was beautifully molded with a teasing suggestion of a dimple; his neck was full, but not too short and bull-like; his skin was what the French term matte, and his closely shaven beard shadowed his cheeks, upper lip, chin and neck in that outline which accentuates and improves masculinity. His lips and the tips of his ears were a deep healthy red. He had been a famous athlete in college the past year.

"Get him over here, Clarence. I'm weak," said Fay as she forced her gaze away from the man.

Clarence officiated. "Hello, stranger. Come over here. Here's an extra seat. Shove this way Fay!"

The man came over. "Have champagne?" asked Clarence.

"Sure, if you've got any to spare," he answered in a deep resonant voice that would thrill any woman.

"Over long?" asked Clarence.

"Ten days."

"Staying long?" Clarence asked with a laugh.

"That depends. I'm starting on a tour of Germany, and it may take some time," he answered in the same bantering spirit.

Then Fay spoke in the voice which so often attracted and held men for some unaccountable reason, "Where are you billeted?"

"Just arrived. Not billeted at all. Thought I'd get the lowdown here, maybe."

"You'll probably draw a haymow over the family dungheap unless you care to accept what I can offer you. You look very tired. I'm rested. You can have my bed and I'll throw some blankets on the floor, or I'll turn in with Clarence here."

"I don't want to drive you out of good quarters."

"Oh, it's not much. Wait till you see the dump. Meantime have a bite and take some more champagne."

They exchanged names. His was Frank. He gave the correct German pronunciation to Clarence Bütsch's, but Fay's last name was difficult for him.

They talked of things in America and of his college life. Clarence knew better than to intrude his own experiences, and Fay followed Miss Savoy's oft-iterated advice, "Keep 'em talking about themselves and when they run down, ask 'em for advice. They need a listener and they'll grow to feel they need you."

Fay cared absolutely nothing about competitive athletics. What she loved was the physical development of the players. A touchdown was a vague football term to her. Nevertheless, she took pains to remember what games he had been in and referred back to them occasionally, expressing regret that something or other had so often kept her from attending the important games of the past.

They discussed the "frogs," their greedy extortions, and the lieutenant touched on their gross sexual immorality, comparing it, erroneously, with the "superior" morality of Americans, at which Fay and Clarence Bütsch discreetly rolled their eyes at each other.

"Yes," lisped Fay, "their immorality must be something shameful, but that could not touch you."

"You bet it couldn't. I'm saving myself, keeping myself clean for the return home." He too cherished the belief that the other man, not he, would stop the bullet. "I've seen all of that kind of stuff I want to see and I'm through, for all time," he announced firmly.

Finally Clarence suggested that they turn in. He escorted Fay and Lieutenant Frank to the little cottage to which Fay had been assigned. "I'll wait below till you two decide what to do," he said, "and day after tomorrow one of you can have my place, for I've got orders."

He had not long to wait, for Fay soon thrust her head out of the window and said, "It's all right. See you at breakfast."

Fay's room had a little offset on one side. Here she hung a sheet for a curtain and with blankets made a bed on the floor. She had long ere that learned to sleep in far more uncomfortable quarters.

The young lieutenant had wrenched a shoulder the day before. Fay volunteered to massage it for him. He removed his coat and shirt, and Fay examined him carefully. With deepest pleasure she observed the beauty of the upper part of his torso. Then she directed him to lie on the bed while she sat on the edge and began a skillful manipulation of the muscles, including petrissage, of which she and Mason had so often joked in the past. It soothed the wearied man, and almost at once he dozed off, murmuring, "My God! That's a relief."

His body was sweet and clean smelling. As she finished, Fay bent and gently kissed him on the neck, that part where the skin is so soft and sensitive, midway between the angle of the jaw and the hair line at the back of the neck. He opened his eyes, startled, then smiled as he murmured, "Oh! It's you. That's all right." He folded his arms about her, bringing her head close to his, then like a contented child sank into a deep sleep.

His clean body odor gave her keenest delight. She hesitated to attempt to alter their relationship, and possibly lose him entirely. He had accepted her as a pal, that she would be.

Gently she disengaged herself.

On her pallet on the floor behind the curtain she lay wakeful a long time, fighting down her desire.

They awakened early. There was a brief note of adieu from Clarence Bütsch, who had hurried away to battle and make the world safe for plutocracy.

Fay and Lieutenant Frank descended to the tiny living room. Madame found some eggs and provided a tolerable breakfast. The two daughters, aged sixteen and eighteen, did their utmost to interest the lieutenant americain, and even madame, whose husband had too long been far away at the front, was perhaps more ardent than was seemly. But the lieutenant americain was indifferent. All through his college years he had been surfeited with the attentions of women. To paraphrase a rough leatherneck expression, his attitude had been, "Use 'em and leave 'em." Besides, he was interested in Fay now. She filled completely that need which he felt for companionship.

The days slipped by. Mostly their duty consisted of standing by to await orders. Fay kept to her corner on the floor, declaring that she had so long slept on a hard bed that she felt more comfortable lying with only blankets between her and the boards. But every night she soothed him to sleep—even long after the strained muscles had ceased to pain him.

One night, when she thought that she had used therapeutics long enough as an excuse for fondling, she omitted her usual massage of his shoulder.

Behind her curtain she prepared for sleep and he, half clothed, had slid under his blankets. She blew out the candle and was startled when he called, "Didn't you forget something!"

"What?" she gasped, her emotion almost overcoming her powers of speech.

"You didn't tuck me in!"

"All right." After pausing a moment to regain self-control, she felt her way across the darkened room.

"That's better," he said as she snuggled down beside him, her lips on his neck and one hand softly caressing his wavy hair. But he made no move to change their relation of warm comradeship.

43

STILL THEY LINGERED IN THE LITTLE TOWN.

Lieutenant Frank had less and less to do with women in general and hurried away from his former companions to be with Fay. With her he was content, content to await any fate. And no one smiled, or looked wise or gossiped as would have been the case back in America. Relations of all sorts, so close to the front, were accepted in those times without comment and without the urge to pry into others' lives and reform every and all things.

Fay made a heroic effort to keep her love for him untarnished, and strangely, she was succeeding, and finding the greatest joy of her life in this idealized relationship. Lieutenant Frank, on his part, did not realize how dear she had become to him. Now they shared every least thing together, a walk to the canteen, to the post, to the laundry woman, to any little shop to buy what offered in the way of trinkets for friends. They read together, each holding a corner of the book and taking a turn at reading aloud.

At this time Fay wrote to Mason.

"I have found the ideal of my life." She gave a lengthy description of Lieutenant Frank, and then continued, "Mason, you and the others may ridicule me, but this love is pure, the purest love possible. Frank needs me and I need him. Every night I cuddle in his arms until he relaxes in sleep, then I go to my own corner of the room. I doubt if I would have the strength of character to keep my love for him the pure sentiment it is; that power comes entirely from him. You realize how suggestible I am. I only know that I wish to be whatever he wishes me to be. That is sufficient." She wrote fully of the little town, of their life there, and then the note of impending tragedy intruded itself: "Mason, I may never return to you. We must all realize that. My will has been made leaving everything to you to do with as you may please. You and Marjorie of course will never have children of your own. Will you, dear, if I never come back, in remembrance of me adopt a little boy and a little girl orphan? Select talented children (for they suffer so much more than the others if neglected), and give them the advantages which would otherwise be denied them. And when they are grown up, tell them of me, all the good if there is any, and all the bad, for I want no fictitious sainthood.

"Frank will soon be sent to the slaughter, and where he goes I shall go.

"I feel very sad tonight, Mason. Whatever happens, my love will ever attend you and Marjorie. I feel it is goodbye, dear. Fay."

Finally came the long-awaited order to go to the front. Fay, with absolute disbelief in combat, succeeded in getting orders juggled so that she could proceed with Lieutenant Frank's regiment. They were sent to a front where the fighting was known to be hot.

Now Fay had no thought of personal danger. It was always of Lieutenant Frank she was thinking. When they came to the trenches, filthy and vile with blood and excrement, holding the overpowering odor of carrion, they were separated. Fay had to remain behind with the hospital unit as the combatants moved forward. She reverted to her profession, forgetful that she was employed by a newspaper as a columnist.

Not long did they have to wait for their baptism of fire! And then the wounded began coming in to the dressing station; mere boys who had gone forth beautiful were hurried back from the hell, some with arms or legs dangling or missing; some with faces shot away. Some bled to death under Fay's hands. Quickly she worked, patching here and there to stop the flow of blood, deciding which, the more hopeful, should be sent further back in an attempt to save them; keeping the half moribund near at hand to see whether they were worth further attempts at salvage. Blood and horror! And the din of battle nearer and nearer. She had almost ceased to feel, only possessed of mad desire to overpower death. Other than that she felt no emotion except worry for the safety of Lieutenant Frank. Someone not hopelessly wounded had seen him still unscathed, but that was early in the day. Another, a brother officer, brought in late in the afternoon, answered her inquiry, "He was all right an hour ago, but he'll get his yet."

"Get his yet!"

There was a lull. She waited in anguish, picturing him brought in dying. Nightfall came on. There was an order to move the hospital unit further back. Fay hastened. A fresh young medical officer had been brought forward to help. Together they worked furiously, and when all was ready Fay suggested, "You follow the litters; I'll remain to dress anything that comes back."

To fall back with Frank still at the front? She could not do it! Madly she started, and in reverse order followed the trail that was coming from the front. The regiment, they told her, lay behind a hill to the left, about half a mile—but a half mile charged with death.

On she went!

A shell hit the road not far in front. That meant the Germans had the range. Quickly she veered to the left, making her way over what had recently been ploughed fields. She waded a filthy brook; then began the ascent of the hill which Lieutenant Frank and his company defended. She made her way to the top and entered a trench, stumbling over dead bodies to do so. Automatically, she stooped to examine them. One was still warm, but there was no pulsation of the arteries. She went on. She recognized the voice of a Polish boy who was in Frank's company, and continued to make her way forward. There was a terrific explosion as a shell broke in front of the trench. In a blaze of light she had a momentary glimpse of Lieutenant Frank, not fifty feet away. He was still uninjured when she reached him. She stood quietly beside him. He turned quickly, did not recognize her and yelled, "Damn you, soldier, why don't you do your part?"

"Noncombatant, Frank!"

"Hell! Did they have to send you here?" Then he continued to direct his men. He gave the order to move forward. The shells were less numerous but still continued to fall near them as they advanced, Fay trudging behind him, obsessed with the idea that she might save him. There was a shriek overhead, then an explosion, the final shell of attack.

Immediately about them was a cessation of movement!

Fay grasped one of her thighs. She fell to the ground. She knew where to compress the artery. In her kit was one remaining tourniquet. Even at that moment she did not forget to look for Lieutenant Frank. He was still standing, a dark shadow before her. She applied the tourniquet swiftly and tightly. Then she dragged herself to Frank. At that moment, he too sank down.

"Are you hurt, Frank?" she asked.

"Here," he said, putting her hand on his left arm.

There were still occasional bursts of flame which revealed them. They sought concealment in a shell hole. There they lay close to each other. It became quieter. With practiced fingers Fay felt his shattered arm. He was bleeding so freely that he must inevitably succumb unless she stopped the flow of blood. It was her life or his, and loving him as she did there could be but one answer.

Hastily she undid the tourniquet from her thigh and transferred it to his arm, charging him, "Pull it tight, Frank, tighter. It will stop your bleeding."

The spurts from her own severed artery weakened her. With one hand she thought to stay the flow of blood, seeking to linger long enough to tell him of her love.

Again she lay against him, her head close to his. The din of battle was ever more distant. With his uninjured right arm he held her close while she spoke into his ear.

"Frank, I am dying; in a few minutes I shall be gone. I want you to know that I love you more than anything else in the world, more even than my own life. I have not lived a good life, according to the standards of others." She did not spare herself. "Till I met you, I was promiscuous. All my life I have been a ———. Before I go, won't you kiss me, dear; kiss me on my lips," she begged pitifully.

As he kissed her he knew that he too loved her.

"Now I am happy. I'm going, Frank," she said as she released her pressure on the artery and threw both her arms in weak embrace about his neck.

Thus, Fay Etrange lay dying on a battlefield in France, dying in the arms of the man she loved—the last man she loved.

The End.

Robert Scully is the unknown author of *A Scarlet Pansy*.

Robert J. Corber is the William R. Kenan Jr. Professor in American Institutions and Values at Trinity College.

www.ingramcontent.com/pod-product-compliance
Lightning Source LLC
Jackson TN
JSHW020208310825
90255JS00004B/6